The Cost of Love

Jenkins & Sons Construction Series

Sharon C. Cooper

Amaris Publishing LLC

The Cost of Love
By
Sharon C. Cooper

Copyright © 2024 Sharon C. Cooper
Amaris Publishing LLC

ISBN: 978-1-946172-53-2
Paperback

Marcella A., it's readers like you who make me want to keep writing!
Thank you for being you!

Much love!

Chapter One

A stab of jealousy pierced through Antonio Jenkins and practically knocked him off-balance. He rubbed his chest as if the motion could straighten him out. It didn't. If anything, it intensified the uncomfortable heat coursing through his body and a tightness that wrapped around him like a steel band.

What the heck was wrong with him? He'd been out of sorts since waking up that morning, and even more so now that he was in the groom's room with some of his family members.

He ran his hand over his low haircut, then tugged on the bow tie, which seemed to be tightening around his neck. Glancing around, he took in the familiar faces. It was Ben Jr.'s wedding day and some of their male cousins were hanging out in the small space, spewing words of wisdom on what Ben could expect from being a new husband.

Antonio had heard enough. Rubbing the tense spot on the back of his neck, he eased away from the group and moved across the room, stopping near a leather loveseat. He knew exactly why he was agitated. He might be happy for his little brother, but a part of him couldn't shake the melancholy swirling inside. All his cousins in the room were married with kids. Now Ben was joining that group, making Antonio the odd bachelor out. As usual.

He perched on the arm of the loveseat and sighed. They were at a large church where the wedding would take place, followed by a sit-down dinner for immediate family. Later, there'd also be a large, adults-only reception at their grandparents' estate for extended family and friends.

As the best man, he anticipated a long day, but what he hadn't counted on was his funky attitude. He was thrilled that Ben and Mahogany found each other and decided to build a life together. But there was a voice in the back of his mind screaming—*What about me? When will it be my turn?*

Not one of the five men across the room ever intended to get married. None of them had mapped out a life plan and probably still didn't have one, but Antonio had. He had created his roadmap during his senior year of high school. At the top of the list had been to attend college while working at their family-owned business—Jenkins & Sons Construction. Next, and maybe most important—get married and have a family.

At thirty-three, he still hadn't found "the one." He wasn't a player and never wanted to be, and even though he'd been in a couple of long-term relationships, neither had resulted in marriage. Antonio had done everything right. Got his education, settled into his job as an estimator, and was financially prepared for a wife and kids. Still...

Someone clapped him on the shoulder, and he glanced back to find his cousin, Liam.

"Mr. Grumpy, can I talk to you for a minute?" Liam asked quietly, humor in his tone as he nodded his head toward the door that would lead them to the private hallway.

Antonio tried not to grumble and feed into the name he'd

been called more often than not by his cousins. "Yeah, I guess, and I'm not grumpy," he mumbled and headed to the door with him.

"*Ant*, where you going, man?" Ben Jr. asked, and Antonio cringed at the nickname his brother used only to get under his skin. He hated nicknames, which only made Ben use them more often.

"Just stepping outside for a moment. Don't worry, I'll be there to catch you when you faint when Mahogany starts walking down the aisle." Everyone laughed as Antonio walked out, closing the door behind him.

"How's Charlee?" he asked, glad to be away from the others. "The baby should be coming any day now, right?"

"Six more weeks," Liam said proudly. They were having a boy, and Antonio had never seen his cousin happier.

Liam was one of his oldest first cousins, and he and Antonio were more alike than any of the others. They both were introverts and serious about every aspect of their lives. But Antonio had seen a change in Liam since he and his wife married a few years ago. He knew it had everything to do with Charlee, who was extroverted to the ninth degree. It was impossible not to like her. Her energy was palpable.

"My wife is over being pregnant and is more than ready for our LJ to be born. She's literally counting down the days, but enough about us. What's up with you? You seemed a little distracted in there. Does this have anything to do with Scarlett? You two have gone out a few times now, but you haven't mentioned her lately."

Scarlett.

Hearing her name twisted Antonio up inside.

Months ago, he had given up on dating. He met his share of nice women, but his dating life hadn't been going as planned. He had to be the problem. Too clingy. Too possessive. Too everything, and he'd decided to take a step back and figure himself out.

That was, until Scarlett Rowsey, Mahogany's sister, caught his attention.

The former model was so far out of Antonio's league, it was almost laughable that she'd even given him the time of day. She also had the cutest little girl, Bella. In his eyes, Scarlett was the total package, and no one had been more surprised than him when she agreed to go out with him—more than once.

Over the last couple of months, they'd spent time together. Dinners. Movies. An art exhibit. They'd had a good time on each outing, and the attraction and chemistry between him and Scarlett was *hot*. Antonio wanted her more than he'd ever wanted another woman, and the fact that he got along great with her daughter was a plus.

Yet, he couldn't get a clear read on Scarlett. She had an invisible wall up that was impenetrable. Antonio was at a loss about how to move forward.

Not ready to discuss his relationship with anyone, he said, "Nah, it's not about Scarlett. I'm..." What could he say without sounding like a punk? "I just have some things going on."

Liam stared at him for a moment in that penetrating way of his. The guy really should've gone into law enforcement instead of architecture considering his intimidating expressions. They were both over six feet tall with broad shoulders and a slight muscular build, but Liam could mean-mug someone into spilling their whole life story.

Antonio chuckled. "Dude, don't look at me like that. As for Scarlett, there's nothing to tell. We're still getting to know each other is all."

"Speaking of Scarlett," Liam said and smiled at something over Antonio's shoulder.

"Uncle Tony!"

Bella's high-pitched voice immediately brought a smile to Antonio's face. He loved this kid. She wasn't his niece, but because Bella was his nephew's best friend, she called him uncle like Jayden did. Antonio loved that she always seemed thrilled to see him.

While his nephew Jayden, Ben's son, loped toward them, Bella ran to Antonio at full speed in her white flower girl dress and white shoes. She was so cute and petite. She looked more like a five-year-old than her actual age of almost eight.

When she was closer, she leaped into his waiting arms.

"Hey, Baby Doll," he said, kissing her cheek as she giggled and tightened her arms around his neck.

"I'm not a baby doll," she said, her soft voice washing over Antonio like a soothing balm. When she rested her head on his shoulder, his heart almost split open. "You smell good," she murmured, pulling another smile from Antonio.

God, this kid. She was a great cure for the blues. His heart seemed to expand whenever he was with her. How was it that he could love this child so much as if she was his own?

"Hey, Uncle Antonio and Uncle Liam," Jayden said, giving them each a fist bump. Liam was Jayden's second cousin, but he referred to all of them as *uncle*. "Have you seen my dad?"

"Yeah, he's right in here," Liam said, opening the door to the groom's room and letting Jayden in before closing the door.

"Are you supposed to be out in the hallway?" Liam asked Bella.

She lowered her eyes and snuggled into Antonio. "I had to ask Uncle Tony something."

Antonio nuzzled her sweet-smelling neck, and she giggled again. He didn't think he'd ever get tired of the sound. "What did you have to ask me?"

She lifted her head and looked at him, her facial expression serious. "Can you dance?"

Antonio chuckled, wondering where this was going. "Yes. Why?"

She leaned in close to his ear and said, "Can you take me to the daddy-daughter dance at my dance school? Mommy said she would take me, but it's for daddies. I don't have a daddy, and I want you to take me."

Her words could've knocked Antonio over with a feather. If he hadn't already been in love with her, that request would've sealed it for him. He hated that this precious little girl didn't have a father—someone to love and protect her—but he'd gladly step in and play the role.

Bella's request might have shocked him, but it also made him feel ten feet tall. She would never understand how much this meant to him.

Her father had died in a car accident before she was born, but as far as Antonio knew, Scarlett hadn't told her daughter the details. Bella just thought she didn't have a father. Once she got older and started asking more questions, he was sure Scarlett would tell her the truth.

"I'd be glad to go to the dance with you as long as it's okay with your mommy," he finally said, feeling a little choked up by the request.

"Yay!" she cheered, then hugged him and placed a kiss on his cheek. "I'm so happy. I'll tell Mommy she doesn't have to go."

"Bella!" Amelia, Bella's grandmother, whisper shouted as she hurried down the hallway wearing a long, pale pink dress. "Young lady, what are you doing out here?"

"I had to talk to Uncle Tony," Bella said as Antonio lowered her to the floor.

Amelia smiled at him and Liam, then shook her head as she reached for Bella's hand. "Well, you'll have to talk to Uncle Tony later. The wedding is starting soon, and we have to finish getting you ready." She glanced at Antonio. "I'm sorry. I hope she wasn't bothering—"

"No apology necessary. She always brightens my day." He winked at Bella, who ducked her head and giggled. As her grandmother guided her away, Bella turned back and smiled at him.

"Uncle Tony?" Liam said when Amelia and Bella were out of earshot. "When we were growing up, you *never* let anyone call you *Ant* or *Tony*. Hell, even now you're ready to murder the first person who dares shorten your precious name. Yet, you let her call you Tony."

Antonio frowned and pointed in the direction Bella went. "Dude, did you see that kid? She's the cutest thing on this side of heaven. Who am I to stop her from shortening my name? With those eyes and that adorable smile, she can call me whatever she wants."

The corners of Liam's mouth kicked up. "Ahh, another one snared by an adorable kid. You know this is exactly what happened to Jerry when Rayne and Stormy moved in next door to him. That little girl had him wrapped around her finger the first time they met, and now? If Stormy asked for the moon, he'd try to get it for her."

Yeah, Jerry was still putty in Stormy's hands, maybe even more so now. But this was different. Though Antonio had gone out with Scarlett several times, and he was crazy about her, he wasn't sure of her interest level.

But if there was a chance for the same outcome—an instant family—Antonio was here for it.

Chapter Two

Scarlett stood behind Mahogany as they faced the full-length mirror while she fastened the pearl necklace—an heirloom from their grandmother—around her sister's neck. The day had finally arrived—Mahogany's wedding day.

Older by two years, Scarlett admired the way her sister never gave up on what she wanted—a family of her own. Even after a broken engagement a year ago, Mahogany had been determined to find her *person*. Sure, there were moments of doubt, but she remained positive and encouraged, and now she was marrying the man of her dreams. Ben worshipped the ground her sister walked on, and Scarlett hoped every woman, including herself, could one day experience that type of love.

"All right, turn around and let me see you," she said.

Mahogany spun, and Scarlett eyed her sister's face critically. When they were growing up, they'd often been mistaken for twins. Their reddish-brown skin tone, dark eyes, and bow-shaped lips were almost identical. So, looking at her sister right now was a little like looking at herself.

She had done Mahogany's makeup, keeping it fresh and natural with a pop of color from the highly pigmented, crimson-red lipstick. As a makeup and fashion blogger and social media influencer, Scarlett received tons of free products. While she loved trying them herself, she also enjoyed testing them out on others, especially her sister.

"This is one of those times when I'm glad you always liked playing with makeup and doing hair when we were kids. Now you're a pro. There's no way I could've pulled this off by myself," Mahogany said, stealing another glance at the mirror. "I almost don't recognize myself."

Scarlett grinned. "You are the perfect canvas, and you're absolutely gorgeous."

Normally, Mahogany wore her hair in micro braids, but today her hair hung loosely around her shoulders in waves, only adding to her elegant appearance.

Her wedding dress was everything she'd dreamed it would be. The scoop neck, asymmetrical, strapless gown was the color of champagne and shimmered under the fluorescent lights. Satiny material draped across the bodice, giving the illusion of a wrap dress where pearls adorned the left side of the garment. The full skirt billowed out, revealing a jaw-dropping, deep split that showcased Mahogany's shapely left leg whenever she took a step. Her tall, strappy sandals matched the outfit perfectly.

Their mother thought the outfit was too risqué for a church wedding, but Mahogany and Scarlett disagreed. The one-of-a-kind gown was a Jada Jenkins-Anderson original. When the fashion designer, who happened to be Ben's cousin, offered to create the dress, Mahogany had leaped at the opportunity. The final result was breathtaking.

Jada had also made Scarlett's outfit, which was a strapless, pale pink dress with a band of jewels around the midsection.

The garment molded over her body like a second skin and also had a daring split like Mahogany's.

"Words can't express how stunning you are, Sis," Scarlett gushed, and joy bubbled inside of her. "Jada should put you in her next fashion show."

Mahogany released a snort, but quickly covered her mouth and chuckled. "You got me mixed up with you. I can barely walk down the street without tripping, and I'm praying I don't face-plant when I stroll down the aisle. There's no way I could model anything."

Scarlett couldn't help laughing. When they were growing up, there was a reason the kids called her sister Misstep Mahogany. She was the clumsiest person Scarlett knew, but her incoordination had played a major role in her snagging and keeping Ben's attention. Now, here she was about to get married.

"Speaking of modeling," Mahogany said, "I heard Jada asked you to be in another one of her fashion shows soon. Are you doing it?"

Scarlett had considered the generous offer, but she could barely keep up with her current responsibilities. No way could she add modeling back into the mix.

Before getting pregnant with Bella, Scarlett had modeled professionally and enjoyed it, but that had been over eight years ago. Now she was a single mom, and she couldn't see herself modeling again. Participating in a fashion show periodically was fine, but Jada suggested she return to the industry full time. Or at least modeling Jada's Fashions exclusively.

"I don't know. My photography business has picked up, and I told you that I recently signed a contract with a jewelry designer. I'll be busy working them into the rotation of the current content on my social media sites. I don't know if I can add more to my days."

Mahogany nodded. "I guess when you're good at everything, you become in demand. It must be rough being you," she cracked, her red lips twitching as she tried to fight a laugh.

"Oh, be quiet. You're just as busy with your interior design business. I guess talent runs in the family."

"Okay, enough about our talents." Mahogany leaned in as if she was going to share a secret. "How was your date the other night with Antonio?"

"Seriously? You're about to get married and you want to discuss my dating life? Shouldn't you be asking me if everything is in place for the dinner and reception later? Or—"

"Stop stalling," Mahogany ground out, her hands on her hips as she glared at Scarlett. "I already know everything is in place for today. What I want to know is why you've been hush-hush when it comes to Antonio. We used to share everything about our dates, but you've been holding out."

Scarlett huffed out a breath and paced away from her sister. She didn't like the route this conversation had taken. Her pulse amped up just hearing Antonio's name. Which was ridiculous, and the intense sensation swirling inside of her made her want to talk about anything but him.

"I know you like him, and he's *crazy* about you and Bella. So why have you been acting so weird? If I've noticed it, I'm sure he has too. What's going on? I thought you were ready to start dating again."

"I am... well, I thought I was, but..." Scarlett's words trailed off as she tried to get her thoughts together to explain what she was feeling. Yes, she liked Antonio. Actually, she more than liked him, but doubts were creeping in.

"What aren't you telling me?" Mahogany moved closer, forcing Scarlett to stop pacing. "Did something happen? Did he do something to you?"

"No! No, Antonio is a sweetheart. He is honestly the nicest

man I've ever met." And the hottest, kindest, and most attentive man, she wanted to add but kept that to herself. Instead, she said, "I've enjoyed our times together."

"*But?*" Mahogany said impatiently.

"But he makes me remember!" Scarlett snapped, catching them both off guard.

She huffed out a shaky breath and took a step back. The room felt as if it was closing in around her. This was so not the time for this discussion, but sometimes her sister was relentless when she wanted answers. Answers that Scarlett wasn't sure she could even make sense of herself.

"I don't know," Scarlett murmured, then swallowed hard as flashes from her past raced through her mind like an old black and white movie. A past she thought she had dealt with years ago, but apparently not. "When I'm with Antonio, he makes me think about my time with Ezra," she said quietly of Bella's father.

Saying his name made her heart hurt. She missed him dearly, but more than anything, the soul-jarring guilt that she'd felt the night he'd been killed was back with a vengeance.

"Aww, Sis." Mahogany reached for her.

Scarlett went into her sister's arms willingly and released a shuddering breath. Between her wonderful dates with Antonio and helping Mahogany plan the wedding, she couldn't help but think of Ezra. Unfortunately, each time she did, a stab of pain pierced her chest.

She blinked rapidly, refusing to let any tears fall and destroy her makeup. But it was hard not to cry for the man who had given her the greatest gift of all—Bella. When all Scarlett had given him was heartache. She hadn't been able to return the type of love he had given her... the type of love that he had craved.

The door burst open, and Scarlett startled.

"Okay, girls. It's time." Their mother hurried into the room, and Scarlett quickly pulled away from Mahogany while discreetly dabbing at the corners of her eyes with the heel of her palm.

"Oh, baby, you look so beautiful."

Scarlett turned back to see her mother hugging Mahogany, but her sister, who was taller than their mom, stared at Scarlett. The pity she saw in her eyes made Scarlett look away. She didn't want her pity. All she wanted was to get through the day and be rid of all the painful memories weighing on her like an oversized refrigerator.

Then again, it wasn't only the memories that plagued her, it was the stupid guilt and regrets of not handling her relationship with Ezra differently. For almost eight years, her family thought she'd been crazy in love with Bella's father. They assumed that was why she'd taken his death so hard. On the contrary. It was because she hadn't loved him enough.

Admitting this to herself had her choked up, but she couldn't cry. Not now. Definitely not minutes before her sister's wedding. Even knowing that didn't stop a runaway tear from racing down her cheek.

Scarlett lowered her head and dabbed at it, willing others not to fall. She needed to get herself together, but she kept thinking about the night that Ezra proposed to her. When he'd asked her to marry him, she hadn't known she was pregnant. Not that it would've changed her answer. She had no choice. She had to turn down his proposal because, though she loved him, she hadn't been *in* love with him. There was no way she could marry someone she wasn't in love with.

She swallowed hard and rubbed her chest. It was as if she could still see the hurt and disappointment in Ezra's eyes. She could feel his anguish when he begged her to make him understand why she wouldn't marry him. By the time they'd finished talking, she had been worn out, and he had left the apartment, saying he needed some air.

Then he was gone... for good.

Scarlett had received a call in the middle of the night saying he'd been in a car accident. He'd been killed by a woman who'd been texting while driving.

"Ben Sr. is waiting for you," their mother said to Mahogany.

Since their father died years ago, her sister had asked her future father-in-law to walk her down the aisle.

"Mom, can you let him know I'll be ready in five minutes?" Mahogany's words punched through Scarlett's thoughts, and she quickly dabbed at her face, hoping their mother hadn't noticed her tears.

"Sure, sweetie," her mom said, but when Scarlett looked at her mother, she was looking at her.

Crap. Scarlett would never forgive herself if she was the cause of Mahogany being late for her own wedding. She braced herself, half expecting their mother to ask what was going on, but she didn't. Amelia Rowsey was nothing if not observant.

But there was one thing in particular that Scarlett loved about her mother, and that was she knew how to read a room. She knew when to ask questions, press for answers, and when to wait to see if her girls would automatically share what was on their minds.

Instead of saying anything, her mom approached her, squeezed Scarlett's arm, and gave her a reassuring smile. Then she kissed her cheek before walking out of the small room.

God, I love that woman.

Scarlett released the breath she hadn't realized she'd been holding, then turned her attention to her sister. Mahogany gave her a small smile.

"I know there's more going on than you're letting on, but I'll let you keep your secrets. Just remember, I'm always here for you. However, before we go, I need to say something. Antonio is one of the good ones. He won't hurt you. He'll treat you like a queen, but if you know you're not interested in him, tell him."

"I am interested in him, but—"

"But you're afraid."

Yeah, she was afraid, but not for the reasons Mahogany was probably thinking. If Scarlett was going to be with any man, it would be Antonio. But what if she really did have a problem? What if history had shown she was incapable of falling in love? Before Ezra, it had been Todd, her high school boyfriend. After graduating high school, he had assumed they'd get married and live happily ever after. But just like it had been with Ezra, she loved him, but she hadn't been in love with him.

"Bella already loves Antonio," she said, wishing her daughter hadn't gotten to know him before Scarlett worked things out within herself. But Bella had met and spent time with Antonio and the Jenkins family before he had even asked Scarlett out.

Mahogany squeezed her hand. "Antonio loves her too. He hasn't said it, but it's written all over his face whenever they're together. I assure you, no matter what happens between you and him, his feelings for Bella won't ever change."

Scarlett nodded. "Yeah, because he's an incredible man."

He was the first man to come along and evoke feelings within Scarlett that she hadn't felt in a long time. If ever. What if she ended up hurting him the way she'd done Todd and Ezra? She wanted to fall in love and live happily ever after, but what if something was broken inside of her? What if she was incapable of those feelings?

It would hurt her more than Antonio if she let things progress only to find out that she couldn't fall in love. Especially knowing he was looking to get married and have a family one day. He deserved happiness.

"Don't overthink whatever is happening between you and Antonio," Mahogany said. "Enjoy the ride. Everything will work out as it should."

"Yeah, I hope you're right."

Chapter Three

"Okay, let's do this," Antonio said to Ben, then opened the groom's room door for them to leave.

It was showtime, and he was glad that Liam had pulled him out earlier to talk. It helped. Between their conversation and the short visit with Bella, Antonio was in a better frame of mind. He was ready to be the best man.

"Wait!" Ben said.

Antonio glanced over his shoulder at his brother and closed the door back. "You better not be getting ready to say something stupid like, *I can't go through with this*."

Ben snorted. "Nah, man. I'm good. Just wanted to thank you for all your help over the last few weeks. I had no idea what all went into a wedding."

"I know, right?" Antonio smiled, thinking about how busy they'd been in the days leading up to this moment. "I want to get married someday, but I can do without all the hoopla that comes with weddings. Glad you're experiencing this first. Now I know what I *don't* want in my future."

Ben chuckled. "Yeah, I know. This shindig was supposed to

be small and intimate, but I should've known that would be impossible with our family." He sobered and glanced down at his shiny, black Stacy Adams shoes before returning his attention to Antonio. "As for you getting married, I have no doubt your day is coming. I know how hard it is for you to witness me taking this next step. When everyone thought you'd be next."

Antonio nodded and felt like an idiot for his funky behavior since they'd arrive. "I owe you an apology. I've been a jerk all day. It had nothing to do with you. I was all up in my head, and I'm sorry."

Ben stuck out his hand, and Antonio grasped it before pulling his brother into a man hug where they clapped each other on the back.

"No apology necessary. I know you're ready to settle down and get married. And though you might not believe what I'm about to say, I'm going to say it anyway. Your woman is out there somewhere. I have no doubt we'll be in these tuxes again soon, and it'll be your turn. Maybe even sooner than you realize."

Antonio was fairly sure Ben was referring to Scarlett, though he didn't feel as confident. He could only hope something more would develop between them, but he honestly wasn't so sure. Until he could get a better read on her, he'd try not to get his hopes up. He had made that mistake too many times with women.

While taking a break from dating, one of the things he realized about himself was he moved too fast. He was so set on obtaining his next big goal of having a family that he wasn't taking the time needed to really get to know the women he dated.

That was going to change, and he'd start with Scarlett if she gave him a chance.

He and Ben walked to the sanctuary, where huge vases of

pink and white roses sat on tall clear stands at the front of the church. Bouquets of the same flowers, held together with black, white, and light pink satin ribbons, graced the ends of each pew along the center aisle leading to the altar.

They nodded and greeted their immediate family, who were sitting in the first few pews on the groom's side of the church.

Antonio took his place next to Ben and nudged him before leaning over to whisper in his ear. "You ready for this?"

Ben flashed him the stupid grin that always signified trouble when he was a kid, and Antonio shook his head and chuckled.

"Hell, yeah," his brother said, then winced. "I mean, yes, I am."

They cracked up, and once again, Antonio was glad he was there.

A short while later, the pianist started playing a familiar melody. Two members of the church, a man and a woman, stood near the piano with microphones in their hands. They'd be singing a few songs that Ben and Mahogany had picked out.

Antonio's gaze settled on the double doors at the back of the church where his stepmother, Makena, stood. She was decked out in a long, pale pink dress, similar to Mrs. Amelia's, and she was holding Jayden's hand.

The singers started singing "Love Ballad" by L.T.D, and Jayden escorted Makena down the aisle. His nephew looked sharp in his little black tuxedo, and if the smirk on his face was any indication, the kid knew it.

Antonio grinned as they got closer. It was almost scary how much Jayden was like Ben when it came to self-confidence and maybe even a little bit of arrogance. The kid had been like that since he was two and started talking. If he was like this now, it

19

was going to be interesting for all of them when he became a teenager.

Once Jayden walked McKenna over to her seat in the front row, he stood between him and Ben.

After Mrs. Amelia, Mahogany's mother, was escorted to her seat, Bella appeared in the doorway with a small white basket. Antonio's heart melted as she slowly made her way down the aisle, tossing a few rose petals along the way. He was so proud of her. Normally, she was shy, and Scarlett had been concerned she wouldn't be up for this task with so many people watching. Apparently, Bella was proving her wrong.

As soon as Antonio had that last thought, Bella stopped. She'd made it halfway down the aisle, and now she was nibbling on her bottom lip, looking as if she was going to start crying. It was taking everything in him not to go to her, but...

Jayden sighed loudly, then walked back up the aisle, and Antonio and Ben chuckled softly. When his nephew reached Bella and gently grabbed her hand, the little girl gave him a timid smile as he guided her the rest of the way.

"My boy," Ben whispered, and Antonio was just as proud of his nephew.

One thing he could say about the Jenkins men, no matter their age, they were taught early on how to be gentlemen.

Jayden walked Bella over to the bride's side in front of the pews where normally other bridesmaids would stand. But she and Scarlett would be the only two standing up for Mahogany. Jayden had barely returned to his position when Bella scurried over to them, and the wedding guests laughed.

She glanced up at Antonio, and he winked at her, making her smile. What shocked him, though, was when she slipped her small hand into his. He bent down to whisper in her ear. "You did great, baby."

She flashed another adorable smile at him. "Thank you."

Ben cleared his throat loud enough for Antonio to glance at him, and his brother motioned with his head for Antonio to look toward the back of the church.

Air lodged in his throat. Scarlett, in all her glory, stood in the doorway of the sanctuary, and Antonio was sure he had never seen a more beautiful sight. As she started down the aisle, stepping to the beat of the music, it was as if everyone in the room disappeared. All he could see was her.

Beautiful didn't begin to describe how stunning she looked with her hair pinned up in an elaborate twist, makeup flawless, and that sexy ass dress had him clutching his chest. Antonio cursed under his breath as a heaviness pressed down on him. Though he was sure no one heard him, Ben chuckled and nudged him with his arm.

Antonio ignored him. He couldn't tear his attention from Scarlett. She commanded the room as she glided toward the front of the church as if being carried on a cloud.

From the first day Antonio met her at Mahogany's birthday party months ago, he had thought her the prettiest woman he'd ever laid eyes on. But it was more than that. She had beauty and brains. A dangerous combination where his heart was concerned.

As his gaze followed her every step, an intense, overwhelming sensation settled around him. There was an electric current pulsing between them even from a distance, and it was taking everything within him to stay up right.

"Goodness," he murmured, suddenly struggling to get air into his lungs.

"Breathe, dude. Can't have you passing out on us," Ben cracked, and Antonio ignored him.

She's the one, a voice in the back of his mind yelled. *She's. The. One.*

The words were blaring in his head like a car alarm in a

21

quiet neighborhood, and Antonio felt them to the depths of his soul. Was his brain messing with him? Or was this some type of premonition? Or maybe he was losing his mind.

"I told you. Your day is coming," Ben whispered. "The Jenkins men's myth is not a myth. Brace yourself. Your world is about to be *rocked*."

"Man, shut up," Antonio said out the side of his mouth.

He had heard about that stupid myth. He didn't believe in such crap, but before he could say as much, Scarlett's gaze slammed into him, and she smiled. The electric current charging through his body was more powerful than being tased, and Antonio stood frozen in place.

He tried to return her smile, but he wasn't sure if his facial muscles were cooperating. He couldn't move, and it was starting to wig him out. It wasn't until she was in her spot on the other side of the aisle across from him and Ben that he snapped out of whatever fog had descended on him.

He swallowed hard and blinked several times before gazing around the sanctuary. Thankfully, no one seemed to be paying him any mind. That was intense and scary as hell. Like nothing he'd ever experienced before. His breathing was still a little erratic, but after inhaling and exhaling slowly, he didn't feel as lightheaded.

Be cool, he told himself, and then Bella squeezed his hand while she was shifting in place. Antonio had momentarily forgotten that she was standing next to him. Yeah, he was tripping, and he needed to pull himself together before he embarrassed himself.

He leaned down and whispered into Bella's ear. "Do you want to go and stand next to your mother?"

She glanced at Scarlett and then back up at him and nodded. After a slight hesitation, she ran to Scarlett's side.

The music changed and as the ushers unrolled the white

runner for Mahogany to walk down the aisle on, the guests stood. Seconds later, Mahogany appeared in the doorway looking like an angel. The two soloists started singing "The Point of It All" by Anthony Hamilton, and everyone *oohed* and *ahhed* at the sight of her. His dad, dressed like him and Ben in a black tux, looked dapper as he escorted Mahogany down the aisle.

Ben tugged on his bowtie as beads of sweat popped out on his forehead. Antonio leaned close to him. "You all right, Bro? You aren't going to pass out on me, are you?" he whispered, and chuckled when Ben growled under his breath.

Unable to help himself, Antonio stole a glance at Scarlett and was shocked to find her looking at him. She dropped her gaze quickly as if surprised to be caught staring. He didn't know what was going through that beautiful head of hers. Did she feel as off-kilter as he'd felt a moment ago?

She's the one, the voice inside his head screamed again.

Jeez, could Ben be right? Was the Jenkins men's myth true? Could his mind, body, and soul really know who he'd end up with? Who his soulmate might be?

Antonio shook the thought free. No way. All types of nonsense went on within his family. He'd lived the craziness for the last thirty-three years. This myth thing was probably another ridiculous conception that some family member made up.

But what if it wasn't? What if Scarlett really was the one for him? And if she was, how would he know for sure?

He had more questions than answers, but maybe if he took his time and didn't scare her off, he could get a better read on her. Maybe.

23

Chapter Four

Wow. Just, wow.

Scarlett tried to stop herself from glancing at Antonio every ten seconds, but she couldn't. It was as if she was looking at a different man than the straight-lace, reserved guy she'd gone out with several times.

This version of Antonio, the version in a black tuxedo with satin lapels on the jacket that emphasized his powerfully wide shoulders and broad chest, was downright *fiiine* with a capital "F." Not that he wasn't handsome on any given day. Normally, on their dates, he dressed conservatively with a button-down shirt, khakis, or dress pants.

Not this evening, though. Right now, he was absolutely scrumptious. He had her lady parts pulsing with need. It had been awhile since she'd been this turned on by just the sight of a man. Antonio favored Charles Michael Davis, her celebrity crush, and she was tempted to do something insane. Like sashay over to where he stood, leap into his arms, and kiss him senseless.

Yeah, that wouldn't be weird at all.

If her sister thought she'd been acting strange lately, that would definitely have Mahogany setting up an intervention. But *dang*, the man was totally lickable. That handsome face with his gorgeous dark eyes, perfectly groomed goatee, and those kissable lips were calling to her. Add all that to the diamond stud earrings glittering in his ears, and he was too sexy to be ignored.

There was another side of Antonio Jenkins which he probably didn't let many people see often.

And I have clearly lost my mind if this is what I'm thinking about during my sister's wedding.

Scarlett quickly diverted her gaze when Antonio glanced over and caught her staring. Forcing herself to stop thinking about him, she tuned back into the ceremony, smiling as Mahogany and Ben exchanged vows. Seeing them so happy made her happy, and she had no doubt that their marriage would last until eternity.

"I now pronounce you husband and wife. You may kiss your bride," the minister said, and as the couple kissed, the room exploded into applause and cheers.

Holding her flower bouquet in the crook of her arm, Scarlett clapped along with everyone else, grinning like a proud mama. If she was this excited, Mahogany had to be even more thrilled about this new chapter in her life.

As if reading her mind, her sister glanced at her with shiny eyes and the biggest smile on her face. She turned fully and pulled Scarlett into a tight hug.

"Thank you for being a part of my special day. I love you."

"I love you too, Sis. I'm so happy for you," Scarlett said, giving her a squeeze before releasing her.

Music started playing and Ben and Mahogany, hand in hand, started strolling up the aisle. Jayden and Bella fell in step behind them.

Scarlett's gaze slid over to Antonio, and when he smiled, flashing twin dimples, a frisson of excitement sent goose bumps scurrying over her body. She was a sucker for dimples, and because he didn't smile often, they always caught her off guard. Even with the light dusting of facial hair, they peeked through as if winking at her.

She couldn't help but return his smile as they moved toward each other. They'd been instructed to link arms and follow behind Jayden and Bella. There would be a receiving line in the hallway outside of the sanctuary, and then they'd go to the lower level for a sit-down dinner.

"You look stunning," Antonio whispered when she slid her hand into the crook of his bent arm.

"Thank you. You do too."

As they strolled up the aisle, his intoxicating fragrance danced around her, and she inhaled deeply. *Goodness,* he smelled amazing. Whatever cologne or aftershave he was wearing had a woodsy scent with a hint of vanilla and something spicy that made her pulse beat a little faster.

When they reached the hallway, Antonio deposited her next to Mahogany, but he didn't release her hand. His intense, dark gaze met hers as he slowly brought the back of her fingers to his gorgeous lips.

Scarlett's heart stuttered, and she swallowed hard as her quivering nerves got the best of her. The tenderness of the kiss was as potent as a hot and heavy make-out session. Then he flashed those damn dimples again and winked at her before taking his spot on the side of Ben. He was really pouring on the charm while she wanted to take things slow with him.

Mahogany cleared her throat, and Scarlett's gaze snapped to her sister's knowing look.

"You clearly left a few things out of our conversation," she murmured with a smirk, and Scarlett sighed heavily as the guest headed toward them.

Yeah, she might've underestimated Antonio's charming ways.

* * *

She's avoiding me.

Hours after the sit-down dinner, Antonio stood near one of the bars set up in his grandparents' ballroom. He was sipping from his glass of Jack Daniels, pondering why Scarlett was avoiding him. He shouldn't have kissed her earlier, even if it was just a peck on the hand. It had been the wrong move.

It was no wonder his cousins used to joke about him being socially awkward. Antonio mostly kept to himself, and when in the presence of an alluring woman, he wasn't as smooth as some of his cousins. If he were, he wouldn't have done something so cheesy as kiss the back of Scarlett's fingers. Not only that, but he also wouldn't have done it in front of others.

But something had come over him in that moment, and he hadn't been thinking straight. It was the only way to explain his need to touch her, hold her, hell, even kiss her. He had brought her hand to his lips before thinking, and now he wanted to kick himself for doing it in front of his brother and sister-in-law. Scarlett's startled expression had quickly turned into embarrassment.

Antonio shook his head in disgust and sipped his drink as he recalled how reserved she'd been during the family's sit-down dinner at the church. They'd had to sit next to each other, and though small talk flowed between them, it hadn't been like their usual easy-going conversations. He hadn't missed her discomfort. Unfortunately, that hadn't been a good place to apologize for making her uncomfortable after the wedding.

Now, after the toasts had been made, the bridal bouquet tossed, and the reception was in full swing, Scarlett had disappeared. She hadn't left the celebration, according to Mahogany, but she had done a good job keeping her distance from Antonio.

He brought his glass to his lips as he watched his cousin Martina approach. Gone was her usual T-shirt, blue jeans, and ponytail. Instead, her hair was loosely curled and hung past her shoulders, and she wore a sleek black, halter jumpsuit with sky-high heels. She sure didn't look like the master carpenter who he worked with every day.

Martina might drive the rest of the family nuts with her snooping and troublemaking ways, but she and he got along great. More like brother and sister than first cousins. Antonio could always count on her for anything whether work related or personal. She always came through.

"So, where's your girl?" she said over the loud music.

Antonio cocked an eyebrow at her. "What are you talking about?"

"Don't play dumb. It's not a good look." She lifted her hand to get the bartender's attention. "You and Scarlett have been tap-dancing around each other all day. The way you guys have been stealing glances at each other when you think no one's looking is almost cute." She made a gagging noise while pretending to stick her finger down her throat, and then rolled her eyes. "You're practically in love with her, and there's no doubt that she's feeling you. I don't under—"

"Wait." Antonio frowned and moved closer, not wanting to have to yell over the music. He also didn't want anyone else hearing their conversation. "You can tell that by just looking at Scarlett?"

He didn't bother correcting her about the *practically in love* comment. Whatever feelings he had for Scarlett were confusing as hell. He was pretty sure it wasn't love, but today, the strange electric currents pulsing between them was unexplainable. It was also unnerving how Martina picked up on whatever was going on between him and Scarlett.

"You cannot be that dense," she said with irritation in her tone. "The sister is straight up feeling you. Although, I'm not quite sure why she's keeping her distance." She shrugged. "No worries. I'm sure I'll figure it out soon."

All Antonio could do was stare at his cousin. It didn't matter how old he got, he would probably never understand how the female mind worked. Unfortunately, there were days when he didn't even want to try, but when it came to Martina, there was no telling what she was cooking up. And he already knew she was up to something.

"Don't give me that look," she said as the bartender approached, and she ordered a glass of cabernet. It had been an open bar until ten. Now it was almost ten-thirty, and everyone was paying for their own drinks.

"Stay out of it, MJ," Antonio said, using her childhood nickname. He slipped his wallet from his pocket and set enough cash on the bar top to cover her drink and a sizable tip.

"Thanks, Cuz. Get Paul to pay you back when you see him," she said of her husband and grabbed her wine. "Oh, and don't move. I'll find Scarlett and send her over here, and for God's sake, ask her to dance. Then make your intentions known."

Antonio growled under his breath as Martina started walking away. "I said stay out of it!" he called after her. She threw her head back and laughed though he couldn't hear the sound over the music.

Martina was a mixed bag of brilliant and irritating. Right now, he might be experiencing a combination of both. But he didn't like the idea of her interfering in whatever was happening between him and Scarlett.

Antonio drained his drink and set the glass on the bar. When he turned, it was as if he was living a Bible story moment —when Moses parted the Red Sea. Scarlett materialized through a throng of people looking like a goddess. And she was headed his way.

Chapter Five

A ntonio's gaze traveled over her hourglass figure, loving the natural sway of her shapely hips as she got closer. When she was within reach, a smile kicked up the corners of his lips. At around five feet eight, she appeared taller tonight thanks to several inches that her high heels gave her. When she stopped in front of him, they weren't quiet eye to eye, but it wouldn't take much to bend down and kiss her gorgeous red lips.

"Hi," she said, barely audible. "Martina said you wanted to talk to me."

Despite his reservations about MJ getting involved in his business, he was going to have to thank her. He might also have to thank the DJ, too, since he slowed down the music. "Let Me Love You," a slow jam by Mario, played through the speakers. It was perfect timing. He wouldn't be surprised if Martina was behind that too.

"Dance with me," Antonio said. Not giving her a chance to decline, he reached for Scarlett's hand and gently tugged her toward the dance floor. He skirted around groups of people until they reached it.

Showing off some of his dance moves, he spun her, then dipped her before pulling her into his arms.

"Sure, I'll dance with you," she said sarcastically and chuckled.

Antonio grinned down at her. "I appreciate that."

He held Scarlett's right hand cradled against his chest while his other arm tightened around her narrow waist and snuggled her close. As the smooth melody filled the crowded space, they swayed to the beat.

This was what he'd wanted all evening. Maybe all his life. Her, fitting perfectly in his arms, pressed against his body. They stared into each other's eyes, and it was as if everyone around them faded away.

"I never would've guessed you were such a good dancer," she said and rested her head against his shoulder.

"I'm full of surprises," Antonio said, but in all honesty, he really wasn't. He was a routine type of guy, but his orderly life had served him well.

He inhaled Scarlett's delicate scent and hummed along as they swayed to the sensual beat. Having her snug against him, her firm breasts pressed into his chest heightened every nerve in his body. Holding her so close had him wound tighter than an extension spring keeping a bed together, and he wanted more. Not just from her, but also for his life. He worked ridiculous hours, and even more since he had taken a break from dating, but Scarlett made him want to live a little.

He spun her again and pulled her back into his arms, then whispered close to her ear, "I'm sorry if I embarrassed you earlier. I would never intentionally do anything to make you uncomfortable."

She leaned her head back slightly as they continued swaying. When she smiled, something brightened inside of him, and heat soared through his body. "I wasn't uncomfortable. Shocked maybe, but not uncomfortable. The kiss was sweet and tender."

That made him smile down at her. Staring into her beautiful brown eyes had his pulse pounding a little faster. Being this close to her, holding and touching her had his body stirring with need. But he promised himself he would take things as slow as necessary with Scarlett. Something was holding her back, and he hoped one day she would trust him enough to tell him. That was assuming he didn't scare her away before then.

"You should smile more often," she said, laying her head back against his shoulder as another slow song started.

"I will as long as you're in my life," he said.

Scarlett slowed, probably surprised by his response, but Antonio didn't release her, forcing her to keep moving. The words had tumbled out of his mouth before he could stop them. Yet, they were true. When he was around her, or even just the sight of her, brought him a certain joy that he didn't feel with anyone else.

Yes, it sounded crazy, but the more he thought about it, he realized her presence in his life had opened a part of him which he usually kept closed off from others. She made him happy.

When the slow song ended, and a faster one started, Antonio guided her off the dance floor. She didn't pull away, and he would count that as a win.

"Thanks for the dance," he said close to her ear when they stood off to the side.

"You're welcome. I enjoyed it." She glanced at the slim watch on her wrist. "I think I should head out. It was good seeing you today. Are we still on for the concert next Saturday?"

"Of course," he said quickly. He couldn't wait to have her

to himself. Spending time with her over the last couple of days was nice, but they'd been surrounded by their families. Saturday, it would be just the two of them.

"I'll walk you out." With a hand at the small of her back, he escorted her out into the hallway. Noting that the area was clear, Antonio backed her against a nearby wall.

With wide eyes, Scarlett stared up at him. It wasn't fear he saw, but surprise and desire radiating in her dark orbs. Probably what she saw in his. The urge to kiss her was stronger than he had ever felt for any other woman in his life.

Let her know your intentions. Martina's words rattled inside his head.

Despite that other voice in the back of his mind, insisting this woman was the one for him, Antonio wasn't a hundred percent sure of his intentions. Not exactly.

"What are you doing?" Scarlett whispered as her hands gripped his biceps in a death grip.

"Probably making a big mistake, but..."

Antonio let his words trail off and wasted no time in covering her lips with his. She gasped into his mouth, but a second later, she kissed him back with an urgency that matched his.

When he had followed her out of the ballroom, this hadn't been the plan. He had wanted to spend more time with her and make sure they were cool about what happened earlier.

But this...

Now that he was tasting her, Antonio didn't want to stop.

One of his hands moved to the back of her neck while the other went to her hip as he deepened their connection. It was easy to get swept away by the sweetness of her lips and the sensual moans she was making as their tongues tangled. Desire thrummed through his veins as their kiss became more needy... frantic.

They'd been on a few dates, and he had kissed her after each one. A platonic peck on the lips or on the cheek, but this? It had been nothing like this. The taste of her, the feel of her softness pressed against him, and the heady scent of her perfume were dizzying—in a good way.

Neither of them could deny their attraction to each other. Yet, the sparks igniting within Antonio had him believing this was much more than attraction. They had a connection. An explosive connection like no other.

He wanted her.

He wanted her in every way a man could want a woman, and if this kiss was any indication, she wanted him too.

As soon as that last thought filled his mind, Scarlett suddenly jerked her mouth from his and gasped. Her eyes, wide with shock, met his as she backed up, only to bump into the wall. "I—I... We shouldn't have, well I shouldn't have... Shoot, I have to go. I'll call you."

She pulled away before Antonio could get his body under control and blood back to his brain. With her long dress hiked up, Scarlett ran down the hallway as if being chased by an assailant.

What the hell just happened? One minute they were kissing and exploring each other's mouths, and the next—

Laughter came from behind him, and Antonio closed his eyes and groaned. He didn't have to look over his shoulder to know who was standing behind him.

"Way to make your intentions known, Cuz. But next time maybe try not to freak her out and have her running for the hills."

He whipped around and growled. "MJ, I'm going to kill you. How long have you been standing there?"

"Long enough to catch you two moaning and groaning. *Yuuuck.*" She gave a mock shiver. "Couldn't you have found a

35

more secluded spot?" she said as she sauntered down the hall in the opposite direction laughing wickedly.

That stupid laugh always meant trouble, and of all the people to catch him getting better acquainted with Scarlett, why'd it have to be Martina? Why couldn't it be anybody but her? He was never going to hear the end of it.

Sighing, Antonio rubbed the back of his neck as he glanced in the direction that Scarlett had gone.

So much for not scaring her off.

Chapter Six

Two days later, as she wiped down the kitchen counter before heading upstairs to retire for the evening, Scarlett thought about Antonio. She wouldn't soon forget that amazing kiss they'd shared at the wedding reception the other night. She also wouldn't forget how freaked out she'd gotten when she opened her eyes to find Martina standing behind Antonio grinning.

Scarlett shook her head and chuckled as she recalled that unnerving feeling, like someone had been watching her. Then to see Martina...

"I probably looked like a total idiot," Scarlett mumbled to herself as she made sure the back door was locked.

The situation was funny now, but that night would go down as one of the most embarrassing moments of her life. Not because she got caught kissing a hot guy. No, it had everything to do with her response—running. She must've looked silly running away in her bridesmaid gown like a scared rabbit being chased by a coyote.

How could she ever face Antonio again? Or even Martina

for that matter. According to Mahogany, MJ was the Jenkins family's busybody who enjoyed stirring up trouble. It would be just Scarlett's luck to be the topic of conversation at the next Jenkins Sunday brunch. She had attended a couple and quickly realized some family members loved stirring up drama.

"*Ugh.*" Scarlett growled thinking about what Mahogany was going to say when she found out what happened. Her sister was never going to stop laughing. "So embarrassing," Scarlett mumbled and strolled through the first floor of the house, turning out lights on her way to the stairs.

She and Mahogany were renting a two-story home that Ben Jr. owned in the Clifton area of Cincinnati. They used much of the lower level of the house for their business ventures. Scarlett used the back room for her photography studio and for creating social media content. Mahogany had claimed the living and dining room for her interior design business. The upstairs housed three bedrooms, two bathrooms, and a loft-like sitting area.

Months ago, it had been the perfect space for the three of them. The home was already great before they moved in, but after Mahogany decorated the first floor, it became a gorgeous showroom.

Now that Mahogany was married and had officially moved in with Ben, Scarlett needed to make some decisions. The convenience of living upstairs from where she worked couldn't be beat. Yet, the place felt too big for just her and Bella.

"I'll worry about that another day," she murmured into the quietness of the house.

She had enough on her mind right now, including thoughts of Antonio. She hadn't heard from him since he texted her the night of the wedding reception making sure she arrived home safely. Even though he probably thought he was dealing with a lunatic, she appreciated the gesture. She hadn't been able to apologize enough for leaving like that, but he told her not to worry about it.

The saying, *don't judge a book by its cover*, described Antonio perfectly. He might come across as a straight-lace, introverted nerd, but there was a sexy, sensual side to the man who was calling to Scarlett. And that kiss? She felt that kiss to the depths of her soul—a first. So lost in the pleasurable moment, she'd been oblivious to everything around her. Which was why opening her eyes to find MJ there had freaked her out.

Gawd, but it had been worth it.

Now she and Antonio needed to talk. Like *really* talk.

They—no she—needed to figure out what she wanted from him besides his sexy body. Maybe if she was upfront about her concerns, they could work something out. Scarlett didn't know how, but she wasn't ready to walk away from him. Still, the fear that she might not be able to give him what he was looking for in a woman was still at the forefront of her mind. The thought of her being incapable of falling in love with a man was a real fear. How the heck would she be able to explain that to him.

"If I say something so absurd like that, he really is going to think I'm crazy."

When she made it upstairs, she strolled into Bella's room. Her daughter was curled up with a stuffed animal in her arms and snoring softly. Scarlett gently tugged the toy out of her grasp. She wasn't concerned about waking her. The kid was such a sound sleeper, she could sleep through a tornado.

After placing a kiss on her baby's forehead, Scarlett pulled the door closed and went across the hall to her own bedroom. Before she could head to the attached bathroom for her nightly routine, her cell phone rang.

"Who could be calling this late?" she murmured and pulled the device from her back pocket.

Cynthia?

It was after eleven. Why was Ezra's grandmother trying to FaceTime this late at night?

Scarlett hurried over to the bed and sat down while grabbing her iPad from the nightstand. The bigger screen would be easier for their chat.

"Cynthia? Is everything all right?" Scarlett asked by way of greeting when she clicked on.

Ezra's eighty-year-old grandmother came into view. The woman, who was lying in a huge bed with tons of pillows propped up behind her, could barely keep her eyes open. She also looked like she had aged twenty years in the past week.

Scarlett wanted to ask about her health, but Cynthia usually responded to the question with, *I'm doing all right for an old lady.* Still, Scarlett worried about her. Cynthia didn't really have anyone to look after her except for hired staff. It wasn't the same as having family around.

She probably had her assistant, Nancy, who was a godsend, set up the call. Whatever Cynthia wanted, she got it, and it helped that she was extremely wealthy and had a full staff. Most lived at the mansion and adored her. Which was good since Ezra's parents, specifically, his mother, didn't come around much. According to Cynthia, the relationship with her daughter was almost nonexistent.

"I'm fine, honey." Cynthia's once strong voice sounded weak and tired. "You and Bella were on my mind, and I wanted to see how you two were doing."

Ezra's grandmother was tough and had probably been a force to be reckoned with in her younger years. She never admitted to having health issues, but it was clear that whatever was going on was getting worse.

"We're fine, but I'm worried about you. You should be asleep. What's going on?"

Ezra had adored his grandmother. She had practically

raised him since he didn't get along with his powerhouse parents. His mother was a well-known corporate attorney in Miami, Florida, and his father was a senator or a congressman. Scarlett couldn't remember which.

She stared at the screen of her iPad, concerned for the woman who had quickly become her friend. Ezra would've been heartbroken to see her in this condition.

"Don't look at me like that," Cynthia said with a ragged laugh. "I look worse than I feel. I've been asleep for the last few hours and woke up thinking about my favorite girls. Oh, and how's your young man? Are you two still dating?"

Scarlett was a little taken back. Since she and Cynthia talked weekly, she told her about the wedding, and the wonderful Jenkins family. A few weeks ago, Cynthia had called when Scarlett was preparing to go to a movie with Antonio. She had made it clear to the older woman that she and Antonio were just hanging out, getting to know each other. Apparently, it hadn't been clear enough.

"Cynthia, he's a friend. A really good friend," Scarlett said.

The last part came out a bit more forceful than intended, and Antonio's intense eyes and gorgeous lips flashed through her mind. Then there was that toe-curling kiss. The kiss which she could still feel on her lips at times.

All right, maybe he was more than a friend, but she wouldn't admit that to Ezra's grandmother.

"Okay, dear. If you say so," Cynthia conceded, humor in her tone before she turned serious. "I'd love to see you and Bella. Will you two come and visit me?"

Scarlett only took Bella to Miami to visit Cynthia once a year, suddenly wishing she'd taken her more often. Unfortunately, Scarlett's busy schedule always got in the way. The older woman adored her great-granddaughter, which was why Scarlett made sure they all video chatted at least once a week.

"Yes. I'll see if I can find some flights for us to come in a few weeks. Bella will be out of school soon," Scarlett said, mentally thinking about the commitments she had over the next few weeks.

"I'd like for you two to come this weekend," Cynthia said, sounding more tired than she'd sounded only minutes ago. "Nancy will make all the arrangements. She'll call you in the morning. Though, I would love for you and Bella to stay at the house with me, I never know when Alberta and Theodore might show up," she said of Ezra's parents who didn't know Bella existed.

Scarlett understood that last part. Ezra hated his parents and often said they were dead to him. Cynthia, for the most part, felt the same way. She didn't want them to know about Bella. Always saying they were money and power-hungry politicians who didn't care about anyone but themselves. According to her and Ezra, it was best Scarlett never crossed paths with them.

"Will you come?" Cynthia asked. "Nancy will make the arrangements for your visit, including hotel reservations nearby and a driver. Say you'll come for the weekend."

Bella would miss dance class, and Scarlett had plans with Antonio Saturday night that she hated to cancel, but he would understand. Hopefully. "Yes, we'll come, but you don't have to have Nancy make arrangements. I can—"

"No, it's my pleasure, dear. The least I can do is make sure you two can get here with no problems and have a nice visit. I also need to speak with you about a few important things that can't wait. Something which can't be discussed over the phone."

Unease clawed down Scarlett's spine at the no-nonsense tone that Cynthia's voice had taken on. What could they possibly have to discuss that was so important?

Chapter Seven

After the conversation with Cynthia, Scarlett hadn't been able to shut her brain off and had tossed and turned for much of the night. Considering she was one of those people who needed eight hours of sleep to function, she wasn't sure how she'd survive with only three. So far, the two cups of strong coffee she'd had before leaving home were helping. But they'd done nothing to calm her worries for her friend. Her overactive imagination had her thinking the worst.

But here she was, sitting in her Nissan Rogue in Antonio's driveway, drinking a mocha cappuccino. As if she hadn't already had enough to drink, she had purchased it, along with bagels, after dropping Bella off at school.

On a whim, Scarlett had shown up at Antonio's place because she had to cancel their date for Saturday night. The initial plan had been to call him first thing this morning and express her regrets about having to bail on him. Instead, since she hadn't been too far from his house, she convinced herself to talk to him in person. In her mind, that would be better than canceling over the phone. Hopefully, he hadn't left for work yet.

"All right, let's do this." She grabbed her coffee, purse, and the bag of fresh bagels before climbing out of the car. Antonio wasn't a coffee drinker, but she hoped he liked bagels.

As she trudged up the walkway, Scarlett glanced around at the charming homes. Everything from Tudor to craftsman style dwellings. No two homes were the same on the tree-lined street with perfectly manicured yards. Antonio had lived in his home for years, and based on one of their conversations, he had no intentions of moving anytime soon.

Who could blame him? The large, stately brick home was lovely on the outside with flagstone pavers as the walkway, flowers which were already starting to bloom, and an inviting porch that she could see drinking coffee out on. The inside was just as impressive.

After climbing the wood stairs, Scarlett readjusted the bag in her hand and rang the doorbell. Seconds ticked by and she fidgeted while waiting for him to answer the door.

I should've called first, she thought and rang the doorbell again. He was an early riser, and it was almost eight o'clock in the morning. Maybe he had left for work earlier than usual, or maybe he was still out for his morning run. Something he usually did before heading into work around nine.

"I should call him." But that would mean returning to her vehicle to get her phone, which she just remembered was in the cupholder.

This was ridiculous. She should have done that in the first place. Her brain clearly wasn't operating on all cylinders yet.

Just as she started down the stairs, she spotted a lone figure jogging up the street. It was Antonio. He almost stopped when he saw her but then picked up speed.

Scarlett took in his appearance and heat rushed through her veins.

"*Ooh wee.*" It was all she could say as he jogged toward her looking like a tasty snack. It was a wonder that women weren't chasing behind him because the man was sex on a stick. If she thought he was smoking hot in a tuxedo, Antonio in running gear was *fire* hot if that were a legitimate description.

The short-sleeve athletic shirt molded to his upper body, hugged his thick biceps, and showcased his wide chest and flat abs. She swiped her tongue across her lips remembering how good it had felt to be in his arms and hugged up to his incredible body the other night. Still, she had no idea he was built like this.

Her gaze traveled to his running shorts that weren't super tight, but she could still make out his thick package as his long, muscular legs and even strides brought him closer. Then there were the aviator sunglasses and the way he was wearing his baseball cap turned backwards on his head. The man was giving off all kinds of bad-boy vibes, and she liked everything she saw.

She wasn't sure what to make of Antonio anymore. He was surprising her at every turn, and the more she learned about him, the more she wanted to know. Mostly. There was still the fear that she was incapable of being more than friends, but her curiosity was piqued.

"Hey, what are you doing here?" Antonio asked as he cut across the grass. "You okay?" he panted, his words coming out in a rush as concern radiated in his dark, amber eyes. He had slipped off his sunglasses and hung them on the front collar of his athletic shirt.

Heart pounding fast, Scarlett shuffled from one foot to the other. Keyed up from the coffee, she couldn't seem to stand still.

"I'm-fine-sorry-to-just-drop-by-I-wanted-to-talk-to-you," she said, her words flying from her mouth in rapid-fire succession. "After-taking-Bella-to-school-I-decided-to-stop-by-I-know-I-should've-called-but—"

"Hey, take a breath," Antonio said, slipping one arm around her waist and guiding her back up the stairs and to the door. "You're always welcome here. No call necessary."

He unlocked the door, then ushered her inside before turning off the house alarm.

"Let's head to the kitchen," he said.

With one hand at the small of her back, Antonio nudged her straight ahead to where the house opened up to the family room, kitchen, and an eating area. Without releasing her, he set his baseball cap on a bar stool and had her sit on the other stool next to it. Then he took the coffee out of her hand.

"Hey!" Scarlett leaped from her seat. "I'm not done with that."

"I'm not sure how much caffeine you've had, but I think it's safe to say you've had enough. Scarlett, you're practically vibrating." He poured the rest of her drink into the sink.

"Maybe, but—"

"I have something else for you. Something that won't have you bouncing around like you're on an out-of-control pogo stick."

A smile played around Scarlett's lips at the visual that his words made. Antonio's sense of humor peeked out occasionally, but not enough to know if he was really funny. Who knows, maybe a funny bone was another one of his wonderful qualities.

She watched as he washed his hands in the sink before moving about his kitchen with ease. A kitchen that was like something out of *House Beautiful* magazine. Mahogany had told her that the Jenkins family all enjoyed cooking, and their spaces reflected that. Antonio's inviting kitchen was no different with its top-of-the-line stainless steel appliances, custom oak cabinets, and marbled quartz countertops.

He pulled a tall glass from the cabinet near the dishwasher, then moved over to the refrigerator, where he took out bottled water and a pitcher of green stuff. Which reminded her.

"Oh, I brought bagels. All different types," she said, temporarily forgetting the bag in her hand. "Wait. Do you like bagels?"

"Yeah. Thanks."

Scarlett placed the small bag on the breakfast bar just as Antonio set a glass of green stuff on the counter, straw and all. Then slid it over to her.

"Drink," he said gruffly, and opened one of the bottles of water for himself.

Scarlett eyed the green concoction warily. "What is it?"

"A smoothie with kale, berries, a banana, Greek yogurt, and flax seed. It'll give you energy without the jitters."

She scrunched her nose, wishing it was just a fruit smoothie, but tried it anyway. Surprisingly, a burst of flavors hit her tongue including strawberry and blueberry. Her favorite fruits.

"Wow, this tastes a lot better than it looks," she commented and flashed him a smile before drinking more.

She sipped, trying not to stare when Antonio lifted the tail of his shirt, wiped his sweat-slicked face, then let the garment fall back into place. But not before she got a peek at smooth dark skin, rippling muscles, and a six-pack that would make other men jealous.

Yeah, there was so much more to Antonio than his brilliant mind and handsome face. He also had a body fit for a god.

After he downed the whole bottle of water, he set the empty container on the counter and gave her his complete attention. He was standing in front of her on the other side of the bar with his thick arms folded across his chest. His legs were spread shoulder-width apart, and his demeanor reeked of power and no-nonsense.

"So, are you ready to tell me what's on your mind?" Then he lifted his hand. "Hold that thought for a minute and don't move. I'll be right back."

He disappeared up the stairs, which gave her time to take a breath. Antonio was probably right about the coffee. Her heart was beating faster than normal, but she wasn't sure if it was because of the caffeine or the fact that she was at Antonio's house. She could've easily had this conversation over the telephone.

Ten minutes later, he returned wearing a gray Polo shirt instead of the running shirt, and a pair of black pants and black work boots. It was clear that he had showered. His fresh, masculine scent was evident the moment he moved past her to reclaim his standing position on the other side of the counter. "Okay, now tell me what's going on."

"First, I need to apologize for the other night," Scarlett started. "I shouldn't have run off the way I did, and I don't have a good excuse. But I will admit, MJ caught me off guard. Your cousin is a trip."

Antonio grunted and shook his head. "You have no idea. She lives to freak people out, and she's like a ghost sometimes in the way she sneaks up on you. So, no apology necessary. If anything, I'm sorry that she interrupted us."

He dropped his arms to his side and slowly moved around the bar. When he stopped next to her stool, Scarlett lifted her head which made the bar stool swivel slightly. Now she was facing him.

"What?" she said when he didn't say anything. Only stood there searching her eyes.

"I thought maybe you had run off because I had kissed you. I told you before, I never want to do anything to make you uncomfortable. If the kiss—"

"The kiss was amazing," she said without hesitation. Yes, it had surprised her, but it was hands down the most toe-curling kiss she'd had in a long time, if ever.

"I'm glad to hear that because I want to kiss you again," he whispered and moved closer, not seeming to care that he was invading her personal space. He didn't stop until he was standing between her legs.

When Antonio cupped her cheek with his large hand, Scarlett leaned into his touch as she slid her tongue out to moisten her lips.

She wanted to kiss him more than she wanted her next breath. Since that night at the reception, she hadn't been able to stop thinking about that kiss. Had the connection she'd felt been real? Or had she just gotten caught up in the moment? It was possible, especially with love flowing through the air after such a beautiful wedding.

Now she was getting a chance to determine if the electric currents that had flowed through her during their intense lip-lock had been genuine.

Antonio lowered his head and covered her mouth with his, and all thoughts of the other night fled her mind. His tenderness when dealing with her since they first met was just as prevalent in the way he kissed her. There was a quiet calmness about him. Yet, his expert lips threw a powerful punch that rocked her to her core, and she yearned to explore every part of this man.

Her fingers gripped the front of his shirt, and she stood on shaky legs, needing to be closer. She slid her hands up his chest, over his shoulders, and wrapped her arms around his neck and held on.

Antonio's hands traveled down her sides until he gripped her hips, pulling her tightly against him. She felt his hardness pressed against her lower stomach as their tongues tangled. Erotic moans filled the air. Lust flowed through her body, and Scarlett could admit this kiss was more intense than the one they'd shared the other day.

This was proof. Their connection was as solid as she'd thought. At least their physical connection was. She still had to be careful with him, with his heart. Hell, with both their hearts. She and Ezra had a similar connection early on, but she never fell in love with him. Would that be the case with Antonio? Or would it be different?

There was something special about this man. Maybe, just maybe, he was the one to prove that nothing was wrong with her. That she was capable of a forever type of love.

A piercing alarm sounded, and Scarlett startled. Panting, they jerked apart, and Antonio mumbled something and moved to the counter near the refrigerator. The alarm was from his cell phone, and he shut it off.

"I should go," Scarlett blurted. She had momentarily forgotten she had bogarted her way into his morning routine. "I don't want you to be late for work."

"No, you're fine. Besides, I'm sure there's another reason you stopped by. Come on."

With a hand on her elbow, he led her out of the kitchen and into the cozy family room. The space was simply decorated with plush, tan carpeting, and a forest-green sectional that sat across from a white brick fireplace. Instead of a mantel, a huge television hung above it. Also, on each side of it were built-in shelves housing photos, books, and other trinkets. A large recliner rounded out the space and sat in the corner near a window.

"Have a seat," Antonio said, nodding at the inviting sectional.

"I don't want to get too comfortable. I've already taken enough of your time."

"Don't worry about that. Sit down."

His tone left no room for argument, and if he wasn't worried about being late, she wouldn't either. He was one of the bosses at his family's construction company and probably could show up whenever he wanted. But knowing Antonio, she'd bet he was one of those people who was never late and rarely called in.

When Scarlett sat down, he sat next to her, their bodies touching. "Tell me what's going on." He pulled her close to him until she was in the crook of his arm, her head resting against his solid chest.

The combination of soap and a woodsy scent wafted past her nose, and Scarlett settled against him and sighed. It had been a while since a man held her like this. It reminded her of what she'd been missing. Someone to cuddle with. Someone, other than her sister or mother, to talk to, and someone to care enough to wonder what was going on with her.

That had been one of several reasons why she had decided it was time to start dating again. She was tired of being alone. Bella might bring her more joy than she could explain, but sometimes it was nice to be with a man.

Then her reason for stopping by bombarded her mind and frustration nipped at her nerves. "I hate to do this, but I need to cancel our date for Saturday night."

Chapter Eight

"Unfortunately, I won't be able to attend the concert with you on Saturday. I have to fly to Miami this weekend. Bella's great-grandmother lives there in Coral Gables."

Scarlett waited for a reaction, but Antonio didn't say anything. Nor did he move. Instead, he continued holding her while his hand gently ran up and down her bare arm. To say it was soothing was an understatement. She felt more relaxed than she'd felt in the last twenty-four hours.

She lifted her head slightly and glanced at him. When she met his intense gaze, those damn butterflies that often took flight in her stomach when he looked at her were back. He really was a beautiful man, but his stare could be a bit unnerving at times.

"Did you hear me?" she asked.

"Yeah, I was waiting for you to finish," he said simply, still caressing her arm.

"Oh." She returned to her position and sighed.

He knew of Ezra. Well, he knew Ezra was Bella's father,

and he had passed away before she was born. He didn't know anything about Scarlett's relationship with him, though, and there was no need to talk about it. Instead, she recounted the conversation she'd had with Cynthia and told him about her concern for the woman. Specifically, that she didn't think Bella's great-grandmother was well.

"The last thing I want to do is cancel on you, but since she asked me to come this weekend, I'm thinking I really should. I'll pay you back for the concert ticket. Unless..."

Unless you want to take someone else, she almost said, but she couldn't make herself finish the sentence. That would be like pushing him into another woman's arms.

Then again, just because she couldn't go didn't mean that he shouldn't, but she doubted he would. Going to a Maxwell concert should be experienced with someone special. Someone you were romantically interested in.

And the thought of him taking another woman was... Well, it didn't sit right with her. Scarlett didn't want to imagine Antonio enjoying the concert with someone else, and that was just selfish. She should want him to go and have a good time.

"Unless what?" Antonio asked, his quiet tone cutting into her erratic thoughts.

"Unless you umm... Unless you want to take someone else," she said quietly, hating to even give him that idea.

"I don't. And you don't have to reimburse me," he said.

Scarlett sighed. She hated this. Sure, there might not be a future for them as anything more than friends, but canceling after promising to go out with him made her feel awful.

Antonio might be a little too serious, rarely smiling, and not a big talker, but he was a sweetheart. He was also a great catch. Any woman would be lucky to snag him. Unless Scarlett got her act together, it wouldn't be her.

"Did Bella tell you that she asked me to go to the father-daughter dance with her?" he asked, switching the subject.

Scarlett smiled. She forgot to thank him for making her daughter so happy. "Actually, she told me that she doesn't need me to go because her Uncle Tony was going with her. She said I can stay home. I'm not sure if I should be thanking you or be offended that she kicked me to the curb so easily."

Antonio didn't say anything, and when Scarlett glanced up at him, he was smiling, dimples and all. She returned her head to his chest. There was comfort in hearing his steady heartbeat against her ear. So what if he wasn't a big talker? His calming presence more than made up for his lack of words.

"She really likes you," she said of Bella. "Outside of Jayden, I have never seen her take to anyone so quickly before."

"My grandmother calls that the Jenkins men's charm." He gave a slight shrug which jostled her a bit. "Women are defenseless against it."

Scarlett snorted a laugh. She laughed even harder when she glanced up to find him with a serious expression on his face. The fact he could say that with a straight face made it even more hilarious.

"What's so funny?" he asked in all seriousness, and she lost it, rolling away from him and laughing harder.

This man. He really needed to lighten up some.

When Scarlett finally pulled herself together, she settled back on the sofa a few feet away from him. "You're something else. You know that?" she said, dabbing at her eyes with the back of her hand. She wasn't worried about smearing mascara since she hadn't bothered putting on makeup.

"Is that a good something else?" Antonio asked, surprising her.

Scarlett searched his unwavering dark amber eyes and got

lost in their depths. He was definitely getting under her skin, in a good way. Some of her concerns about allowing him to get closer were easing.

"It's a very good something else," she finally said. "Would you be interested in going to Miami with us for the weekend?"

Wait! That's not what she'd planned to say. Hell, she wasn't sure what she'd been about to say.

Antonio's left eyebrow shot up, and his expression said, *seriously?* Her expression probably telegraphed the same message, but now that she had posed the question, inviting him wasn't a bad idea.

"Yeah, come with us. We're leaving Friday and returning Monday evening. I can ask Nancy to get you on our flight and reserve another hotel room. Or we can see about finding a two-bedroom suite. I know Bella would be thrilled if you spent the weekend with us."

"You said Bella would be thrilled to have me on the trip, but what about you Scarlett? Do you want me to go?"

"Yes," she said without hesitation. "I want you to go. Besides, a little birdie told me that you need a vacation."

Antonio snorted. "With my family, that could've been any one of them."

"If you can't go, I understand, but—"

"I would love to spend the weekend with you and Bella, but we won't need hotel rooms. I have a vacation home in Miami that I don't use nearly enough. We can stay there."

* * *

They landed in Miami over an hour ago, and Antonio still couldn't believe Scarlett had invited him to vacation with them. The invite the other morning had been one of several surprises by her that day. Finding her on his doorstep after his run, had rocked him. At first, Antonio thought he was seeing things, but when the shock wore off, concern took over. His blood pressure had skyrocketed until he was assured she was all right.

Antonio smiled as he glanced at her in the passenger seat sound asleep and then through the rearview mirror at Bella, who was asleep in the back. Nothing could get him down today. Spending time with the most exquisite woman in the world and her precious daughter was the boost he needed. Add to the fact that they were making a long weekend out of this Miami trip, and he felt like he was floating on air.

Scarlett mumbled something in her sleep, and Antonio glanced at her. They'd left Cincinnati at the crack of dawn, and after being on a flight for a couple of hours, she looked totally pulled together. Her hair was twisted in individual medium-size braids, with one side covering her right eye and the rest hanging to her shoulders. Her makeup, though she didn't need any, was flawless as usual.

Then there was her outfit. The outfit that made him have to glare at a few guys who thought it was okay to check her out. The stylish olive-green jacket and pants set seemed a little dressy to Antonio, but if Scarlett had been trying to catch attention, it worked. Men shot appreciative gazes her way, and there were several women at the airport who stopped to compliment her. To his surprise, his cousin Jada had designed the outfit.

The jacket hung just below Scarlett's shapely ass and belted around her narrow waist. The loose-fitting pants had two huge square pockets down each leg, and a rope-like string which tied at her ankles, bringing attention to her high-heeled sandals.

Antonio had initially thought it was a two-piece suit, but now that she had the jacket hanging open, he noted the sports bra-like top in the same color and material as the jacket and pants.

The woman was already sexy, but her stylish outfits took her appearance to the next level. She looked as if she had just stepped off a fashion runway. If she planned to dress like this for the whole trip, he would have to do some shopping. Otherwise, his polo shirts and khakis might make her embarrassed to be seen with him.

Antonio pulled onto the circular drive of his single-level concrete home and parked in front of the door. He had gotten the three-bedroom, three-bathroom home five years ago for a steal. It had needed a little work, but with the help of his brother and father, they'd renovated it to his specifications. He loved the place, but other family members used it more than he did.

Scarlett jerked awake suddenly and looked around. She and Bella had fallen asleep within minutes of getting into the rental car.

"We're here, Sleepy Head," Antonio said. "Are you feeling okay? You slept the entire flight, and you barely had your seatbelt fastened before you fell asleep again."

"I'm sorry. I'm fine, and I know I'm horrible company today. The last few days have been super busy because I had to move up a couple of photo shoots with some new clients. I've been getting to bed late and getting up early."

"I'm glad Bella insisted on sitting next to you on the airplane. Otherwise, she would've been whining about me dozing off." Scarlett glanced out the passenger side window at the house. "This is lovely, Antonio. I can't wait to see inside."

"Sit tight, and I'll get your door for you. Then I'll get Bella," he said and climbed out.

He and his male cousins had been taught from an early age the importance of being a gentleman. That and learning how to cook were nonnegotiable in their family, and he and his cousins were passing what they knew down to the next generation.

Antonio opened Scarlett's door and extended his hand to her. She took it and smiled up at him, and it was as if someone had pulled open the curtains and let the sunshine in. He wanted to take things slow, but when she looked at him with such adoration, it made him weak in the knees.

She climbed out of the vehicle like the regal queen she was, and it was taking everything within Antonio not to pull her against his body and taste her luscious lips again. He wouldn't. He couldn't mess this trip up by moving too fast. The restraint would test his patience, but in the end, it would be worth it.

But when he started to release her hand, Scarlett held on and smiled at him as she moved closer. He stood still, willing to let her do whatever she had in mind, and his patience paid off. She lifted up on tiptoe and placed a lingering kiss against his lips.

"Thank you for coming with us and for letting us stay at your place."

Antonio gently eased some of her braids away from her eyes. "Believe me when I say it's my pleasure. Oh, and feel free to kiss me whenever you want. My lips are yours."

Dammit. Did that line sound as cheesy to her as it did to his own ears? When she burst out laughing, he got his answer. Smoothness with the women wasn't one of his strengths, but if he could keep her laughing, maybe she'd overlook his weak pickup lines.

"Noted," Scarlett said grinning. "I like kissing you."

"The feeling is mutual."

He wanted to do much more than just kiss her. If he had his way, she'd be officially his by the time they left Miami. Whether the Jenkins myth was a real thing or not, Antonio believed in his heart that Scarlett was his. He had to show her how good they could be together, and this trip was the perfect time to do that.

He just had to stay away from cheesy pickup lines and become a smooth operator.

Surely, it couldn't be that hard. Could it?

Chapter Nine

A sweet thrill pulsed through Scarlett as she followed Antonio who was carrying Bella into the house. It wasn't just because of the tender kiss they'd just shared, but it was also the sight of his firm ass in the khakis he was wearing. His backside was so perfect. She was tempted to reach out and grab his butt cheeks with both hands, then squeeze.

Ha! That wouldn't be weird at all, would it? Who knows, maybe before the trip ended, she'd get to do just that.

Then a thought came to her, she pulled out her cell phone and snapped a few pictures. Not just of his backside, but of Antonio and Bella. She loved how peacefully her daughter slept in his arms, her head resting on his broad shoulder. Scarlett had brought one of her cameras and planned to take plenty more pictures while they were there.

When Antonio picked her and Bella up from home that morning, Scarlett had made a decision. Whatever developed between them this weekend, she was going with it. No overthinking. No second guessing. No letting fear control her. Antonio was too good of a man to not see where this could go.

"All right, here we are," he said as he opened the door to his vacation house and ushered her in.

Scarlett gasped. "Oh, wow. Antonio, this is gorgeous."

The living room and dining area made up the open floor plan, but it was the view beyond the kitchen that caught her attention. A patio door and a wall of windows overlooked a swimming pool and beautiful backyard.

"I'm glad you think so. Come in and make yourself comfortable. I'll lay Bella down in her room, then go back for our luggage."

Her room. Those two words warmed Scarlett from the inside out. Knowing Antonio had designated a room for her daughter might seem small to some, but it meant everything to Scarlett. Bella adored him, and Scarlett loved that Antonio felt the same about her.

She had always wanted her child to grow up with a loving father like she and Mahogany had. Her dad was the best man Scarlett knew, and if Bella could have that...

Whoa. "Just slow your roll, woman," she told herself before her imagination got the best of her.

Yes, Antonio was going to make a wonderful father, but Scarlett didn't want to get ahead of herself. This was new for all of them, and she wanted each one of them to enjoy the journey without any expectations. Antonio made them both happy, and she hoped they brought him some joy too. For now, that was enough.

Instead of dwelling on their relationship, Scarlett shrugged out of her jacket and laid it across the back of an overstuffed floral chair. Everything was different here from his home in Cincinnati, but just as warm and inviting. The walls and furniture were white with various shades of blue and yellow accents throughout the open space.

Scarlett strolled into the kitchen, which wasn't as big as the one in his other home, but it was just as nice and functional. The stainless steel and black appliances gleamed against the pale-yellow walls.

As she approached the patio door and looked outside, she already knew where she'd be spending most of her time. Tall cypress trees along the wood fence provided privacy and framed the perimeter of the yard. The kidney-shaped swimming pool with lighting along the inside edge was definitely the focal point. Well, that and the gurgling waterfall in the far corner.

Her gaze took in the partially covered patio made up of stamped concrete. The stainless-steel outdoor kitchen sat perpendicular to the house, and the table for six, along with cushioned lounge chairs, took up the rest of the space.

"What do you think?"

Scarlett yelped, swung around, and almost slammed into Antonio. "Oh my God, you scared me," she said, her hand on her chest to keep her heart from leaping out.

"Sorry. I thought you heard me come back in." He opened the sliding glass door, and Scarlett realized what she thought was a wall, was accordion glass doors.

"Okay, now I'm really impressed. Talk about indoor-outdoor living. Antonio, this is spectacular."

"Thanks, it took me, my dad, and Ben years to get the place just right, and I like the way everything turned out. The house isn't huge but let me show you the rest of it."

Holding her hand, he took her through the place, explaining what parts were renovated. Which sounded like most of it. She loved the choices they made, and the more she saw, the more she fell in love with his space.

He took her to the guest room where she'd be staying, and it was perfect—like a classy hotel suite. The queen-size bedroom set took up most of the space, but there was a cute reading nook near the window. She also had her own bathroom.

When they reached the room that Bella was in, Scarlett fell a little harder for Antonio. Knowing how much Bella loved pink, there were various shades of it everywhere. He had even managed to add a hanging canopy over the full-size bed. The room was too girly for it to have already been like this. She knew he had done it especially for his *Baby Doll*, as he liked to call Bella.

Her child was going to be thrilled when she woke up. There were even stuffed animals strategically placed around the room, and one on the bed next to her.

"Antonio, I don't know how to thank you for all you've done for me and for Bella. It was enough that you traveled with us, carried our bags, *and* you're letting us stay with you. When did you even have time to arrange this?"

"The day after you invited me on the trip. I wanted to make sure you two were comfortable here. So, I had the house cleaned, stocked with food, and I might've gone a little over-board where Bella is concerned. I hope she'll be happy with the room. Jayden on the other hand will probably be pissed when he visits. This is normally the room he stays in." Antonio shrugged and flashed Scarlett a sexy grin, rewarding her with a peek at his adorable dimples.

They backed out of the room with him still holding her hand. When she invited him on the trip, she had no idea what to expect. She just thought it would be fun to have him come along and hang out so they could get to know each other better. So far, the visit was exceeding her expectations.

"Thanks for everything you've done," she said and squeezed his hand.

"It's my pleasure. I love having you here."

The lust radiating in his dark orbs sent warmth rushing through her body. Their attraction to one another was definitely on the rise, and Scarlett was curious about whether he'd make a move on her.

Did he want to kiss her, touch her, and explore her body as much as she wanted to do to him? She wasn't sure, but if his heated gaze was any indication, he was thinking along those lines.

"Show me your room," she said, her voice low and seductive, though that hadn't been her intent.

His eyebrows shot up in surprise, but then a slow smile crept across his sensual lips. "Right this way."

As they headed in that direction, giddiness bubbled inside of Scarlett, and she almost laughed out loud at herself. She felt like a kid on Christmas morning, anxious to see what presents Santa had in store for her. She was acting as if getting a tour of his bedroom was code for rendezvous, kissing, and hot, sweaty sex. When in fact, Antonio probably only planned to walk her around the space and point out the changes that he'd made since buying the house.

They moved slower than necessary with each other, unsure of how to proceed or even if they wanted to. Considering how she'd kept him at a distance the last few months, Scarlett might have to make the first move.

They reached the master bedroom at the end of the hallway, and she stepped into it and glanced around. Like the rest of the house, the bedroom was bright and airy, and it gave her that warm, cuddly feeling like a cashmere sweater on a chilly day. The room was double the size of the other two, with large, dark masculine furniture that contrasted with the brightly painted walls but together it worked.

When she turned back to Antonio, he was standing with

his shoulder propped against a nearby wall and his muscular arms folded across his chest. He watched her intently, and his smoldering gaze only added to his sexiness.

The man was just too fine. He seemed so cool and comfortable in his skin, and he was tempting as hell.

Scarlett approached him, her gaze volleying between his eyes and his mouth. She was never bold when it came to asking for what she wanted from a man, but this man was different. With Antonio, she felt comfortable, and she knew he would never deny her anything.

"Remember when you said I can kiss you anytime?" she said as she stood before him.

Antonio straightened. "I remember."

He slid his arm around her waist and crushed her against his hard body. His touch ignited like liquid fire against the bare skin between the band of her sports bra and the waistband of her pants.

Goodness, this man had her all twisted up inside—in a good way. She loved that, though he came across as a little grumpy and introverted, he definitely wasn't shy.

Scarlett gasped and her pulse accelerated when he suddenly turned her and backed her against the bedroom door. She hadn't even noticed it was closed, and the moment his mouth covered hers, she didn't care about anything but him.

Her arms went around his neck as his tongue snaked between her lips, and fireworks exploded through her brain. Antonio kissed her with a hunger that she hadn't experienced with him before, and she loved this strong, take-charge side of him.

Yeah, this was what she wanted—his mouth on hers and his hands squeezing her ass.

Pleasure radiated through Scarlett's veins, sending shock waves to every cell in her body. With each lap of his tongue, her senses reeled, short-circuiting her brain as she felt his erection pressed against her lower body.

"Tony," Scarlett moaned, realizing she had shortened his name. She wasn't thinking straight as her desire for him surged.

Antonio growled and ripped his mouth from hers. Before Scarlett could form her next thought, he gripped the back of her thighs and lifted her off the floor. She gasped and held on tightly.

"I promised myself that I would go slow and get to know everything about you," he said, "but you're too damn sexy."

Their mouths met again. Teeth gnashing, tongues tangling, and their groans mingled and pierced the quietness of the bedroom. With her legs wrapped around his waist, Scarlett felt no shame in grinding against him. She was already wet for him. The sensualness of his mouth on her body and how good he felt between her thighs was almost too much.

If only their clothes weren't in the way. She wanted Antonio bad enough to beg for him to take her. Right then. Right there.

"Scarlett," he growled under his breath, frustration in that one word as he pressed harder against her.

His mouth went to her neck, and her eyes slammed shut as the back of her head brushed against the door. He kissed, sucked, and ravished her neck while the pulsing ache between her thighs grew more intense.

"Tony, I—"

"I know, baby," Antonio murmured against her skin, his breaths coming in short spurts.

He lifted his head and held her against the door with one arm.

The man was hella strong. With his other hand he pushed up her sports bra, and her breasts spilled free. Antonio wasted no time latching on to one of her nipples, and a shock wave of need shot straight to her core.

"*Oh, my goodness. Ohh,*" she whimpered. "More. I need more."

His tongue teased her mercilessly as he swirled the tip around her sensitive nipple before gently biting down. Scarlett moaned at the delicious pain. When he was done with that one, he went to the other, inflicting the same sweet torture.

Still grinding against him, she needed to be closer. She wanted to feel him. Not just chest to chest, but everywhere else. Her response to the way he kissed her, touched her, groaned her name, was so intense it wouldn't take much for her to come.

"Okay, okay, okay," she panted, arching into him as he feasted on her breasts. "I—"

"Mommy," Bella's small voice could be heard in the distance, but Scarlett tried to block it out.

She needed Antonio to keep going. She wanted more. She *needed* more. But then she heard Bella again, and apparently Antonio did too. He froze.

Noooooo! Her brain screamed.

Just when things were heating up, they'd been dosed with a big hunk of reality. Scarlett wanted Antonio so bad, she hated to admit it had slipped her mind that Bella was in the house.

How could she forget that? How could she forget about her number one priority?

She was sex starved. That had to be the reason she'd temporarily forgotten about her baby.

She couldn't remember the last time she'd been intimate with a man, but Antonio wasn't just any man. He was the first man in a long time to tempt her in every way possible. Yet, Bella had to come first.

Still breathing hard, Scarlett dropped her forehead to Antonio's shoulder and whimpered as he slowly lowered her to her feet. He made quick work of pulling her bra back into place.

"I'm sorry," he said, panting near her ear. "I didn't mean to go at you like this. I—"

"Stop," Scarlett said, holding his face between her hands. "Don't apologize because I want this as much as you do."

Antonio smiled.

"But having a child—"

"I know. I get it." He gave her a quick peck on the lips. "We'll pick this up again... soon."

"I'm holding you to that."

"Why don't you check on Bella, and once I pull myself together, I'll make lunch. Unless you prefer to cook."

"Umm, we'll enjoy your cooking more than we'll enjoy mine. Let's just say I wouldn't burn down the house, but I can't cook as well as Mahogany."

"Ahh, gotcha. Sounds like I'll be the chef in this relationship." And before she could mentally play around with the word *relationship*, he said, "And yes, *what we're building is a relationship.*"

Scarlett smiled up at him and nodded as she fumbled with the doorknob behind her.

Yep, they were definitely on the same page. In the meantime, she needed to get her libido back in check, and after that make-out session, it wouldn't be easy.

Chapter Ten

Struggling to get his body under control, Antonio ran his hands down his face. It was safe to say he and Scarlett's attraction to one another was intensifying. That wasn't good. Well, it was good in one sense. When they finally got together, they were going to burn up the sheets.

What wasn't good was how he had promised himself to take things slow. Something might have shifted for the good between them since arriving in Miami, but she'd been holding back for the last few months. Why? He wasn't sure, but he planned to find out before they went any further.

Antonio left his bedroom still thinking about Scarlett. He wouldn't turn down sex with her, but he wanted more. Antonio wanted all of her. Not just her body. If that was all she'd be willing to give, he'd have to move on.

But it would be damn hard to move on from her, especially after the little taste he'd had. Had they not been interrupted, he had no doubt that he would've taken her right up against the door. They would've both enjoyed it, but that wasn't what he wanted for their first time. When they eventually got together, he wanted it to be a beautiful night to remember. Not just some quick fun.

"Uncle Tony!" Bella yelled just as he was walking past her bedroom. "I like my room."

"I'm glad, Baby Doll." Antonio strolled inside and sat on the bed next to her. She had her iPad in her hand, and three stuffed animals surrounding her.

"Where's your mom?"

"She told me to stay right here until she changed clothes. She doesn't want me to get your house dirty."

Antonio chuckled. "Well, I'm not worried about that, but how about you and I go and make lunch?"

"Yes!" She grabbed the stuffed elephant that she'd been sleeping with earlier and leaped off the bed. "I want to learn how to cook like Jayden. He said he would teach me, but I want you to teach me."

Antonio shook his head. That nephew of his was eight going on thirty and thought he could do anything. Sure, he could make a few dishes, and he had some baking skills, but he still had a lot to learn.

Antonio stood and headed to the door. "I think I can handle teaching you a few things in the kitchen. How about we start with grilled cheese sandwiches?"

"Yes. I like those," she said and slipped her hand into his.

"What would you like to go with them?"

"Potato chips and Twizzlers."

Antonio laughed. "I was thinking more like a salad or some other vegetables. We'll see what's in the refrigerator."

As they made their way through the house, he remembered she was seeing it for the first time. He gave her the ten-cent tour along the way.

"You live in two houses?"

"I only live here some of the time. Mainly when I need a vacation."

"Oh. Can I come with you every time you need a vacation?"

God, he loved this kid.

"We'll see." Was all he said, but if he had his way, Scarlett and Bella would be on every vacation he took.

When they reached the kitchen, Antonio checked the refrigerator and cabinets. He had a management company take care of the place, but a friend of the family helped him with the extras for this trip. That included decorating Bella's room and stocking the kitchen. He planned to make some of his specialties for his girls.

My girls.

That's what they had become to him, and he was going to do his best to make it a permanent situation.

* * *

Later that night, after tucking her daughter in, Scarlett huffed out a breath as she closed Bella's bedroom door. The older her child got, the more questions she had, and they were getting harder to answer.

Does Nana Cynthia have any kids? Does she have kids my age? I never saw any.

Why does my great-grandmother want to talk to you? Don't you talk to her on the phone all the time?

Why do I have to go to Nana Cynthia's house with you? I want to stay here with Uncle Tony.

Can we live in Uncle Tony's house forever?

There was one question Bella had never asked, but Scarlett knew it was coming one day. *Why is my daddy in heaven?*

Leaning against the wall outside of the bedroom, Scarlett

released a long sigh. It was only a matter of time before Bella asked more questions about her dad.

When she'd started school and saw other children with fathers, she'd wanted to know why she didn't have one. Scarlett hadn't had a clue on how much to tell her but decided to give her the basics. He had gone to heaven before she was born.

Scarlett wasn't ready to share more.

Bella knew Ezra's name and that Cynthia was her father's grandmother. Surprisingly, she hadn't asked about Ezra's mother or father. She also hadn't asked how he died. All she knew was that she didn't have a daddy because he was in heaven.

She wasn't sure how Bella would handle knowing he'd died in a car crash. No, that would probably scare her baby, and the last thing Scarlett needed was for Bella to be afraid to ride in cars.

"You okay?"

Scarlett glanced up to find Antonio standing in the hallway. She pushed away from the wall and headed toward him.

"I'm fine. It's just been a long day, and Bella decided she wanted to ask me fifty-million questions before falling asleep."

Antonio draped his arm around her shoulder and pressed a kiss against her temple as he guided her to the kitchen. After their make-out session in the bedroom earlier, he had put a little distance between them. Nothing uncomfortable, but it had been noticeable that he'd made Bella the center of attention.

"How about a glass of wine? I have chardonnay and pinot noir, unless you want something a little stronger," he said and released her when they reached the kitchen island.

"You are too good to me," Scarlett said, weariness settling into her body. "Red would be great."

Antonio had catered to her and Bella's every need since they'd arrived. After lunch, they went on an amazing boat tour

The Cost of Love

and then played video games at Dave and Buster's. Scarlett enjoyed bowling and arcade games as much as the next person, but after the first couple of hours at the arcade, she'd had enough. Thank goodness Antonio had enough energy to keep Bella entertained the whole time. It was nice having someone to tag-team with parenting for the day.

"How about we go out back?" Antonio suggested, holding their drinks. "We can keep the doors open in case Bella wakes up."

"Okay." She followed him outside and over to the loungers tucked in the corner of the patio.

It was a perfect night at seventy-two degrees with a light breeze. The gurgling waterfall added to the peaceful sounds of the evening, and Scarlett released an exhausted sigh when she sat down.

"It's wonderful out here."

"It's one of my favorite spots. When I visit, I do my best thinking here," Antonio said, taking a long drag on his beer. "I should come here more often."

"Why don't you?"

It was dark out with only the light from the kitchen spilling into the yard, and a few spotlights strategically placed near the fence. Scarlett could only see a silhouette of his features, but she saw him shrug.

"Work and just not taking time off. I love coming here, but not too much by myself. You and Bella help give the space... life. I've enjoyed you two today."

"The feeling is mutual. Oh, and just a heads-up, Bella will probably ask you to bring her here every weekend."

He chuckled. "Yeah, she told me she loves it here. I hope to bring you both back here sometime."

"That would be nice," Scarlett said quietly.

"Before we came to Miami," Antonio started, his voice

73

barely loud enough for her to hear, "I sensed you keeping distance between us. What was that all about?"

Scarlett stared out at the pool, debating on how to respond. She had promised herself she'd go with the flow this weekend, and that included not holding back on her feelings for Antonio.

"Fear," she said, matching his voice level. "I'm afraid. Or at least I was afraid of us getting too close."

A long silence fell between them. She had learned earlier in the week that Antonio liked to mull over what's said before responding, but she kept going.

"I've dated a little off and on over the years. But it's been a long time since I've been in a relationship."

"I'm not going to hurt you Scarlett," he said. "I would never do anything to hurt you. I hope you know that."

She stared into her glass of wine. "I know, but I'm more afraid of hurting you."

"Why do you think you'll hurt me?"

How could she explain? If she told him that she was afraid that she wasn't able to fall in love, would he think her weird? Or would he even take her seriously?

It's Antonio. Of course he'll take you seriously.

"I think I'm incapable of falling in love."

Gathering her courage, Scarlett told him about her relationship with Todd and how he had assumed they'd marry after high school. She adored him and told him that, but he wanted more. At the end of her freshman year of college, he'd given her an ultimatum. Marry him or they were over. She said no, and that had been the last time she'd seen him. He changed colleges.

But it was her relationship with Ezra which had changed her life forever. They had met when she had spent spring break in Miami during her junior year of college. The two of them had hit it off immediately and managed to sustain a long-distance relationship for almost two years.

After graduation, she moved to Miami to be with him. Those years they shared had been fun and exciting. She had started her modeling career, and Ezra was working at his grandfather's investment firm while attending grad school. Their lives were busy, but they always found time for each other.

"We lived together, and everything was great. Perfect actually. Next to Mahogany, he'd been my best friend, and I loved him."

"But?" Antonio prompted when she stopped talking.

"But he asked me to marry him, and I said no. Then hours later he was dead," Scarlett choked out.

"Ahh, baby," Antonio murmured, and before Scarlett realized he had moved, he joined her on the lounger.

He was a big guy, but he managed to squeeze in next to her and pulled her into his arms. "God, that had to be awful, but I hope you know it wasn't your fault."

Scarlett wiped frantically at her eyes. "I know, but still it was awful, traumatic even. At first it didn't seem real, and I didn't want that to be my last memory of him. He wouldn't have left the apartment had I not turned down his proposal. I knew how much he loved me. He told me all the time, and he showed me in everything he did. I really did love him."

"Then why did you say no?"

"Because I wasn't *in* love with him. I was caught totally off guard by his proposal. Yes, I cared about him, but we were so young and just starting in our careers. Even if we got along great and enjoyed each other's company, we weren't nearly ready for marriage.

"Besides that, I didn't love him enough for the type of commitment a marriage requires. I couldn't marry him, and it broke his heart. After our conversation, he left the apartment because he said he needed air. Then he never came back."

"Damn," Antonio said under his breath and held her tighter.

"I still feel awful that I hurt someone who I cared deeply for, and I never got the chance to say, *I'm sorry.*"

Antonio cradled her in his arms for what seemed like hours, and for the first time in a long time, Scarlett felt safe and cherished. It was as if a weight had lifted from her shoulders, and the pain that usually came with discussing Ezra didn't feel as crippling.

"After that, I found out I was pregnant, and I haven't been in a serious relationship since then."

"Has that been by choice?"

Scarlett had to think about it for a minute. "Yes. I'm not able to fall *in* love. And I can't risk you falling in love with me. I won't be able to return your feelings. At least not in the way you deserve. I'm not trying to make it seem like I'm all that because I know I'm not. But if I couldn't fall in love with a man who treated me like the most important person in his world, then I don't think it's possible."

"How do you know you weren't *in* love with him?" Antonio asked after a long hesitation.

"I just knew. I loved every minute we were together, but something was missing. My parents were my role models. My mother once told Mahogany and me that her heart always felt like it would beat out of her chest when my dad walked into a room. Tony, you should've seen them together. When you saw one, you saw the other, and they even completed each other's sentences sometimes. This might sound crazy, but I could feel their love for each other. If that makes any kind of sense."

"It does. My grandparents have been like that for all my life, and they've been married sixty years. Now I see the same type of love with my dad and stepmother. So yeah, I know what you mean."

"Well, I didn't feel that with Ezra. Even though I cared about him, I feel awful that I couldn't love him like he deserved."

Scarlett snuggled against Antonio and let his fresh scent and strong arms ground her. Peace settled over her and she closed her eyes, allowing the comfort he provided and the sound of the gurgling waterfall to relax her.

It felt good to get that off her chest, but a hint of fear lingered. She prayed she would never cause Antonio the pain that she had caused Ezra. She would never forgive herself if that happened again.

"Scarlett, not to sound insensitive, but I don't think you should be afraid to give our relationship a try. Because maybe Ezra just wasn't your person."

Chapter Eleven

"Can you pick me up?" Bella said as they stood on the walkway to Cynthia's front door.

Antonio's heart flipped when she gazed up at him with those big, gorgeous brown eyes. How could he deny this kid anything when she looked at him like that? Like he hung the moon or like he could fight off dragons for her? Having her and Scarlett in his life was becoming one of the greatest gifts he had ever received. If she wanted him to carry her around, no problem.

"Bella, you can walk," Scarlett said, cutting into his thoughts as she started up the walkway to Cynthia's front door. "You're too big for someone to be carrying you around."

Bella continued gazing up at Antonio, and he laughed as he lifted her into his arms. "Are you trying to get me into trouble with your mom?" he whispered and placed a kiss on her soft cheek and started after Scarlett.

"No," she said innocently. "I just like it when you carry me, and you smell really good."

As if to punctuate how she felt, she rested her head on his

shoulder. That move alone was worth the wrath, which Scarlett might leash on him when she realized he was carrying Bella. Once again, he had fallen for her cuteness.

"Tony, you're spoiling her. She's not a baby, even if she acts like one sometimes," Scarlett grumbled when she glanced back at them.

For a person who wasn't a fan of people shortening his name, Antonio loved when his girls called him Tony. It might not seem like a big deal to some, but it felt intimate... special. Like something that was just between the three of them, and he cherished it and them.

He hadn't planned to join them at Cynthia's house this afternoon. He only planned to drop them off and then pick them up after their visit. However, Bella's great-grandmother had other ideas. She called Scarlett that morning and insisted she bring him to meet her.

When Scarlett mentioned it to him, he had declined. No way did he want to infringe on their visit, but Scarlett and Bella wanted him there.

Seconds after Scarlett pushed the doorbell, the large oak door swung open, and they were greeted by Cynthia's assistant, Nancy. The tall, rail-thin woman was dressed in a crisp white, short-sleeve blouse and navy-blue pants with matching flats. This woman was all business. Her fair complexion gained a little pink in her cheeks when her lips formed into an infectious smile.

"Come in. Come in. Welcome back," she said and hugged Scarlett like they were old friends, then turned to Antonio and Bella.

"Nancy, this is Ton—I mean Antonio," Scarlett said and slipped her hand into the crook of his arm. It was interesting how neither Scarlett nor Bella seemed very comfortable in the stately home.

Nancy gave him a slight nod and a warm smile. "Nice to meet you, Antonio. Glad you could join us."

"It's my pleasure. Thanks for making the arrangements."

"No problem." She smiled warmly. "And hi there, Miss Bella. You're growing up so fast."

Bella gave Nancy a shy smile and said hi as she held on tighter around Antonio's neck as if making sure he didn't put her down.

"Mrs. Cynthia is anxious to see you all and has arranged for a lunch buffet on the lanai."

As they strolled through the stately home, Antonio admired the detailed architecture and twenty-foot ceilings. The space had an old-world charm with wood detailing everywhere, including the beams overhead and the dual, spiral staircase. Shiny travertine floors, antique furnishings, and oil paintings filled the enormous space.

The size of the mansion reminded him of his Jenkins family estate, but this place lacked the warmth of his grandparents' home. There were no personal photos lining the walls, no kids of all ages running through the hallway, and the house was eerily quiet.

Was this why Bella and Scarlett didn't visit often?

"Here we are," Nancy announced, stopping after what seemed like a mile of walking. "Mrs. Cynthia, your guests are here."

The smell of barbecue permeated the air, and Antonio realized just how hungry he was as they entered the lanai. The massive screened-in area held an outdoor kitchen and a buffet table loaded with various dishes. He looked left to spy a cozy sitting area in front of a fireplace as well as a dining table. Straight ahead his gaze took in the lap pool, and just beyond that was a man-made private lake.

The space was more welcoming than the rest of the house,

and he assumed this was where Cynthia spent much of her time. The older woman sat on the edge of the lanai, close to the pool, in a shaded area. Huge sunglasses covered much of her face, and she wore a short-sleeve, stylish floral dress that flowed to her ankles.

Cynthia removed her shades and a slow smile kicked up the corners of her pinkish-red lips. Considering Scarlett had mentioned the woman was eighty, her sepia-tone skin gleamed, and her face wasn't as full of wrinkles as one would expect. Her silver-gray hair was pulled back in a tight bun, and there was a regalness about her that showed even in the way she tilted her head slightly.

"My girls are here." She beamed but didn't stand.

Scarlett reached for Bella, then set her on her feet before guiding her closer to the woman. Antonio gave them space to greet Bella's great-grandmother alone. The moment after hellos and hugs were exchanged, Cynthia glanced at him and smiled.

"This must be Antonio. Welcome to my home," she greeted. He moved closer, prepared to shake her hand, but she said, "I only accept hugs."

He grinned and obliged. "Thank you for the invitation. You have a beautiful home."

"Thank you, dear." She patted his arm. "But you're too kind. You probably felt as if you were walking through a museum of classical antiquities," she cracked, and he chuckled. "I've thought about having the place remodeled, but these days, I spend most of my time out here or in my bedroom. So, I figure why bother."

"Understandable," Antonio said and gave the area a cursory glance. "It's very peaceful out here."

"It is, especially in the early mornings and late evenings." She adjusted in her seat as if she were about to stand. "If you don't mind helping an old lady to her feet, we can go ahead and eat," Cynthia said.

"It would be my pleasure." Antonio helped her stand, and she held on to his arm as she shuffled alongside of him until they reached the table. He pulled out the chair for her and helped her sit down.

When Cynthia glanced up to thank him, Antonio could see features of Bella around her eyes and nose. Though Bella was a splitting image of Scarlett, she clearly must have inherited some of her father's features.

A short while later, with plates piled high, the conversation flowed easily. Cynthia did a masterful job in including all of them in the chit-chat. Clearly she adored Scarlett and Bella, constantly referring to them as her girls. She asked about everything they'd been up to and what they had planned for the summer. She hinted about the trio visiting more but quickly backed off, understanding that they had their own lives to live.

Antonio could only imagine how lonely it must get in such a huge home, with no one but the hired help fluttering around. Though he was a part of a close-knit, large family, he was concerned about growing old alone. But now with Scarlett and Bella in his life, hopefully, that wouldn't be the case.

The meal, including barbecue ribs, roasted chicken, a green salad, a potato salad, and other dishes, could easily feed twenty people, though it was just the four of them. Antonio wondered if she entertained often, considering how perfectly everything was laid out. His grandmother, who loved hosting gatherings, would be impressed.

He lifted his glass of water and drank heartily until Cynthia asked, "What are your intentions with my girls?"

Water spewed from his mouth, and Antonio choked-coughed as he struggled to recover from the question. Bella, sitting next to him, cracked up, but Scarlett, who was directly across from him, appeared to be as surprised as he was.

Are you okay? she mouthed.

He gave a jerky nod and hurried to wipe up his mess with the cloth napkin that had been in his lap.

Instead of looking at Cynthia, he directed his attention to Scarlett when he finally responded. "I assure you Mrs. Cynthia, my intentions are honorable. Your girls are in good hands with me."

After a slight hesitation, the woman said, "That's the perfect answer, Antonio. I'm sure time will tell if it's accurate though."

Antonio's gaze snapped to Cynthia's. There was a note of *something* in her tone that set him on edge. Was she pissed that he was getting a shot with Scarlett when her grandson should be the one sitting at the table? Or was he just reading too much into her words and her tone?

By the ambivalent gleam in her eyes and the firm set of her mouth, he didn't think so. Then again, he wasn't sure what to think since the conversation had veered so suddenly.

All Antonio knew for sure was he wouldn't let Bella's great-grandmother or anyone else come between him and Scarlett. She was a woman he'd fight for... her *and* Bella.

Chapter Twelve

After a delicious lunch, Nancy helped Cynthia to her living quarters on the second floor. While she did that, the housekeeper escorted the rest of them to a small theater room. For Scarlett, it brought back fond memories of Ezra and how they occasionally hung out, watching one movie after another while snacking on whatever the cook created.

She still remembered the first time he brought her to meet his grandparents. Scarlett liked them from the start. From day one they treated her as if they'd known her forever, and she loved visiting them. She and Ezra would go there for dinner a couple of times a month, hang out, and play games. They might be up in age, but they were a lot of fun.

After Ezra's grandfather died of a heart attack, Scarlett and Ezra made it a point to visit Cynthia even more, hoping to somehow fill the gap. She'd always been a strong woman, and though she grieved for her husband, she stayed active with various organizations. Continuing to live a full life. It wasn't until after Ezra died that it seemed a part of Cynthia had died too. Still, the older woman remained kind to Scarlett, and their relationship continued to grow, especially after Bella was born.

"Scarlett, Cynthia would like for you to come upstairs," Nancy said from the doorway of the theater room.

"Thanks, Nancy. I'll head up shortly."

"We don't have to go, do we, Mommy?" Bella asked, a small tub of popcorn in her lap as she stared at the big screen. They'd been watching *Shark Tale*, one of Bella's favorite movies, and Scarlett was thankful for the reprieve.

"No, honey. Tony's going to stay down here with you."

Before standing, Scarlett leaned over and gave Antonio a slow kiss. When she pulled back slightly, she licked her lips, tasting the butter and salt from his popcorn, then smiled.

The only problem with being this close and kissing this gorgeous man was she wanted to do it again, but next time with a little tongue. Hell, she was ready to do way more than just kiss him. Stripping him out of the Henley shirt that molded over his muscular body and showed off his wide chest, thick biceps, and flat abs would be a good start. Then, she'd work her way down.

Whoa. Don't go there.

From the moment she'd opened her eyes that morning, Scarlett had been anxious to meet with Cynthia. Having Antonio along eased her anxiety. However, being so close to him throughout the day had wreaked havoc on every other part of her body. It started when he walked out of his bedroom that morning looking like a delicious snack. The shirt was one thing, but the nicely worn blue jeans seemed to highlight his tree-trunk-like thighs and long legs and had an effect on her that she hadn't expected.

There was no question that she was attracted to his sharp mind, his kind nature, and his handsome face, but that body? *Good Lord!* The man had her insides quivering with need and arousing her sexual desires, which had been dormant for too many years. Each passing day had her looking forward to getting to know every aspect of Antonio Jenkins.

Unable to help herself, she kissed him again, then stood and headed for the door.

"Mommy kissed you," Bella said to Antonio in a conspiratorial whisper as Scarlett walked away.

"She did, didn't she?" she heard Antonio say, and then he and Bella laughed.

Scarlett shook her head and smiled. She thought Bella would be too engrossed in the movie to catch that. Apparently not, but how she and Antonio moved forward was going to be tricky. Dating as a single mother wasn't be easy, and at some point, she needed to talk to Bella. She already knew her daughter would be all in for having Antonio around more, but Scarlett wanted to make sure.

A few minutes later, she entered Cynthia's bedroom and glanced around the enormous space. It was more like a two-room hotel suite. She crossed the sitting room area that included a sofa, loveseat, and an upholstered chair. The furnishings faced the wall-to-wall shelving unit which not only held a television, but also books and personal items. Including photos of her, Bella, Ezra, and Cynthia's late husband.

The woman spent the majority of her time up here, usually hanging out in the sitting area. Scarlett had been surprised to find her sitting on the lanai when they arrived. She half expected Cynthia to be propped up in bed looking unhealthy like she had days ago. That hadn't been the case at all. Instead, she was beautifully dressed and appeared well. During lunch, she'd been her usual sharp, witty, and charming self. Except for when she'd put Antonio on the spot regarding his intentions. That had been uncalled for, and Scarlett planned to tell her so.

Now, Cynthia was tucked in bed with mounds of pillows

propped behind her. She seemed exhausted, as if the afternoon of entertaining them had worn her out.

Cynthia nodded toward the comfy looking recliner next to the bed. "Have a seat. I'm so glad you all were able to come for a visit. I've been looking forward to it all week."

"I'm glad you asked us to. I really should've gotten us here sooner. I'll try to bring Bella more often."

"I hope you do, and feel free to bring Antonio as well. He's extremely handsome. He reminds me of my Ezra," Cynthia said, a wistfulness in her tired voice. "He's as charming as I expected him to be, and a perfect gentleman. I can see why you're so taken with him."

Scarlett smiled. She was crazy about Antonio and the more she got to know him, the more she liked him. No doubt Cynthia had noticed how much she and Bella adored him.

"Why'd you ask him about his intentions?"

"I wanted to see how he'd handle himself. There's no doubt in my mind that he really cares for you and Bella. By the way, I had my assistant look into the Jenkins family," Cynthia said, as if she was telling Scarlett that she'd had her assistant search for the closest restaurant.

"Excuse me? What are you talking about? Why would you do that?"

"You've talked about the Jenkins family during many of our conversations. I got curious, and when you kept bringing up Antonio in conversation, I knew I needed to check them out. In all the years since Ezra died, you've *never* mentioned a boyfriend. Once you even said you'd never get married. That it will always be just you, Bella, your sister, mother, and your Aunt Rita, but now you've included Antonio and his family. I wanted to know more about him and his people."

Scarlett struggled to remain calm, but anger stirred in her

gut. "Why would you dig around in their lives? They are none of your business!"

"Did you know Toni Jenkins-Logan's husband, Craig, is a former detective turned law enforcement consultant?" Cynthia continued as if Scarlett hadn't spoken. "Or that Luke, Christina's husband, used to be the most sought-after defense attorney in Manhattan?" she said of Antonio's cousin-in-law, who some members of the family referred to as the Thug Lawyer.

"Oh, and we can't forget Ben Jenkins Sr. and his accomplishments. Antonio's father is one hell of an attorney who does extremely well for himself and not just in the legal field. The real estate development company that he owns with his sons and some of his nephews has acquired some very valuable land recently."

Cynthia recited more of her investigator's findings regarding the Jenkins family and those who'd married into the family, including Martina's husband Paul. He came from a long line of state senators and was a state senator himself until he got into the restaurant business.

It was frightening how much she knew about them, including the net worth of some of the family members. Scarlett hated how invasive the woman and her team had been, but she shouldn't be surprised. With Cynthia's wealth and connections, she could find out anything she wanted to know.

"If the Jenkins family is as impressive as the reports I've read, I'm glad you and Bella have them in your life."

Scarlett stood, staring at the woman who she called a friend. There was no remorse in Cynthia's tone. As if poking around in people's lives was no big deal. Well, it was a big deal to Scarlett, especially since the Jenkins family were her family now. She knew for a fact that they were private people and wouldn't like this one bit.

"You are way out of line, Cynthia," Scarlett growled. "It's

one thing to be curious, but it's another to invade someone's privacy. How could you? What if they find out and think I had something to do with your snooping?"

"When I die," Cynthia said. Scarlett opened her mouth to tell her to stop talking like that, but Cynthia lifted her hand. "Hear me out. I don't know when I'll take my last breath, but I'm tired. I'm also old as dirt, and I know my days are numbered. I want to make sure you and Bella are taken care of. I want to make sure you two are prepared for what's to come."

"What's to come?" Scarlett returned to the recliner and perched on the edge of the cushion. "What are you talking about?"

"I told you about Ezra's parents. They are not nice people. The two of them are money hungry, power hungry, and will do *anything* to get ahead. I'm telling you this because I want you to have an idea of what you'll be facing when I die."

Scarlett's pulse amped, and she tried to push down the unease clawing down her spine.

"Bella will inherit the majority of my estate, and it's substantial. But when Alberta and her husband find out that all they're getting is this property, they will be livid. They will do everything in their power to find out what happened to my money and assets. There's no telling how far they'll go to get what my daughter thinks she deserves."

The unease Scarlett felt moments ago suddenly turned into fear. "What are you saying? Is my daughter in danger?"

"No, they might try to use her or get to her money, but they would never hurt a child. At least not physically."

Cynthia repositioned in bed, and it looked like she'd fall asleep at any given moment.

"Ezra's father, Theodore, is a state senator running for reelection. That costs money. Don't get me wrong, he and my daughter are doing well for themselves, but they are never satis-fied. They always want more.

"As for Theodore, he will be seeking out any leverage, espe-cially something that will make him more relevant and relat-able. Like having a cute, smart, adorable granddaughter who will make him look good to his voters. He's the type of person who won't think anything of shoving Bella in front of the media, pretending to dote on her. When I tell you they are uncouth and only care about themselves, I'm not exaggerating."

With her heart pounding hard enough to explode, Scarlett lurched out of her seat. Her mind reeled as she moved over to the large bay windows on shaky legs. As she stared out at the rose garden, a colorful sight that should bring her peace, all she could think about was how much Ezra disliked his parents. His description of them was similar to Cynthia's, and Scarlett trusted their judgment.

Returning to Cynthia's bedside, Scarlett released a tremu-lous breath. "I appreciate all you've done for Bella over the years, but please don't think you have to do anything else for her. The college fund you set up for her when she was born was extremely generous. And I've been able to create a nice comfortable life for us, and I'm giving her everything I think she needs. Cynthia, Bella is fine. She doesn't need a ton of money or properties or whatever you're planning to leave her."

"As far as I'm concerned, Bella is my sole heir. She deserves everything I have and more. You both do. I'm only leaving Alberta and her loser husband this house because my husband told her that it would one day be hers. But she'll get *nothing* else from me."

Scarlett didn't know what to say. She rubbed her temples, trying to make sense of all this. She didn't know exactly how much money Cynthia had, but Ezra once joked that his grandparents were wealthier than Oprah. That was over eight years ago. She couldn't imagine the value of Cynthia's estate now.

"You once said you'll probably never get married, and that's your right. You young women today are so independent and don't *need a man*," she said that last part with air quotes, and Scarlett remembered spewing those words more than once. "But what about Bella?"

"What do you mean?" Scarlett wasn't following, which seemed to be the case with most of this conversation.

"That girl needs a father and someone who can protect her."

Anger boiled inside Scarlett's gut. "Cynthia, I give Bella everything she needs, and I'm capable of protecting my child!"

Yes, Scarlett wished her baby girl had a daddy and lived in a two-parent household, but not because she didn't think she could give her daughter what she needed. No, it had more to do with wanting Bella to grow up with a loving father the way she and Mahogany had.

"I appreciate what you're trying to do, Cynthia, but if it means my child could be in danger, I won't be able to accept your generosity."

Cynthia waved her off. "Don't worry, dear. You two will be fine, and I have an idea to ensure that."

Scarlett was almost afraid to ask, but said, "And what's that?"

"Ask Antonio to adopt Bella," Cynthia said as easily as if she was ordering a pizza. "She'll become a Jenkins. They are a formidable family, and I have it on good authority that they protect their own."

Chapter Thirteen

Miniature golfing should be fun, but Scarlett's mind was everywhere but on hitting that tiny yellow ball into an equally tiny hole. After leaving Cynthia's house over an hour ago, all Scarlett could think about were those unbelievable five words—Ask Antonio to adopt Bella.

No matter how many different ways the words sounded in her mind—the idea was ridiculous. At least that's what she kept telling herself. Yet, as she glanced at her baby girl grinning up at Antonio after he helped her sink the ball into the fifteenth hole, the idea didn't seem so crazy.

"Yes! I did it!" Bella screamed, jumping up and down as if she'd won a million dollars for her efforts. Then again, to let Cynthia tell it, Bella might become a multimillionaire before she was an adult.

Ugh!

How has this become my life?

Scarlett was thrilled Bella's great-grandmother wanted to leave her a sizable inheritance, but not if it came at the expense of Bella's childhood. But no matter how Scarlett pleaded with Cynthia not to put her or Bella in a compromising position, the woman didn't listen. She insisted Bella deserved her inheritance, and Scarlett shouldn't worry.

How could she not? The woman tells her that Ezra's parents are ruthless and money hungry, yet she still insists on leaving Bella practically her whole estate. There's no way those people won't contest the will or, worse, come after them. Especially when or if they find out that Bella is their grandchild. They might insist on being in her life.

Scarlett didn't want that. She didn't want them anywhere near her child.

If Bella became a Jenkins, would they still be able to find her?

Ugh, stop!

"I need to stop thinking," Scarlett murmured under her breath. She was going to drive herself nuts. She needed to focus on enjoying the evening with Bella and Antonio, and nothing else.

"Scarlett?"

Scarlett jerked her head up and met Antonio's concerned gaze. He pointed to her yellow ball that was at least six feet from the hole. Even Bella was beating her, and this was her daughter's first time playing miniature golf.

"Oh, sorry," Scarlett said and moved up to her ball.

As she stood above it with her putter in hand, she glanced from the ball to the hole several times, hoping it was lined up perfectly. Trying not to hit it too hard, she tapped the ball, careful not to put too much power behind it.

Go. Go. Keep going. She willed the ball to keep rolling.

"Yay, Mommy! You..." Bella's words trailed off when the ball curved sharply to the right, then stopped a foot away from the hole. "Oh, that's okay, Mommy. You can hit it again," her sweet baby said encouragingly.

Three tries later, and holding up the people behind them, Scarlett finally sank the ball in the hole. She couldn't wait until this little adventure was over, even if Bella was having a blast.

When they'd finally made it to the last hole, Scarlett had had enough. The last hour or so had been pure torture, and it didn't help that Antonio was watching her intensely. He'd been trying to get her to tell him what was wrong since they left Cynthia's place. Scarlett assured him all was fine, but it was clear that her acting skills needed work. She had no doubt that the moment they were alone, he'd want answers.

That was one difference between him and Ezra. While Ezra wasn't the most observant, Antonio noticed everything. Her moods, how she was dressed, if she had something on her mind, hell, he even knew when she wanted a kiss. Scarlett didn't have to say a word. He was attuned to her as if he had some sixth sense where she was concerned.

If she was honest, it was a little creepy. Okay, maybe not creepy but... *different.*

"Now what are we going to do?" Bella asked but got distracted when a family with five kids entered.

All Scarlett wanted to do was go back to the house, pour herself a stiff drink, and hide out in the bathroom. It would be the perfect time to try out Antonio's soaking tub.

As they were walking to the rental car, Antonio slid his arm around Scarlett's waist and pulled her close. She liked the way his hand rested on her hip as if he had every right to have it there. She also loved being hugged up against his hard body.

"I don't know what happened back at Cynthia's, but you and I are talking once Bella goes to bed. All right?"

Though his tone was authoritative, there was also concern in his voice, and it made Scarlett teary eyed. God, she was falling hard for this kind, generous man. He popped into her life only a few months ago, and he was already chipping away at her defenses.

She really liked and cared about Antonio. As of late, he was the person she wanted to tell everything to, even about the conversation with Cynthia. Not just because he was at the center of it, but mainly because she trusted him.

Instead of speaking, Scarlett nibbled on her lower lip and nodded. Yeah, they needed to talk. Sooner than later.

"Whatever's going on, we'll work it out. I promise," Antonio said, patting her hip while placing a kiss on the side of her forehead before releasing her.

It might have been a simple peck, but in that moment, Scarlett felt cherished. Like she was important to him. It had been a long time since someone made her feel this way. What surprised her more was she wasn't tempted to run mentally or emotionally at what this meant. She truly wanted to see where things went with Antonio.

On the way to the house, Scarlett debated on how to tell him about the conversation from earlier. She still thought Cynthia's idea was overkill, and Cynthia might be exaggerating her concerns regarding Ezra's parents.

But what if she wasn't exaggerating? What if Theodore and Alberta tried to use Bella for their own gain? Or attempt to steal her inheritance? Or worse, what if they were crazy enough to try to somehow take Bella from her?

Theodore was a politician and Alberta was a defense attorney. They had as many connections, good and bad, as Cynthia. But unlike Cynthia, they'd use their power for evil.

Then there was Antonio.

Scarlett had always wanted Bella to have a father. Someone to love her, protect her, and someone to scare knuckle-headed boys away when the time came. She had also wanted her to have a father like the dad she and Mahogany had growing up.

He was the best, and he always put her, Mahogany, and their mother's needs first. Her dad had been the type of man who worked a nine-to-five instead of having a ton of jobs that kept him away from his family. He worked a regular job, with regular hours, and always came home for dinner. He also made it to every one of their dance recitals, soccer practices, and anything else they were involved in. No, they hadn't been rich, but they'd been financially comfortable and wanted for nothing.

That's the type of dad Scarlett wanted for Bella.

That was the type of father—and husband—Antonio would be. He might have grown up without a mother, but his dad and extended family were there to fill the gap. He had learned first-hand the power of having strong family bonds and being there for each other when needed.

Yep, that was the type of man Scarlett would love to raise her child with, but there was one big problem. Well, there were several problems, but the first one which came to mind was that Antonio wanted kids of his own, as well as marriage. No way would he ask someone to marry him who wasn't *in* love with him.

Then there were the cons of asking Antonio to adopt Bella. Scarlett would have to share her daughter. Adoptions were permanent. Was she willing to share her baby girl?

"I had fun, Uncle Tony," Bella said from the back seat, her sweet voice cutting into Scarlett's thoughts.

"I'm glad, Baby Doll. I had fun too, and the day isn't over. How about we order pizza for dinner and play Uno?"

"That sounds awesome! I love pizza, but I only played Uno one time. I can't remember how to play."

"No worries. I got you," Antonio said. "I'll teach you every-thing you need to know."

Damn this man and his ability to say just the right words at any given time. Sure, he wasn't talking about what she'd been thinking, but Scarlett knew he would always look out for her child. He would always treat her like his own no matter the relationship.

But how would he feel about being a father to a child who wasn't biologically his?

* * *

Later that night, Antonio eased out of Bella's room and closed the door behind him. She had insisted on him being the one to tuck her in. When she announced that after playing several rounds of Uno, his mind had been blown. Sure, they'd had a connection from the start, but to ask him to read with her until she fell asleep had been huge. It was something he fantasized about doing with his own kids one day.

He and Bella took turns reading a page, and it felt like the most natural thing to be doing together. They cracked jokes, laughed, and like she'd done to Scarlett the night before, Bella peppered him with questions.

Did you ever want a sister?

How many cousins do you have?

Can you teach me how to make my own birthday cake?

Do you have a YouTube channel?

Some of the questions were random. Still Antonio enjoyed every minute of their time together. He even learned some of her likes and dislikes when it came to food, kids in her classroom, and clothes. It was safe to say she would be into fashion like Scarlett.

Now that he and Bella had bonded, Antonio needed to

work on creating that same bond with her mother. He wasn't sure what Cynthia had said to Scarlett earlier, but he was sure it had something to do with him. He hoped the woman wasn't trying to break them up.

When Cynthia had asked about his intentions toward Scarlett and Bella, he thought he'd given a good answer. What he'd wanted to say was that he planned on marrying Scarlett, and the three of them would live happily ever after. But lunch with Bella's father's grandmother hadn't seemed the time or the place for that type of declaration. Especially before he had a chance to win Scarlett's heart. Antonio just hoped he'd get that chance.

Standing in the hallway outside of the bedrooms, Antonio listened, trying to determine what part of the house Scarlett was in. He and Bella had left her in the kitchen cleaning up, but that had been an hour ago. Maybe she'd still be in there, or better yet, maybe she was waiting in his bedroom for him.

Antonio almost laughed out loud at the thought. If Cynthia had tried talking Scarlett out of dating him, the last thing she'd be thinking about was getting naked with him. Then again, when she asked to use his tub, he had joked about washing her back. She hadn't said no. Instead, she kissed him so thoroughly he almost forgot his name.

Had it not been for having Bella in the house, Antonio would've followed through on the backwashing offer and more. However, it was probably good Bella was there because he had to keep reminding himself to go slow with Scarlett. He didn't want to scare her away, and more than anything, he wanted their relationship to progress naturally without him pushing her toward something she might not be ready for.

When Antonio made it to the living room, he found Scarlett on the sofa with her legs tucked beneath her, and a glass of dark liquid in her hand. There wasn't much left in her glass, and he didn't know if that was how much alcohol she'd started with, or if she had already begun drinking.

What really surprised him was seeing the bottle of Hennessy on the table in front of her, as well as a glass for him.

Ahh, damn. It's going to be that kind of conversation.

Might as well get this over with, but Antonio should warn her. If she was thinking about breaking things off with him, he wasn't going to make it easy. Two days of claiming her as his own wasn't nearly long enough. He wanted forever.

He poured himself a shot of the cognac, thinking a bit of liquid courage wouldn't hurt. Bringing it to his lips, he tossed back the alcohol and cringed at the way it burned on its way down his throat.

Goodness. He wasn't a big drinker of hard liquor, but tonight he'd make an exception.

Antonio poured another and took a sip as he sat next to Scarlett. "I'm not letting you go," he said. "If Cynthia thinks I'm not the right person for you, she can take it up with me. You and Bella are *mine.*"

Scarlett, eyes wide with her mouth hanging open, looked at him as if seeing him for the first time. Antonio didn't know what was going through that gorgeous head of hers, but this was nonnegotiable. He planned to fight to be with her. If it made him come across as nuts, so be it. He knew without a doubt that she was the one for him, and he wanted her and Bella in his life.

"Say something," he said, the words coming out more aggressive than intended. His ass was supposed to be taking things slow, and here he was telling her that he was playing for keeps.

Way to go, Antonio. If this doesn't have her running for the hills...

"I-I... wow," Scarlett stuttered and slammed back the liquor that had been in her glass and coughed. "Good Lord!" she croaked. "How'd you do that when it's so strong? I think it burned a hole in my throat, my esophagus, and my stomach."

Antonio couldn't help it, he burst out laughing. The two of them were something else. Like inexperienced teenagers trying liquor for the first time and attempting to drum up enough courage to ask the other to go steady.

After a brief coughing fit, Scarlett cleared her throat. "Okay, I'm just going to ask. Will you adopt Bella?"

Chapter Fourteen

S till chuckling, Antonio smirked at Scarlett, but then her words bounced around in his mind. *Wait.* He blinked several times, wondering if he'd heard her right. No way. No way had she said what he thought she said.

"Say what now?"

"I asked if you would adopt Bella. I know this sounds crazy, but will you adopt her and become her father?"

Antonio stared at the beautiful woman sitting next to him, waiting to see if she'd say more. Surely, she was joking, but when she didn't laugh or crack a smile, he knew she was serious.

"Umm..." was the only word he could form, and he was fairly sure that wasn't even a word. His thoughts were jumbled, but he somehow managed to say, "Maybe you should start at the beginning."

Scarlett sighed loudly, then reached for the liquor bottle, but Antonio stopped her from pouring more into her glass. Taking the bottle from her hand, he set it out of reach.

"I have a feeling this conversation should be done sober. Tell me what brought this on. All this time, I assumed Cynthia was trying to get you away from me."

Scarlett snorted, then quickly covered her mouth with her hand and released a nervous laugh. "Sorry, and no, on the contrary. Asking you to adopt Bella was her idea, and the more I think about it, the more I think it's a good idea. It all started when Cynthia mentioned she was leaving her estate to Bella. Or at least most of it, and it's on the high end of multimillion dollars."

Antonio listened as Scarlett told him about the conversation that she'd had with Bella's great-grandmother. After leaving Cynthia's house, he'd known the woman had said something troubling. From the moment Scarlett had climbed into the car, she'd been distant and quiet. Even Bella had noticed and asked if she was all right. Now he understood why she'd been distracted.

He leaned forward and set his glass down, then propped his elbows on his thighs as Scarlett continued. Her recap of the conversation was all over the place, but he managed to understand a couple of things. Ezra's parents were losers. Cynthia obviously was in a league of her own.

But Antonio didn't care how wealthy the woman was, she had no right to snoop into his family's life. On the other hand, his dad would have done the same thing if he was concerned about the people his kids, or his grandson, was involved with.

"I was so angry to know that she had dug into you and your family. I am so sorry, Tony. I promise I didn't share any personal information with her. Heck, I don't know enough about them to share much of anything. I hope you believe me."

He shot her a glance and frowned. "Of course I believe you. Did she say why she was interested in us?"

"We talk at least once a week, so I can make sure she's

doing okay. She always asks about me and Bella, and sometimes Mahogany, wanting to know what we've been up to. She knows we spent Christmas with your family, and then there's the wedding. I shared some of the preparations that were going into the event, and just stuff like that.

"Apparently, I've mentioned the Jenkins family more than I realized. It was enough to make her curious. Then she made a comment about how much I talk about you and..."

Antonio had been looking down at his interlocked fingers, but when her words trailed off, he turned to her. "What about me?"

Scarlett inhaled deeply and released the breath slowly. "She said you're the only man I've spoken of since Ezra died. I hadn't realized that, but it's not like I've been out with many men since Bella's been born. A date here and there, but nothing serious."

Did that mean she hadn't been intimate with a man since Ezra? Antonio hated it was the first thing that popped into his mind, but he couldn't help it. He wanted her for himself. So of course, he wondered if she had been with many others, especially lately. She was a gorgeous, intelligent, creative woman. Of course, men would be interested in her.

What he should've been asking was—*what did you tell her about me?* But he had learned a long time ago not to ask questions unless you were prepared for the answer. For Cynthia to suggest he adopt Bella meant Scarlett must've spoken highly of him. Still, that didn't mean she was ready for what he wanted—*her.*

"Anyway, she said she had checked out you and your family. Supposedly, it was to protect me and Bella. She wanted to know what type of people the Jenkins were, and then she suggested I ask you to adopt Bella."

Antonio shook his head, still not totally comprehending

Sharon C. Cooper

that logic. Clearly, he had missed something because this just wasn't adding up.

Unable to stay seated, he stood and paced in front of the cocktail table, trying to wrap his brain around this crazy request. He slowly ran his hand over his short hair and let it slide to the back of his neck. As he massaged his tight muscles, several questions bombarded him at once. He wasn't sure which one to ask first.

"This is a lot to take in," he said. "Help me understand. Even if Cynthia is concerned her family might try to contest her will, how does me adopting Bella fit in?"

"Like me, she doesn't want Ezra's parents to know about Bella. She figures if you adopt her and give her the Jenkins name, they'd never know she's their grandchild. In all the years of knowing and visiting Cynthia, I've never run into Ezra's parents. I plan to keep it that way because of what Cynthia and Ezra have shared about them."

"What beef did Ezra have with his parents?" Antonio asked and returned to his seat.

Though he couldn't imagine being estranged from his father, he didn't have a relationship with his mother. She left him and Ben when Antonio was five, and they hadn't seen her since. He planned to keep it that way.

His mother had never wanted kids. She'd only had babies to please his father, but after trying to embrace motherhood, she realized it wasn't for her and left. At that age, Antonio remembered a little about her. Her scent, how quiet she was, and he remembered a few occasions when she got frustrated with him for being a typical preschooler who failed to do what she said.

Though his father had her contact information and said Antonio could reach out to her when or if he was ever ready, he

104

hadn't. She never tried to contact them, and he had made peace with not having her in his life.

Had something similar happened to Ezra?

"He never had anything good to say about them. He once told me that his father was verbally abusive, and he and his mom always made him feel as if he was a burden. Like they couldn't reach their goals with him in tow. It sounded like they were rarely home, leaving him with a nanny. When they were there, they rarely talked to him.

"In middle school, he ran away to his grandparents' home, and his parents never came for him. From then on, Cynthia and his grandfather raised him. They adored him, and the feeling was mutual.

"It sounds like Cynthia has loathed them from that point on. She hates that they put their careers before their own child, and more than once, she's mentioned they only care about themselves and appearances."

"That's too bad," Antonio said.

"Yeah, it was, but he was happy, and his grandparents doted on him. He was their everything. The only times his parents came around where he was concerned was when something big was happening in his life. Like when he graduated valedictorian of his high school, and when he graduated from college with honors. I think one of those years was an election year, and his father had the media there to capture the moment."

Antonio shook his head. Coming from a supportive, loving family, it sickened him to hear stuff like this. He could understand why Ezra kept his distance from his family and why Scarlett didn't want them near Bella.

"Cynthia doesn't think they'd ever cause Bella physical harm," Scarlett continued, "But she fears they might try to use her for their benefit, specifically Theodore's benefit. He's a U.S. Senator, and it's an election year. I can't let them find out they have a granddaughter. Another reason why I want Bella to take your name."

Antonio had heard enough. They definitely sounded like people who would use a child to make themselves look more relatable. He also could understand Scarlett's concerns.

Still...

"You know this idea is insane, right?" Antonio said, but deep down, he secretly loved the idea. Nothing would make him happier than to have a child, especially Bella. Except he wanted a family. Besides that, he was fairly sure adopting Bella wouldn't be as easy as Scarlett was making it sound.

"I know. It's a little out there, but I already know you'd make an amazing father. Besides, if Bella got to choose her dad, I'm a hundred percent sure she'd choose you. Tony, you've only known her for what, maybe six months, give or take? Yet you have treated her like your own from the first time Jayden introduced the two of you."

Antonio smiled at the memory. Bella had attended Sunday brunch with Mahogany and they both were introduced to the family. But for whatever reason, Jayden had sought him out to introduce him to Bella personally. He'd said she was his best friend, and he wanted her to meet his Uncle Antonio.

Antonio picked up his glass of brandy and chuckled as the memory bloomed fully in his mind. Though Bella had heard Jayden call him Uncle Antonio, she called him Uncle Tony. It didn't matter that Jayden chastised her for calling his uncle the wrong name. Bella had smiled up at Antonio and said, "Can I call you Uncle Tony?" He had probably fallen in love with her in that moment.

"Why is Cynthia giving you a heads-up about all this? Is she dying?"

"She hasn't said, but I have noticed a difference in her health. She looks like she's aged considerably over the last couple of weeks, and she just seems tired. But let her tell it, she's just getting old. I think something is going on. I'm planning to stop by and see her Monday morning before we leave town. Maybe I can get her to tell me then."

"Who else knows Bella will be the main heir to Cynthia's estate?" Antonio asked. He wanted as much information as possible as he seriously considered this proposition.

"I have no idea. She's a private person. Besides her lawyer, I'd be surprised if anyone knows, but maybe Nancy. *Maybe.*"

Antonio drained his glass and set it on the table. He was still trying to come to terms with this unusual request.

"Bella needs you, Tony. We both do. I don't know what these people are capable of, but I want my child protected. Even if Theodore and Alberta never seek us out, I still want you to be Bella's father."

"You already know how much I love that little girl. I will always protect her. No matter what happens between you and I, I will always be there for both of you." He took a breath, trying to get his words to match his thoughts. "Scarlett, do you understand what you're asking?"

"I know I'm asking a lot, and I don't expect you to give up your life. You can be as involved as—"

"Stop," he interrupted. "Do you *really* understand what it'll mean if I adopt Bella as my own? She'll be my daughter, and you and I will have the same rights as it relates to her. I suggest you think long and hard. I'll be her father in every sense of the word. Is that really what you want, Scarlett?"

The worried look in her eyes told him that she hadn't thought this all the way through. Problem was, the more he thought about becoming Bella's father, the more he wanted to make it a reality.

But what about Scarlett? She trusted him to take care of Bella, but what about her? What would it take to get her to trust him with her heart?

Chapter Fifteen

Scarlett laid her head back and stared at the coffered ceiling as she sat in the recliner next to Cynthia's bed. The older woman had been dozing off and on since they'd eaten breakfast an hour ago. Scarlett couldn't much blame her. Considering how much she'd eaten, she felt as if she could use a nap herself.

It was Monday morning, hours before she, Antonio, and Bella were scheduled to head back to Cincinnati. Scarlett had come alone to visit with Cynthia in hopes of talking some sense into her about her will. It had been pointless. Cynthia's mind was made up, and she insisted her great-granddaughter was her only heir and deserved every penny she'd get. Scarlett didn't bother telling her that Alberta was also her heir.

Scarlett shook her head. Most people would be thrilled to know their child would inherit a fortune, but she couldn't get excited about that news. Especially not knowing if it would create family drama which could put her child at risk of physical harm or emotional trauma. Nope. Scarlett would rather forego millions and they live a comfortable lifestyle with love and peace.

And why am I even tripping over something that may never happen?

Ezra's parents might not even care if Cynthia gave others a portion of her estate. Besides, Scarlett had to keep reminding herself that they didn't know about Bella. From day one, Cynthia had been adamant about them not finding out. She insisted they didn't deserve to know about their grandchild since they hadn't given a damn about their own child.

I'm worrying for no reason.

"I can hear you thinking all the way over here."

Scarlett lifted her head and smiled. "I find that hard to believe since you can barely hear me when I'm talking."

The older woman's tired, rusty-sounding laughter was like that of a three-packs-a-day smoker. Still, it was good to hear her laugh. Scarlett never really thought about it, but she couldn't imagine her life without Cynthia in it. They'd grown close over the years. She was more than Bella's great-grandmother. She had also become a good friend and like a grandmother to Scarlett. Not only that, but she was also a connection to Ezra.

He might be gone, but whenever she looked at Cynthia, she saw traces of him in her eyes and her smile. Also, being around her brought back fun memories of her and Ezra and his grandparents hanging out eating, laughing, and enjoying each other's company. If Cynthia died... *When* she died, so would that connection. Then again, she still had her most precious gift—Bella—to remember all of them by.

Cynthia glanced at her. "We've talked about everything but Antonio," she said, her voice low and sounding tired. "Does that mean you didn't heed my advice? You didn't ask him?"

Scarlett straightened in her seat and released a noisy sigh. "I asked him."

"What did he say?"

"After his initial shock, he said a lot."

Ever since the conversation with him, Scarlett realized how irrational she'd been in asking him. How had she let Cynthia's concerns about Theodore and Alberta freak her out enough to ask him to become the father of her child? It hadn't been until he started pointing out the obvious that she put the brakes on the idea. An adoption was permanent. That meant he would be a part of Bella's life forever and included in all the decisions regarding her upbringing. Meaning Scarlett would be sharing her child with a man she was still getting to know.

On the other hand, she knew Antonio well enough to know he would be an incredible father. Any child would be lucky to have him in their life. If Scarlett was looking for someone to raise her child with, he'd be her first choice. Heck, right now, he'd be her only choice.

Then there was the Jenkins family. They were a force to be reckoned with, and the most amazing group of people she'd ever met. They had welcomed her and Bella into their lives without question. Her daughter would be lucky to be a Jenkins.

"Well?" Cynthia prompted. "Did he say he'd do it?"

"He said that there was nothing he wouldn't do for me and Bella."

"Hmm, I knew I liked that boy. Well, it's settled. Bella will officially be a Jenkins. The sooner you and Antonio make that happen the better. There won't be any reason for anyone to link her to Ezra."

There wouldn't be any reason at all. Ezra wasn't listed on her birth certificate. Scarlett had left that line blank. The only way someone *might* suspect Bella was the great-granddaughter of Cynthia Armani was if they saw Bella in person. She favored Ezra and Cynthia enough to know she was related to them.

Instead of telling Cynthia that no one would be adopting

Bella, Scarlett stood next to the bed with her arms folded. "Are you dying?" she blurted.

"Aren't we all?" Cynthia shot back.

It was hard not to notice Cynthia's sunken eyes and the sallowness of her skin. She had looked a bit worn out the other day and even more today. Granted, it could be a natural part of aging, but Scarlett sensed the woman wasn't well. That would explain her discussing her will lately.

"Cynthia—"

"Ezra called me an hour before he was killed. He told me he asked you to marry him, and you turned him down," Cynthia said, talking over Scarlett and jolting her with her words.

Shock slammed into Scarlett like a steel weight that she couldn't get out from under, and it left her speechless. Until this moment, she thought only her mom, sister, and Antonio knew about the proposal. Cynthia knew and had never said a word.

The guilt that always hovered in the background surfaced and Scarlett stumbled backwards until her leg bumped the chair. She gripped the arm of it, barely managing to stay upright. If only a black hole could swallow her up. It would be better than having to stand before Cynthia, who lost her beloved grandson, and explain why she couldn't marry him. How could she tell this woman that it was her fault that Ezra had gone out that night?

"Cynthia..." Scarlett's heart was pounding loud enough to be heard on the next street, and she struggled to get it to beat at a normal rate. "I—I don't know what to say," she sputtered.

"I don't expect you to say anything. It's good you turned him down," the older woman said, surprising the heck out of Scarlett. "You two were way too young to be thinking about marriage, and that's what I told him. You guys were just starting in your respective careers, but Ezra didn't want to hear it. He insisted you were it for him. Something about wanting to lock you down before some other guy made a move on you."

"I'm so sorry, Cynthia. If it weren't for me, he might still be alive."

"Scarlett, my dear. It is not your fault that someone who wasn't paying attention to the road slammed into my grandson that night. Besides, I've learned a long time ago that when the good Lord is ready for us, there is nothing we can do to stop *His* will.

"If you're carrying around guilt, let it go now and move on with your life. *Live!* That's what he would want for you. That's what I want for you. Enjoy the time you have left on this earth with no guilt and no regrets. You hear me?"

Too choked up to speak, Scarlett swiped at her eyes and nodded.

Cynthia reached for her. "Now, give me a hug."

Scarlett smiled. "I'm so glad you're in my life," she whispered as she hugged Cynthia. "I pray you'll be around for years to come."

"Me too, but always know you and Bella have brought so much joy to my life. I love you girls."

Scarlett felt as if her heart would explode. She hoped this wasn't their last time together, but she was old enough to know none of them would be around forever.

"We love you too," she said, tightening her hold on the woman who was so dear to her.

"What's going on in here? Get away from my mother!"

Scarlett startled at the harsh tone and quickly released Cynthia. When she turned to face the owner of the voice, her breath caught. It was an older, female version of Ezra standing in the room, and the resemblance was unsettling.

Alberta. She and Ezra shared the same chestnut brown skin

tone, dark, almond-shaped eyes, and similar mouths. As if heading to court, her hair was pulled back into a tight bun at the nape of her neck. Scarlett recognized the navy-blue skirt suit as part of the Michael Kors Spring collection. It was tailored perfectly for her pear-shaped figure. Matching three-inch pumps completed the ensemble.

"Alberta, sometimes you act like you were raised by wolves," Cynthia said. "That is no way to enter *my* home or my bedroom. I know you have better manners than that."

The woman didn't respond, she just continued staring at Scarlett. Then again, the look was more of a glower. They had never met, and considering this first encounter, she was glad they hadn't. Any decent person, especially an attorney who was often in the public's eye because of high-profile cases, would at least pretend to be nice and approachable.

"Scarlett, you'll have to excuse my daughter. She's clearly forgotten all her home training." Cynthia lifted slightly, struggling to adjust the pillows behind her until Scarlett helped.

"How's that?" Scarlett asked.

"Perfect. Thanks, dear. Oh, and Alberta this is Scarlett. She was a good friend of Ezra's."

"Hi, it's nice to meet you," Scarlett said, her heart pounding double time.

She couldn't believe she was face-to-face with Ezra's mother. It was good to finally put a face with the evil stories she'd heard. Since Ezra didn't have pictures of his parents, Scarlett had done an internet search years ago to quell her curiosity. The only picture she had seen, not online, that included all of them was a family portrait hanging over the fireplace in Cynthia's library downstairs. Ezra was around four or five when it was commissioned.

"Since Ezra's death," Cynthia continued, "Scarlett has

managed to stay in touch, calling weekly and visiting often. Unlike *some* people," she said pointedly.

Alberta picked up a magazine from the table in the sitting room and thumbed through it. "Hello, Scarlett," she finally said and glanced up.

The woman's gaze did a slow crawl down Scarlett's body. From her braids to the light-gray, bell-sleeved jumpsuit she wore with matching sandals. At least the woman was no longer glowering, but she was surely judging if the distaste in her expression was any indication.

She dropped the magazine onto the table. "Are you here for a handout?" she asked, her words cut like a whip cracking through the air, slapping Scarlett across the face. "That has to be it because I can't see why else you'd be here. Mother's probably the one funding your expensive taste. Donna Karan attire and that Chanel bag and shoes must have set you back pretty good."

"*Wow.*" The word slipped through Scarlett's lips before she could stop it.

This woman was a real piece of work, and Scarlett was so tempted to stoop to her level and say something equally nasty back at her. Something like, *I didn't know Jimmy Choo high heels came in a size twenty-two* because the woman's feet were as huge as Shaquille O'Neal's.

No, Scarlett needed to keep her mouth shut and not bring any more attention to herself. So instead of saying anything to Alberta, she turned to Cynthia whose eyes were shooting daggers at her daughter.

"You were right, Cynthia. Your daughter is *something else.*" It sounded lame even to Scarlett's own ears, but she was at a loss on anything positive to say.

"Get the hell out of my house, Alberta!" Cynthia snarled and pointed to the door. "You're not welcome here, and just to be clear, everyone who visits me is not out for money. Some enjoy my company. Some even stop by because they care about my well-being."

"Well, I couldn't tell by looking at her why she was really here, especially since Ezra is *dead*."

Though her words were cold, Scarlett didn't miss the sadness in Alberta's eyes, but just as fast, it disappeared. Could this cold-hearted woman still be grieving her son's death?

"As for visiting you," Alberta continued, her tone as haughty as Cynthia's was sometimes, "I've been busy, Mother. With my long work hours, you can't expect me to drop everything and be here all the time. That's why I sent people over here for you to interview. People who could help you with your day-to-day needs and—"

"Stop it! You don't give a damn about my needs. You wanted me to hire those people, so they'd be your spies. I'm not stupid, Alberta! I see right through your schemes and don't worry, I don't need you to visit. I'm doing just fine."

With the way the two women glared at each other, the temperature in the room dropped fifty degrees. It was definitely time for Scarlett to make an exit.

"Oh, Mother, please don't start. Especially since you have company," Alberta ground out as she picked invisible lint from her dark-navy skirt. Her lips were pursed as if trying to keep her anger under control.

Scarlett cleared her throat. "Well, Cynthia, it's always great seeing you. I'm heading out, so you and your daughter can spend time together." Scarlett hugged Cynthia tightly and kissed her cheek, something that she always did before leaving. "Take care of yourself. I'll give you a call later."

Scarlett said her goodbyes and couldn't get out of the room fast enough. The dislike between the two women was palpable.

She couldn't imagine speaking to her mother like that or any elderly person for that matter.

Maybe Cynthia and Ezra hadn't exaggerated. It was clear that Alberta wasn't a likable person, and if her husband was anything like her, Scarlett wanted nothing to do with either of them.

She didn't know what it would take, but she was ready to do whatever necessary to keep Ezra's parents out of Bella's life. Even look into the adoption idea.

Chapter Sixteen

"Let me make sure I understand this," Ben Sr., Antonio's dad said. He was seated behind his desk and looked from Scarlett to him and back to Scarlett again. "You want my son to adopt Bella, so she can have the Jenkins name?"

Antonio didn't miss the incredulous tone in his father's voice. Hell, Antonio was still trying to make sense of everything too. After Scarlett returned from seeing Cynthia on Monday morning, she was adamant that he become Bella's father as soon as possible.

While they were waiting for their flight, and Bella had fallen asleep, Scarlett explained what happened at Cynthia's house. Whatever Ezra's mother said or did made Scarlett believe the woman wasn't above coming after them if she found out about Bella.

Though Antonio wanted nothing more than to have Bella as his daughter, this was a rash decision. He wasn't sure this drastic move was necessary, but Scarlett was adamant that this was what she wanted and what Bella needed. Even if Alberta had no legal rights to her granddaughter, Scarlett wanted to do as much as possible to shield her daughter from people who could cause her emotional harm.

Scarlett had surprised Antonio even more when she'd told him that even if things didn't work out between him and her, she wanted him to be Bella's father. She might not realize it yet, but Antonio wanted Scarlett too—eventually as his wife. For now, though, they'd focus on one thing at a time, and then he'd do everything in his power to make Scarlett fall in love with him.

He had called his dad's office first thing that morning to try to get on his schedule. As a defense attorney who owned a large law firm, Ben Sr.'s days were usually swamped. Thankfully his assistant had been able to juggle his schedule. Otherwise, Antonio would've called him directly. One thing about his dad was he *always* put his kids first. It had been like that all their lives, and Antonio tried to never abuse that privilege. Although today he would have done whatever necessary to get his father to meet with him and Scarlett.

"I know it sounds crazy Mr. Jenkins, but..." Scarlett stopped abruptly and glanced at Antonio.

If the way she was nibbling on her lower lip was any indication, she was nervous. Was she having second thoughts? Was there something she hadn't told him? Without thinking, Antonio reached over and wrapped his hand around hers. Her small hand was cold, and he held it tighter.

"You can still change your mind, Scarlett," Antonio said as he gently caressed the back of her hand with the pad of his thumb. He didn't want her having any regrets, and that's what he'd told her on their way to his father's office.

His dad sat back and studied them. "For what it's worth, Scarlett, I can't think of a better father for Bella. You've made an excellent choice in picking my son."

A slow smile punched up the corners of Antonio's mouth, and then he chuckled. "Don't listen to him, Scarlett. Not only is he biased, but he wants more grandchildren."

They laughed.

"Guilty," Ben Sr. said, still smiling before turning serious. "I've heard everything you've said, and I understand your concerns. I'm going to get someone to poke around in Mrs. Armani and her family's life." His attorney demeanor was firmly in place as he continued, "I'm not saying your reasons for wanting Antonio's help in this situation are not legitimate. However, let's make sure that Mrs. Armani's concerns about her daughter and son-in-law are warranted."

Scarlett squeezed Antonio's hand and scooted to the edge of her seat, putting her closer to the large desk. "Mr. Jenkins, I've thought about this long and hard, and I think Antonio adopting Bella is in the best interest of my daughter. Especially since I know how much he loves her. Besides that, I've met Alberta. There's no doubt in my mind that she'll seek out her mother's benefactor and try to contest the will."

"If Mrs. Armani is as smart as I think she is, and as wealthy as you think she is," Ben Sr. said to Scarlett, "she probably set up an irrevocable trust. Her daughter and son-in-law wouldn't be able to touch the estate."

"It's not just about the money, Mr. Jenkins, I don't want them to know about Bella. If she has a different last name, that'll be one way of protecting her from them."

"I understand why you feel you need to protect Bella. They can definitely make your life miserable," Ben Sr. said as he nodded slowly. "Even if her grandparents can't get their hands on her inheritance, they'll want to know everything about the person who was awarded the estate. They might find out about Bella even if Antonio adopts her, especially if they are as powerful as Mrs. Armani claims."

Scarlett rubbed her forehead, then met Antonio's gaze. Warmth spread through his body at the tenderness in her eyes. She regarded him with so much trust and something else that he couldn't quite identify. She had faith in him that there was nothing he wouldn't do for her or Bella.

She's. The. One.

The words screamed inside his head, and a calm settled over him. Yes, Scarlett was the one for him, and adopting Bella would just be the beginning to forever for all of them.

"I want to move forward," Scarlett said, her attention still on Antonio.

An electric charge pulsed between them as they continued to stare into each other's eyes. Did she feel what he was feeling? Did she understand he'd do whatever necessary to make her his?

If she didn't, she'd know soon enough. She was *the one*, and he'd pursue her the way he went after everything else he wanted. He'd make a plan and execute it.

Ben Sr. cleared his throat, breaking whatever electric current flowing between Antonio and Scarlett.

Antonio turned his complete attention to his father, watching him carefully. He could tell when Ben Sr. was working out a strategy because that vein on the side of his forehead was visible. His dad wouldn't steer them wrong.

"I'm not a family law attorney," his dad said, "but I'll set you two up with one of the best in our firm. However, you two have another problem."

His light-brown hazel eyes bore into Antonio, sending unease coursing through his veins. "What type of problem?"

"Ohio has strict rules about adoption, especially when it comes to second-parent and stepparent adoptions. Antonio, the only way you can adopt Bella is if you and Scarlett are married."

Chapter Seventeen

"**M**arried?"

"*Married?*"

Scarlett and Antonio said in unison, then looked at each other with wide eyes.

"Dad, you can't be serious. Adoptions happen all the time," Antonio said before Scarlett could form similar words.

"You're right, they do, but they happen with children who *don't* have parents. Or they happen when parents give up their rights. And they can also happen when a single parent marries, and their new spouse wants to adopt the child. That's the only way a child can be adopted in Ohio."

If Scarlett didn't know Mr. Jenkins better, she would think he was making this up. What he was saying made sense, but there was no way she and Antonio could get married. She might care for him, but she wasn't in love with him, and that was the only way she would marry anyone.

Wait. Had Cynthia known this when she suggested Antonio adopt Bella? Did she know they'd have to get married for any of this to work? How many times over the years had the woman casually mentioned it was time for Scarlett to settle down?

She shook the thoughts free. No way. Cynthia would've just pushed her to marry Antonio without mentioning the adoption idea. But Scarlett wouldn't put anything past the old lady. She could be manipulative when she wanted certain results, but this?

Nah, she wouldn't have suggested marriage. She knew Scarlett wasn't planning on getting married. At least not any time soon, but this information was a curveball Scarlett hadn't seen coming.

The only way Antonio can adopt Bella is if I marry him.

Crap. Why couldn't anything ever be easy? She could admit to being impulsive at times, but this... *I can't do it.*

She'd finally come to a decision that she was one hundred percent sure of, then *bam!* It's all shot to hell. It was one thing to ask Antonio to become Bella's father. It was another to rope him into marriage to make that happen.

"I can't. I can't use him like that," Scarlett said, then snapped her mouth shut. She hadn't meant to verbalize that thought out loud.

She glanced at Antonio, and her breath caught. The compassion in his eyes was powerful enough to send shivers down her spine. There was no doubt he cared about her, and that pleased and terrified her. Why'd he have to be such a sweetheart? Why'd he have to make it so easy to like him?

I'd do anything for you and Bella, he'd said more than once, and Scarlett believed him. The only reason he had hesitated on saying yes to the adoption was because of her. Even then, he was looking out for her well-being wanting to make sure she understood what she was giving up.

This was... this all was too much. Whoever said adulting wasn't easy knew what they were talking about because some decisions felt almost impossible to make. Bella deserved a man like Antonio in her life. Granted, Scarlett didn't have to marry him to make that happen, but she'd do anything to ensure Bella's happiness and safety.

Almost anything.

But what about Theodore and Alberta? What if they found out about Bella and came after them? As her biological grandparents, they might not only come for the inheritance, but they might also want to be in Bella's life. With the latter, they had a right to get to know their own flesh and blood.

Thoughts of Ezra and the way his parents abandoned him came to mind.

No, she couldn't let them into Bella's life. She also couldn't use Antonio like this.

"Antonio deserves to marry someone who is *in* love with him," she said to his father, then turned to Antonio, realizing she should be saying these words to him. "It's bad enough I asked you to adopt Bella. I can't marry you for the sole purpose of you adopting my child. It's not fair to you." Asking him to adopt Bella hadn't been fair either, but that was different. He loved her daughter, and the feeling was mutual.

Antonio searched her eyes, for what, she wasn't sure. He didn't say anything, and his facial expression was unreadable. Which wasn't new considering he rarely smiled and always seemed to be in deep thought. Actually, it was in this moment that he looked a lot like his father. The intensity in their serious expressions were identical.

Antonio reached over and linked his fingers with hers but looked at his father. "Dad, can Scarlett just add my name to Bella's birth certificate and then change Bella's surname?"

"Not without consequences. Adding you now after seven or eight years would look suspect. You guys would have to prove you're the father, which would be impossible."

Scarlett sat back in her seat and sighed. She hadn't thought about any of that. She didn't have any other ideas, and now she was sorry she'd pulled Antonio into this. She had started imagining a future with him in their lives—as Bella's father. Granted, her imagination was all sunshine and rainbows even though that's not how her life had been. Why would it change now?

Mr. Jenkins lifted the handset on his desk phone and typed in three or four numbers. Someone picked up immediately.

"Can you come to my office?" he said before hanging up, and Scarlett wondered who he'd called. Maybe he had another idea.

Seconds later, there was a quick knock on the door, and they turned just as Luke Hayden, Christina's husband, strolled in.

Though he was dressed in an expensive-looking suit and appeared every bit the white-collar role, there was an edginess about him. Maybe it was the bold pattern on his tie and the diamond stud in his left ear. No, that wasn't it. It was the swagger in his walk, the intensity in his eyes, and his confident demeanor. Maybe that's why some of the family thought of him as the thug lawyer. The handsome man looked as if he could handle anything that came his way—good or bad. No doubt his clients loved that about him.

"What's up, man?" he said to Antonio.

"Not much." Antonio stood to shake his hand, and they pulled each other into one of those man hugs.

Luke glanced at Scarlett and extended his hand. "Hey, Scarlett. Good seeing you again."

"You too," she said as they shook.

"Thanks for coming in here," Mr. Jenkins said to Luke while scribbling something on a notepad. He ripped off the top sheet and handed it over. "I need you and Michael to dig up everything you can on those individuals. I want *everything*, and I only want the two of you working on this. I need the information ASAP. Charge any time or fees to the family account."

Luke glanced at the paper, then folded it, and stuffed it into his pants pocket. "You got it." He said his goodbyes and strolled out just as gracefully as he'd entered.

"Michael, as in Peyton's husband?" Antonio asked.

Peyton was one of his older first cousins who used to run Jenkins & Sons Construction before she got married and moved to New York.

"Yes. We hire him for special assignments."

Turning to Scarlett, Antonio said, "Michael Cutter is one of my cousins-in-laws, and he's the best private investigator in New York."

Scarlett nodded. Cynthia was right about one thing. The Jenkins were a formidable family with some impressive connections. But Scarlett didn't want to waste any more of their time.

"Since we can't move forward with the adoption, there's probably no reason to have Cynthia and her family investigated."

"Who said we weren't moving forward?"

Scarlett's head whipped around to Antonio. "We can't since we're not married, and I already told you that I couldn't ask that of you."

"Maybe I'd offer," he said as if this were an invitation to go grocery shopping.

Her heart raced. What was he thinking? "Tony, we can't get married just so you can adopt Bella. That's crazy! That's not a good reason to marry someone," she insisted, even though what she had proposed was just as insane.

"Actually, you'd be shocked at how common marriages of convenience are. My law firm has written up plenty of contracts," Mr. Jenkins interjected and gave a slight shrug.

"People get married for all types of reasons, and some of those reasons are less noble than this one."

Surprise plowed through Scarlett. *Seriously?* She thought that only happened in romance novels. No doubt her disbelief showed on her face, and when she opened her mouth to speak, Mr. Jenkins lifted his hands.

"I mean, this is something you and Antonio should discuss privately before any decisions are made. In the meantime, I have to get to court. Once you two talk this over, if you need me, you know where to find me."

* * *

As they walked out of the building, Antonio's mind was whirling. He couldn't remember ever playing hooky from work, but today warranted it. Even more so now that there was a wrinkle in the adoption situation, but he wasn't discouraged. He would have never considered a marriage of convenience. However, if it meant getting the family he'd always wanted, he wouldn't rule it out.

"I was thinking we could go around the corner to the coffee shop and plan next steps," Antonio said as they stood in front of his dad's office building. "I know—"

"Tony." Scarlett squinted against the sunlight. "You're not much of a coffee drinker. Why would you want to go there?"

"Because you are, and I want us to figure out what we're going to—"

"I don't want to," she said. "I don't want to discuss the meeting, adoption, nor marriage. Let's just... not think. Hey, wanna go to Smale?" she said of Smale Riverfront Park about ten or fifteen minutes away.

They were definitely not on the same page. It was becoming abundantly clear that, though they had several things in common, he and Scarlett also had their differences. One being—he was a planner while she was more impulsive. Too bad Antonio wasn't good at going with the flow or letting things happen at will. He liked to take action and get ahead of a situation.

Scarlett on the other hand was apparently a wait and see type person and was okay with putting things out of her mind for a later time. She jammed her fist on her hips and flashed a cute frown that nearly made him laugh.

"Well, are you going with me? Or do I have to go by myself?"

"I'll go wherever you go," he said, meaning it. He was prepared to do whatever it took to show her that he was in this for the long haul. Her frown disappeared immediately, and she grinned up at him.

"Good. Let's go."

A short while later, they roamed the park, and he admitted, not out loud, that this was the perfect idea. Sunshine and seventy-degree weather with a slight breeze made it a perfect day for a stroll. He couldn't remember the last time he'd walked through the park holding hands with a gorgeous woman.

As they passed the Great Adventure Playground near the base of the John Roebling Bridge, Scarlett slowed.

"It's a beautiful day out," she said smiling and turning her face up to the sky, allowing the sun to kiss her smooth, brown skin.

Sometimes he still found it hard to believe this former model was interested in him. He'd gone out with some nice-looking women, but Scarlett was breathtaking, even with very little makeup and her braids in a sexy-messy ponytail.

"Thanks for agreeing to come out here with me," she said as they took in the sights.

"It's my pleasure. I love spending time with you, and this

The Cost of Love

place was a good choice. I forgot how nice it is out here. Has Bella ever been here?" If she hadn't, Antonio would want to bring her one day, maybe when school was out for the summer.

"Once, a few years ago. Now that she's older and not as scared of a little adventure," Scarlett chuckled, "I'll have to bring her back. Last time she was too afraid to try out most of the activities like the rope bridge and the log climbers."

They walked and talked for the next few minutes about nothing and everything, and Antonio knew more than ever that he wanted this in his life. He wanted to have someone to play hooky with. He wanted someone to hold hands with on a beautiful day. More than anything, he wanted to share his life with a special woman who was easy to be with. A woman who cared about him as much as he cared about her.

"What's your favorite way to unwind after a long day?" Scarlett asked as they walked.

"It used to be having a beer and watching a game. Now, after spending the weekend with you and Bella, it's snuggling with you two on the sofa while watching a Disney movie. I think I can name all the Disney princesses. Quite an accomplishment for a guy who barely paid attention to Cinderella."

Scarlett sputtered a laugh. "If I remember correctly, you fell asleep during the movie."

Antonio shrugged. "It's still my favorite way to unwind. What about you?"

"Well, it used to be soaking in a bubble bath with a glass of wine. Now I'd have to say it's watching you cook dinner for me while I drink a glass of wine."

"Good to know," Antonio said, and the smile she cast on him was as intimate as a sweet kiss. His heart squeezed as he continued to watch her, loving the way her eyes glittered under the sunlight. "We'll have to agree on a set number of days a week that I cook dinner for you."

"I wouldn't say no to that. Next question. How do you cope with stress?"

Antonio pondered the question for a minute before saying, "I usually go somewhere quiet, like my office or my back patio to think about the situation. Time alone usually helps me get clarity. What about you?"

A couple of birds chasing each other and flying erratically practically crashed into them before he and Scarlett ducked.

"Geez, they need to watch where they're going," she joked and chuckled. "Okay, so I do my best coping with anything dark chocolate. Also, taking a walk helps. Oh, and retail therapy. Nothing says relax and breathe like buying a gorgeous pair of shoes. Here's another question. What's most important to you—emotional or physical intimacy?"

Antonio blew out a breath. "That's a hard one. I'd have to say both. Being able to emotionally connect with someone is major for me. I need to be able to trust the person I'm with enough to share my thoughts, fears, and even my dreams. *However*, life without some form of physical intimacy would be impossible. I'm not talking just sex, but also touching. I couldn't imagine not being able to hold your hand." He brought the back of her hand to his lips and kissed her warm skin.

Scarlett visibly shivered, then giggled like a schoolgirl. "I agree, but I think physical intimacy is most important to me. At least right now because without it, I wouldn't be able to do this," she said and kissed his lips.

Antonio smiled, and he could've sworn she whimpered. "I can see what you mean. I wouldn't want to miss out on those sweet kisses."

"I really have to keep you smiling and flashing those dimples," she said barely above a whisper, then asked, "How many kids do you want?"

Antonio pulled up short, shocked by the question but ready with an answer. "As many as you'll give me."

Her mouth dropped open, then she threw her head back, and laughed. "Has anyone ever told you that you have a great sense of humor? And how do you keep a straight face when you say stuff like that?" she asked, still laughing.

"Because I'm serious. I want a big family, Scarlett, and I want you to be the mother of my children."

She lifted her hands. "I'm sorry, Tony. I shouldn't have asked that, especially since I insisted on us not discussing any of that. I guess I was just curious."

"Okay, what else are you curious about? Actually, I have a question. If you ever decided to have more kids, how many would you have?"

"Two. I want two boys. My turn. Have you ever been in love before?"

"I thought I was in love once, but lately I've been questioning whether that was love. Because what I feel for you is like *nothing* I've ever felt for anyone else, *ever*."

That was the truth, and considering the way her mouth was hanging open again, she hadn't expected that answer. He just hoped his responses weren't freaking her out.

"Come on, Scarlett. You know not to ever ask a question unless you're prepared for the answer," he said and gently grasped her hand again.

"Umm... yeah. I'll have to remember that in the future."

For the next few minutes, they walked in silence, but it wasn't an uncomfortable silence. Antonio loved the random questions, and more than anything, he loved learning more about her. Like the fact that she wanted more kids.

"I wonder why they didn't just make this a maze," Scarlett said as they slowed near the edge of the labyrinth. This one was made up of concrete slabs and grass, and the meandering paths were wide enough for two people to walk side by side.

"Because labyrinths are used symbolically as a form of moving meditation. Unlike trying to get through a complicated maze, that might stress you out before you reach the exit, this is meant for you to stroll through and meditate."

Scarlett chuckled. "Of course, you'd know that. Well, we can't let this opportunity go to waste. Let's follow the path and ponder the meaning of life."

They joined a handful of people who had already started around the circular pattern. Antonio had never walked through one before, but he could see how the process could be calming. It was all about the journey and not about figuring out how to exit because there was only one way in and out.

They'd barely gone halfway through the circular pattern, and Antonio could already feel his mind relaxing. All seemed well in the world, and he wished he could go through every moment of the day like this, slowly. He wouldn't have any stress in his life.

After they reached the center, they went back the way they'd come until they were once again standing on the edge of the labyrinth.

"That was cool," he said, thinking how doing something so simple could actually be fun.

Scarlett agreed, and they started back on their stroll. Antonio guided her to the railing that overlooked the river.

"The park's summer concerts start in a week or so. We should try to catch one. This year they're on Thursday nights, and it'll include all types of music genres," Scarlett said.

This was a good sign. She was planning for them to continue dating.

"Sounds like a great idea. I haven't attended one before, so it'll be a nice change of pace." Anything would be, considering he usually worked until eight or nine at night. The long hours were mainly due to not wanting to go home to an empty house. Now that he was dating again, maybe he'd have a reason to cut his workdays shorter.

"Let's get a picture or two," Scarlett said, her cell phone in hand.

She positioned them in front of the water and snapped several selfies. With each photo, she adjusted their positions or turned the phone this way and that, getting different poses with each. Antonio couldn't help laughing when she insisted on them taking a photo with silly faces.

He had never posed for photos as much as he had since dating Scarlett, and it pleased him that she wanted pictures with him. She promised not to put them on social media, though he didn't care. Who wouldn't want to be photographed with such a sexy woman?

It also surprised Antonio that she even thought to take pictures. She seemed to always be ready to whip out her camera or her cell phone to capture the moment. To capture memories. Something he never thought to do.

When she was done, they leaned against the railing and stared out over the calm water. A peace settled over Antonio. "Thanks for suggesting we come out here," he said. "It's a great place to think and just be." He needed and wanted more of this, and he was ready to come up with a plan to make it happen.

"I agree," Scarlett said, flashing him another one of her sweet smiles, and his heart flipped inside of his chest.

Unable to resist, Antonio did something he'd wanted to do since they left his father's office. He backed her to the railing and crushed his mouth to hers. Scarlett moaned in pleasure when he slipped his tongue between her sweet lips and held her close around the waist.

She always felt perfect in his arms, but kissing and holding her always made him want more. A whole lot more.

Her arms looped around his neck, and her hand went to the back of his head, deepening their connection. Antonio would never get tired of kissing her, and the park offered the perfect backdrop. He loved on her mouth, savoring this moment as the river babbled in the background, birds chirped in the distance, and a gentle breeze flowed around them.

This was a perfect way to spend the day with the woman he could see a future with. His hands slowly roamed over her body before settling on her perfect butt as he drank in her sweetness. The sensual sounds she was making with every lap of their tongues had his body stirring with need. Maybe starting something out here hadn't been the best thing because what he really wanted to do was take her back to his place and love on her whole body.

Soon. They'll be together soon.

"Get a room!" someone yelled, and Antonio heard what sounded like roller skates roaring down the sidewalk.

He slowly eased his mouth from Scarlett's but kept his arm around her waist. He placed a kiss against her temple. "I know we agreed to table the conversation about the adoption and marriage, but don't rule any of it out just yet. Okay?"

Scarlett's beautiful dark eyes met his, and it was as if he could see his future deep in the depths of them. After a long moment of searching his eyes, she nodded.

"Okay. I won't rule anything out. Now, how about we go find a room?"

Chapter Eighteen

The drive to Antonio's house seemed to take forever, but the wait made Scarlett want him that much more. Their day definitely hadn't gone as planned. Yet walking and talking with him shed a light on just how much she enjoyed being in his presence. He was so easy to be with, even if this next step in their relationship was a little scary.

But with the magnetic connection between them, Scarlett felt ready. Besides, his potent kisses had her body pulsing with need, yearning to have his hands and mouth all over her. They couldn't turn back now.

"Are you sure about this?" Antonio asked the moment they entered his kitchen from the attached garage.

She glanced at him and didn't miss the heated desire in his eyes. Reaching for his belt buckle, she started undoing it. "I have never been more sure about anything in my life."

This was new for her. Not sex, but the boldness of taking the lead. Anxiousness rumbled inside of her, and Scarlett felt as if she was going to leap out of her skin. When she realized

Sharon C. Cooper

Antonio hadn't said anything else, her hands stilled on his belt, and she met his eyes.

"Tony, don't overthink this. I want you. You want me. I say let's get naked and do what comes naturally, but if you're—"

Scarlett shrieked in shock when he suddenly lifted her onto his right shoulder and stumped out of the kitchen. She burst out laughing. Where had this caveman behavior come from? It seemed a little out of character, but it was turning her on even more. If he was like this in the bedroom, rough, tough, and unpredictable, they were going to have a blast.

Yikes! She held on to the back of his shirt, praying he wouldn't drop her, but he carried her as if she weighed nothing.

"Is this your way of showing off how strong you are?" she asked as she held on tighter while he climbed the stairs. "Or are you trying to make it clear who's in charge?"

She yelped, then laughed again when he started jogging up the rest of the stairs without responding. Watching the floor go by from her upside-down position was making her dizzy, but still, excitement bubbled inside of her.

Once in his bedroom, Antonio didn't give her time to glance around and check out his space. The moment he set her on her feet, he crushed her body to his and took her mouth with a hunger like no other.

Yes! They were doing this. With each stroke of his tongue, liquid heat pooled between her legs, and Scarlett had to squeeze her thighs together to keep from squirming. Part of her wanted them to take their time and explore each other's body. The other part of her, though, was totally open to a quickie.

His drugging kiss and the way he held her close with his large hands gripping her ass stirred her inner temptress. She wanted him more than she wanted her next breath, and her hands went back to his belt. Without breaking their kiss, she finished unfastening it, then went for the clasp on his pants.

136

Was she in a hurry? Yes. Did Antonio seem to care? No.

Still kissing her, he gripped her hands and moved them behind her back as he ground against her. Scarlett moaned with pleasure at the way every part of their bodies touched, but their clothes were in the way.

"Tony," she mumbled against his lips.

"Hmm," he said, breaking their kiss and moving his mouth along her jawline, her cheek, and working his way down her neck, all the while maintaining the hold on her hands.

Her senses reeled and her thoughts spun out of control. They were still fully dressed, but his mouth on her heated skin was doing wicked things to her.

"I want to touch you," she said, moaning as they continued grinding against each other. "All of you. Like... without clothes on."

"That's what I want too," he said and kissed her. He finally released her hands and started unbuttoning her blouse. "Let's get you out of these clothes."

"Great minds think alike," she said and tugged his shirt out of his pants. Their hands were all over each other, and they made quick work of getting undressed until they were standing before each other naked.

Heat raged through her at the sight of him. Even knowing Antonio had an incredible body underneath his clothing, Scarlett hadn't been prepared for the pleasure of seeing him undressed. Between his chiseled chest and rippling muscles, there wasn't a lick of fat anywhere on his body. Her gaze went lower. Long, thick, and hard, his penis stood at the ready, and the way her body yearned for him, Scarlett knew without a doubt their first round would be quick. She didn't require foreplay or an exploration of their bodies. She just wanted him inside of her. Now.

Her sex clenched with need at the way Antonio's gaze took

her in. He had barely touched her, and already he was awakening parts of her body that were starving for attention. It was impossible to miss the lust radiating in his dark eyes.

"Wow," he said huskily. "My imagination didn't do you justice, Scarlett. You're perfection personified." He didn't take his attention from her as he pulled back the covers on the bed. "I have wanted you from the moment I saw you at your sister's birthday party last year, and now you're mine."

Scarlett's heart was beating so fast, and a mix of emotions swirled inside of her, but the main one was impatience. "I am, and now that we have that out of the way, what are you going to do with me?"

"Oh, I have a few things in mind." One of his rare smiles and those adorable dimples made an appearance, and he pulled her against his hard body.

Damn, he felt good, Scarlett thought seconds before he lifted her and laid her on the bed. She had never been one of those women who liked being carried around by a man, but that had changed as of today. She had a feeling every experience would be different with Antonio.

He climbed onto the bed and gathered her in his arms before covering her mouth with his. The kiss started tenderly but as their hands roamed each other's bodies, an electric jolt arced through her. This man. Their relationship might have started slow and steady, but within the last few hours, Scarlett felt closer to him than she'd felt with any man in a long time. And she was here for it. She wanted him. She wanted all of him.

"Damn, you smell good," Antonio murmured against her lips.

He kissed the corner of her mouth, then her chin, and as his chest grazed over her sensitive nipples, Scarlett sucked in a breath. His lips seared a path from her collar bone to the swell of her breasts, on down to her stomach as he whispered his love for each part of her body.

Pleasure pulsed through her, and heat sizzled along her spine with every feather-like kiss over her skin. The delicious torture of this man's lips on her heated flesh sent her arousal to new heights and had her groaning with pleasure.

Goodness. Scarlett's thoughts stalled. She squirmed beneath him as he worked his mouth back up her body, taking his time as if determined to kiss, lick, and touch every inch of her.

"I'm in love with these," he said of her full breasts as he stroked one of her sensitive nipples with his talented tongue.

She gasped and her insides quivered as he sucked one of them into his mouth. An electric current surged through her from her nipples to the tips of her toes. Considering how long it had been since she'd been with a man, at this rate, it wasn't going to take much to make her come. Especially when one of his hands slid intimately down her body until he reached the apex of her thighs.

Multitasker? Check.

Hard, hot, and quick. That's what she wanted this first round to be, but before she could voice her request, Antonio pinched her clit. Scarlett cried out, but it caught in her throat when he slipped a finger inside of her, then another.

"Ohhh." She slammed her eyes close and gritted her teeth as pleasure pulsed through her. Unable to control her hips, she bucked against him and rode his hand as he pumped his fingers into her. Pressure continued building inside of her as the pad of his thumb teased her clit. Her senses were on overload.

"Tony. Oh my... goodness, Tony, I..."

"You like that?" he crooned close to her ear.

"Y—yes, yes. Oh yes," she gasped, and she fisted the covers

while squirming, struggling to hang on as he continued to pleasure her. She couldn't take much more.

"Okay. Okay, Tony, I—I... Oh my... I'm coming... *arghhh!*" she screamed as her muscles tightened.

Omigod. Omigod. Omigod. Her orgasm hit hard, rocking her to the tips of her toes as she vibrated with pleasure. It was like free-falling over a cliff at rapid speed without a care in the world.

Scarlett's breaths came in short spurts while she fought to get air into her lungs. She barely registered Antonio shifting on the bed until she heard a drawer open and then the sound of foil ripping. Bone-weary, she watched him through half-opened lids as he moved back to her and quickly sheathed himself.

Not giving her time to come down from her high, he nudged her legs apart and positioned his large body between her thighs. Raw lust clawed through her. The man was beautiful inside and out.

As he hovered above her, Antonio kissed her sweetly, then stared into her eyes. "You're mine," he said, the intense heat brimming in his dark eyes held her gaze captive.

"Yes," she said. In that soul-stirring moment, she couldn't help but agree to anything he said. "Yes. I'm yours, and you're mine."

Not breaking eye contact, he slowly entered her, inch by delicious inch. Scarlett sucked in a breath as her interior walls tightened around his penis. Damn, he was big, and thick, and hard as granite, and she was more than pleased.

Antonio held still for a second allowing her body to adjust to him. He lowered his head and kissed her. "You okay?" he whispered as he eased in deeper.

"Better than okay," she breathed.

Cupping his handsome face between her hands, emotions suddenly bombarded her. Scarlett wanted to say something.

She *felt* as if she should say something, but the words didn't come.

As Antonio began moving inside of her, he nipped at her top lip, then her lower one, and Scarlett melted when he kissed her tenderly. She had wondered what it would be like when they got intimate, but being with him like this was exceeding her expectations. Their bodies moved in perfect sync as if made for each other.

"Damn, you feel good," he said gruffly and picked up speed.

Scarlett met him stroke for stroke as his thrusts grew more intense. She gripped his firm butt, squeezing him as he went deeper and harder and their moans of pleasure filled the quietness of the room.

A growl rumbled from Antonio and pressure quickly built inside of Scarlett, and the sound of flesh slapping against flesh filled her ears.

"Ohhh," she moaned, her nails digging into his skin as her release grew closer. A swirl of sensations charged through her as Antonio kept driving into her, but one more powerful thrust and Scarlett lost it. She couldn't control the outcry of satisfaction that turned her world onto its axis as an orgasm hurtled her to a point of no return.

Antonio cursed under his breath and picked up speed. His body drove into her over and over and over again uncontrollably until his muscles grew taut and he stiffened. And when he roared her name, the boom of his voice ricocheted around the room as his release shook his whole body.

"*Oh, my God,*" he cried out hoarsely and collapsed on top of her.

Scarlett wrapped her arms around his neck as aftershocks shook them both while their chests heaved against one another. Them being together like this was wild, and she was savoring every minute, reveling in the intensity of what she'd just experienced with this man.

Antonio was surprising her at every turn.

* * *

A short while later, after getting cleaned up, Antonio held Scarlett against his body as they lounged together in bed.

"That was incredible," he said and kissed the top of her head.

"It really was," she whispered and snuggled closer.

She lay halfway on top of him with her arm across his waist and her right leg over his thigh. He marveled at how perfectly she fit against him. Like she was made for him.

This was what he wanted. Scarlett with him like this all the time. He knew when they got together it would be spectacular, but what they just experienced was beyond his imagination. His body was still humming with pleasure, and he looked forward to another round with her before he took her home.

He could admit to loving what they'd done this afternoon, but what was developing between them was so much more than physical. Their connection was like nothing he had ever shared with another human being, and he had to do whatever necessary to keep her in his life.

"Thanks for playing hooky," Scarlett mumbled, sounding half asleep. Her head rested on his chest as he stroked her bare back. She sighed wistfully and said, "It's been an amazing day."

"Yeah, it has, and I'm planning on us having many more days like this."

Antonio wasn't sure if she'd heard him because minutes after he spoke the words, her light snores reached his ears. He lifted his left arm and glanced at his wrist. She needed to pick

Bella up from school by three-thirty, and he wanted to make sure they allowed enough time for her to get there.

As he lay with her in his arms, he was more determined than ever to keep her in his life. She hadn't wanted to discuss their proposed marriage of convenience since leaving his dad's office, and Antonio respected that. But just because she didn't want to talk about it didn't mean the subject was over. Now that he'd had a taste of her, he couldn't let her go. He also couldn't accept them being just friends. They were way beyond that. He wanted to be her husband, her life partner.

He just had to figure out how to make that a reality and sooner than later.

Chapter Nineteen

Later that night, Antonio rang the doorbell to his parents' house. He hadn't been able to stop thinking about the situation with Scarlett and he hoped to get some perspective from his father. His dad was the best man he knew, and in the last thirty-plus years, he hadn't steered him wrong.

The front door swung open just as he was about to ring the bell again. He could use his key, but he preferred to only use it in case of emergency.

"Hey, son," Ben Sr. said and opened the door wider. "Come on in."

"Thanks for being okay with me stopping by this late," Antonio said as he shrugged out of his jacket and hung it in the coat closet. It was around nine o'clock at night, probably too late for a visit, but he needed to talk.

"I always have time for you. Come on, we can talk in my office." Ben Sr. started for the hallway leading to the back of the house but slowed. "Are you hungry? There's lasagna in the refrigerator."

"No, I'm good. I don't plan to stay long, but I wanted to talk more about what we discussed this morning." As they moved farther into the house, Antonio noted how quiet it was. "Where's Mom?" he asked of his stepmother who had been more of a mother to him than the woman who'd given birth to him.

He had known of Makena for as long as he could remember, but it wasn't until he was an adult that he actually met her. She and his father had grown up together, but after high school graduation, their lives went in different directions when they attended different colleges out of town. They'd both majored in law, got their degrees, married other people, and had families. Unfortunately, and fortunately, they both got divorced.

After Antonio's mother left, his dad rarely dated, and it was years later that Antonio knew why—Makena. He'd been in love with her since they were kids, but he never pursued her the way he should've. At least not until several years ago, after her divorce when she moved back to Cincinnati. Now they were married, sharing a law practice, and Antonio had never seen his father as happy as he was since Makena came back into his life.

"She's at a fundraiser, somewhere downtown that Ava is hosting," Ben Sr. said of Antonio's stepsister.

Antonio followed him down the long hallway to the back of the house where his office was located. "I'm surprised you didn't go. You usually attend her events."

"I would've, but I worked late and knew I wouldn't get there in time. Thankfully, Ava was okay with me writing a *fat* check to the organization."

Antonio laughed. "Yeah, I bet she was."

His sister was always volunteering and supporting one nonprofit organization after another. She had a big heart for giving, and made sure to rope all of them, one way or another, into some of her charitable campaigns. Antonio was surprised she hadn't hit him up for a donation or to attend. Maybe because she'd gotten him a few months ago.

When they entered the office, his dad sat behind his desk, and Antonio dropped down on the leather sofa that was off to the side. Not wanting to waste his father's time, he got right to the point.

"Were you serious about what you said, regarding marriages of convenience? Do you really see that a lot?"

His father studied him a long time before nodding. "Yeah, more often than you would believe. I've done contracts for people who had to be married in order to gain an inheritance. Some who married to help keep someone else in the country. There were even a few who married in order to get onto someone's health insurance.

"Many of the marriages have been successful, but there are a few which ended at an agreed time. Usually after two or three years. Are you and Scarlett considering that option?"

"Me more than she is."

"I see." His dad rocked slightly in his seat as he continued to study Antonio. "Even though I think it's a bit extreme, I understand why Scarlett wants you to adopt Bella. What I don't understand is why you're agreeing."

"I love both of them," Antonio said without hesitation. "Besides, you know I've always wanted to get married and have a family. When Scarlett asked me to be Bella's father, even though she said nothing about marriage, I couldn't pass up the opportunity to have them in my life. And Bella..."

His dad smiled. "Yeah, she's a little sweetheart, and you two get along like you've been in her life since birth."

"I feel like I have. As a matter-of-fact, I can see myself spending the rest of my life with her and Scarlett."

He told his father about the eerie feeling he'd gotten as

Scarlett walked down the aisle during Ben Jr.'s wedding. Antonio would never forget that moment when he could've sworn he heard the words: *She's the one.*

"I know it sounds strange," he said. "But it was as clear as day. Dad, I've *never* experienced anything like it, and I'll admit, it shook me."

His father chuckled, a knowing look on his face. "Been there. Done that, and if you ask any Jenkins man who's married, he'll tell you the same thing. We all have similar stories. Don't ignore the feeling, Antonio. I really do believe—"

"Do not say you believe in that Jenkins men myth. Even with that experience at the wedding, I still find it hard to believe our mind, body, and soul can know a woman is *the one.*"

His dad grinned and shook his head. "Son, believe what you want, but I'm telling you, so far, it's been true. And before you ask, the situation with your birth mother was different. She might not have been the woman I was destined to live the rest of my life with, but she gave me the two most incredible gifts I've ever received in my life—you and your brother."

"So when you married the first time, was it for love?"

His father rubbed his short beard as he considered the question. "I loved your mother. She was a good friend, but..."

"But?"

"But I never felt the *'can't live without you'* love that I feel for Makena. She's my heart, and I can't even imagine my life without her."

As his father tried to explain his truth, it was as if Antonio was hearing Scarlett's confession all over again. She'd basically said the same thing to him about her feelings for Todd and Ezra. How she'd never felt like she was *in* love with either.

"I'm sure everyone's *falling in love* experience is different," his father said. "But I'm a true believer that when you find that one woman, the one who feels like your other half, you're going to know. Follow your heart and try not to overthink and over plan in this case like you do with everything else."

Antonio laughed. Everyone knew he could ruin a good time in any aspect with overthinking the hell out of something.

They were interrupted by the house alarm chime, announcing someone had entered.

"That must be your mom. I'll be right back," his dad said before leaving the room. A short while later, they both entered the office space.

"Well, hey there," Makena said. "This is a pleasant surprise. What's going on? A meeting of the minds?"

Antonio chuckled and hugged her. "Something like that. You look nice."

"Thank you, sweetie."

Her golden-brown skin seemed to glow under the fluorescent lights. Or it could be her warm smile causing it. His stepmother always looked classy, and tonight was no different. Her long hair was in an elaborate twist on top of her head, and the short, black cocktail dress made her look as stylish as usual.

"I heard you were at the office this morning. I hate that I missed you."

"Yeah, your assistant said you were in a meeting. I told Dad he could fill you in on why me and Scarlett were there. Did he tell you?"

Makena was an estate planning attorney and had joined his dad's practice a year after they'd married. Their offices at work were on different floors, but whenever he visited one of them, he usually tried to see the other while he was there.

"Yeah, I told her," Ben Sr. kissed Makena's cheek before returning to his seat at the desk. "Babe, tell him what you said to me."

"I told him if you're anything like your father, you've probably already determined Scarlett is the one for you. And you'll stop at nothing to make that happen, even convince her to marry you before she's ready."

Antonio grinned and glanced at his dad, who smirked and rolled his eyes.

"I also told him Scarlett seems like an intelligent woman, who is quite smitten with you. I didn't miss how she kept looking at you during the wedding. She knows you're a sure thing and will do right by her and Bella. However, getting married when you're not in love is a whole different beast."

Makena approached him and cupped his cheek.

"You've shown her who you are. I say ask her to marry you and see what happens. I love you, and you know we're here to support whatever decision you make. And don't worry, I've been told that this stays between us."

Antonio's heart swelled, and he hugged Makena. "Thanks, Mom, for everything. You always know exactly what to say. I'll keep you posted."

"You do that and have a good night."

When she left the room and closed the door behind her, his dad said, "I can't say I agree with the idea of you and a marriage of convenience. However, if you believe in your heart Scarlett is *the one*, go for it. If things don't work out the way you want them to, at least you'll know you gave it your all."

Antonio nodded, feeling surer about this than he had about anything else in his life. "She's the one."

"What if you marry and she never feels the same as you? Are you prepared for that?"

Antonio had thought about that since dropping Scarlett off at home hours ago. She may never love him the way he loved her, but he had to go for broke. He had faith that she'd fall in love with him. When? He wasn't sure, but he was going to love her so good she wouldn't want anyone else.

"I'm prepared to do whatever I have to do to make Scarlett my wife."

"In that case, I suggest we start working on a marriage contract."

"With no expiration date," Antonio added.

His father looked at him doubtfully. "I can tell Scarlett cares about you, but I don't know if she'll go with a contract that doesn't have an end date. But you'll never know until you ask."

"I'm going for it." Antonio ambled to the desk and folded his arms across his chest. "What do I need to do?"

His dad grinned. "Well, since I know my son, I took the liberty of starting a contract for you."

Antonio laughed as his father turned his computer screen around for him to see.

"One thing, though. This afternoon, I talked with one of our family law attorneys. She mentioned that in some cases, it can take up to a year for an adoption to be finalized."

Just when he was getting hopeful about his future, another wrinkle made an appearance. "What?"

"Every case is different, but Luke *knows* people," his dad said with air quotes. "He claims, if necessary, he can get the adoption application expedited when or if you and Scarlett get married."

Antonio frowned. He had no idea it could take that long, and it was safe to say Scarlett didn't know either. "How can he expedite it?"

"I didn't ask, and as your attorney, I suggest you not ask either—plausible deniability. Just know, it'll be legal. Or it'll at least look legal."

Antonio didn't miss the way his dad cringed after those last words. Still, he wouldn't allow Antonio to move forward if he had any concerns.

Antonio rubbed his hands together as excitement swirled inside of him. "All right, let's fine-tune this contract. I have a woman to propose to and a daughter to adopt."

Assuming Scarlett says yes.

Chapter Twenty

Antonio was never late for work, and he never overslept. Until today. This morning had been thrown off from the start, and he hadn't even been able to get his run in. Surprisingly, he didn't care about any of that now. Today he was a man on a mission, but first, he needed to catch up on some work.

He smiled as he exited the elevator on the top floor of Jenkins & Sons Construction where the administrative offices were located. Nothing could get him down today. Spending time with the most amazing woman in the world yesterday had been just the boost he'd needed. Add that to the fact that he planned to propose marriage in a couple of days, and he felt like he was floating on air.

As he ambled down the long hallway, muffled chatter sounded behind closed doors, but thankfully no one was around to see him sneaking in late. He'd never hear the end of it. His family always found something to harass him about, and him deviating from his usual schedule would give them too much ammunition. That was the problem with being predictable. Everyone noticed when you changed things up.

I need to be less predictable.

Antonio approached the last door on the left and unlocked his office before strolling in. His work boots sunk into the thick carpet as he headed across the room. This was his happy place. A space that was calm, yet conducive to getting a ton of work done.

Setting his laptop bag on the desk, he went about his usual routine. Turn on his desk lamp. Open window blinds. Check voice messages and unlock the filing cabinet. In that order. He was pulling out files when a sound came from the opened door.

"What's gotten into you?" his cousin Nate asked.

Nate was a few years older, but they were around the same height and size. He was the chief financial officer for J & S, and it was clear he had meetings today if his stylish, three-piece suit was any indication. The brother looked totally professional except for a small handprint on his pants leg. Clearly, one of his twin boys, preschoolers, had tagged him.

"You might want to wipe that off before your next meeting," Antonio said, nodding at the small powder-like handprint.

Nate glanced down. "Damn, I didn't even notice it. Powdered sugar," he said, trying to brush it off, but it was taking some effort. "I can't believe Martina or Nick didn't say anything," he said of their cousin and his twin brother. "But anyway, what's going on with you?"

Antonio frowned. "What do you mean?"

"First of all, you're late. Secondly, you missed a meeting and didn't call. And lastly, you're whistling. I've never heard you whistle. *Ever.*"

Whistling? Antonio hadn't realized he'd been whistling, but what was the big deal?

"So, what? People can't whistle? It's a gorgeous day." He

gestured to the windows where the sunny spring day was on full display, then shrugged.

He took the files back to his desk and set them next to the telephone. He'd go through them shortly, but first...

"Ahh, let me guess. It's Scarlett, isn't it? Y'all did look pretty cozy on the dance floor at the reception. I take it that things are going well. Does this mean we'll have another wedding to attend soon?"

Apparently, Martina had kept her mouth closed. Otherwise, Nate's questions would've included something about the kiss that Martina had interrupted.

"Everything is fine with Scarlett," Antonio said without elaborating.

He had no intentions of discussing his marriage plans with any of his extended family, at least not yet. Except he planned to get Martina's help with a little project, but he'd have to swear her to secrecy.

"Did I miss anything important at the meeting?" Antonio asked. He was totally off his game today because he hadn't even noticed the meeting on his calendar.

"Yeah, we wanted to run a staffing change by you. Do you have time now to talk?"

"Sure. My first appointment isn't for another couple of hours."

"Okay, let me see if MJ and Nick are available," Nate said.

Nick oversaw operations of the entire company, and if he needed to be a part of this conversation, they were looking at making a major change.

"Where were you this morning?" Martina asked as she barged into the office. "Since when do you come in late without giving notice at least months in advance?" she joked.

"Since today," Antonio growled, and Nate chuckled.

"What do you want MJ?" he asked, even though Nate was getting ready to call her.

"I want to know where you were this morning."

"See, you can't just up and change your routine without everyone noticing. Otherwise, folks will worry," Nate said as he typed something into his phone, probably a text message to his brother.

"Like either of you would worry. So where are we meeting?"

Nate's phone buzzed. "We'll meet in here. Nick is on his way."

A few minutes later, Nick walked in with a file folder. Unlike his twin, his casual attire—a T-shirt, jeans, and work boots—fit in with how most of the people in the office dressed. A sheet metal worker by trade, Nick preferred to be in the field, but his responsibilities kept him in the office most days.

Small talk traveled around the table before Nick started explaining what they were thinking as far as changes to the administrative roles.

"Since Nate is playing a more active role with the property development company, he needs to relinquish some of his responsibilities around here. So we're working on creating a couple of new positions," Nick said.

Nate might be the CFO of Jenkins & Sons, but he was also part owner of a property development company he started with Antonio's dad. The business was several years old, and Antonio was glad he'd gotten in early on as an investor. Already he was reaping the financial benefits.

"One of the new positions will be VP of operations, which I think you'd be perfect for," Nick continued. "Responsibilities will include some financial tasks, as well as tasks on the builder side of the business. Basically, the role will be in line with your business and engineering background. Martina's new role will comprise some of the estimator's responsibilities."

Antonio listened as Nick and Nate explained what they envisioned for both roles—the VP position, as well as the estimator manager role, which Antonio currently held. He had no doubt he could do the new job. He just wasn't sure if he wanted to. The first few months or maybe even a year in the position would require long days to put systems in place. He wasn't sure he wanted to commit to that.

There was also the matter of salary. Neither Nick nor Nate had discussed money yet, but Antonio was fairly sure they would meet his financial requirements if he took the job. But it wasn't just about money. He had others to think about now. Even if he wasn't a hundred percent sure Scarlett would say yes to his proposal, he was planning the next few months of his life around the fact that she might.

Nate handed him a sheet of paper. "That's the salary."

Antonio scanned the document. Jenkins & Sons Construction might be a family-owned business, but their salaries were competitive. The amount was in line with what he'd require from any company he worked for.

"What do you think? We can hash out the details and adjust responsibilities if needed," Nick said, smiling as if knowing Antonio would jump at the opportunity.

A few weeks ago, he probably would've, but things had changed. He didn't want to be a workaholic anymore or the person everyone came to for help.

"What's the backup plan if I don't accept?"

They all stared at him as if he had lost his mind. This was the type of role he had wanted since graduating from college. But like everyone else, he'd had to do his time and prove how valuable he was to the company. Of course, the three of them knew this was what he'd wanted. So, for him to not jump at the opportunity was throwing them off balance.

"You need to take this position because I want your job," MJ said, humor in her tone.

Antonio grinned. As a master carpenter by trade, like Nick, she hated office work, which was mainly what she was doing these days. Occasionally, if there was a problem on a job site, she'd be the one called to check it out. With the estimator's job, she'd get the chance to be in the field more.

"Are you saying you're not interested?" Nick asked.

"I'm not saying that. I'm asking if you have a backup plan."

Nick and Nate glanced at each other.

"Actually, Royce might be returning to Cincinnati," Nate said of their cousin, Royce Garrison, who owned a technology company in Chicago along with his two brothers. "He's thinking about selling the tech company. Or he's interested in merging with J & S. If that happens, he wants to be over the engineering and tech department, but we could possibly move some of the VP of Operations responsibilities to him. Basically, we'd do some shuffling of tasks."

"*Again*," Nick added. He was the least patient of the twins. It worked in his favor, though. He was a get shit done kind of guy and hated delays. More than that, he detested doing something more than once—like shuffling responsibilities.

"Does Liam know about the possibility of Royce moving back?" Antonio asked.

Liam and Royce might be cousins, but they were sworn enemies, and the thought of the two of them in the building at the same time was a disaster waiting to happen. It all started when the guys were in their twenties. Liam had brought his girlfriend to Sunday brunch, and she ended up screwing around with Royce. When Liam caught them together, he went in on Royce and the worst fistfight in Jenkins's history happened that day.

"Remember, Liam is a freelancer now. He doesn't get a say in how the business is run anymore," Nick said.

Liam was an architect by trade and had a waiting list for people who wanted to hire him. He was that good.

"Besides, he's married. I'm sure his issues with Royce are a thing of the past."

"I wouldn't be too sure of that," Antonio said, "But okay. Let me think about this new position. I appreciate the opportunity. When do you need to know my answer?"

"Today."

"No later than a week."

Nick and Nate said at the same time.

Nick frowned at his twin before returning his attention to Antonio. "What's keeping you from saying yes now?"

"The time commitment mainly. I've been thinking about cutting back my hours to a normal eight-to-five. A new role might hinder that goal but let me think about it. In the meantime, is there a job description for the position?"

"We're working on it. I'll make sure it's done in the next day or two and email it to you," Nick said as he stood. "I hope you take the job, though, because it's perfect for you."

"Yeah, it sounds like it, but let me think about it."

Antonio also stood. The position was perfect for what he once wanted to do. Now? Not so much. He was about to get the family he'd dreamed of, and the job didn't seem as important.

When Nick and Nate walked out, Martina pounced.

"What's wrong with you? That job is everything you've been working for. Why didn't you take it?" When he hesitated, she snapped her fingers. "I know. It's Scarlett, isn't it? You've been different ever since you came back from Florida. What happened?"

Antonio closed the office door, and Martina followed him to his desk. He nodded for her to take the seat across from him, but she remained standing and frowned.

"Why do I have to sit down for this conversation? What the hell have you done?"

It was risky telling her about the situation with him and Scarlett, but he trusted Martina. They'd come through for each other too many times not to. Still, she was a wildcard, which was why most of the family didn't share secrets with her. Hopefully, opening up to her wouldn't come back to bite him in the ass.

"I have a plan," he said. "It's a secret, and I'm going to need your help pulling it off."

Chapter Twenty-One

Saturday night, Antonio entered the Contemporary Arts Center excited about the plans he had pulled together for Operation Marry Scarlett. But first, he was attending a fashion show where she would be one of the models.

"May I help you find something?" a big, burly security guard asked just inside the lobby.

"Yes, I'm here for the fashion show." Antonio showed him the VIP ticket that his cousin Jada had texted him. She was one of three featured designers for the event.

After glancing at the ticket, the security guard directed him to the Black Box Performance Theatre. Antonio thanked him, and a short while later, he was standing in the Lower Lobby Lounge, which was being used in addition to the theater.

The Arts Center might be closed to the general public, but there were plenty of people connected to this event who were rushing around to get everything in place. The lobby was set up with a long bar for cocktails and several tables strategically placed throughout the space. He thought he'd be the first to arrive, but others apparently had the same idea of getting there early.

Antonio readjusted the two-dozen pink and red roses in his arms and pulled out his cell phone. First, he texted Scarlett to see if there was a chance she could step out of the changing room. When she didn't respond, he texted his cousin, Jada.

JJ, I'm here. Any chance I can see Scarlett for a minute?

She responded within seconds.

For you? Yes, but only for a minute, two max.

Antonio smiled at the message. He and Scarlett had already had plans for dinner when Jada begged Scarlett to fill in for her tonight. One of her models couldn't make it. That left Jada scrambling to replace her with someone who was similar in size. When she first called Scarlett to ask the favor, Scarlett had said no because she had a date with him.

That's when Jada reached out to him to beg him to tweak his plans with Scarlett for the evening so she could fill in. This was the second time Scarlett, a former model, had stepped in to help Jada. Once his cousin promised to give him a VIP ticket, putting him in the front row, Antonio conceded.

The change in plans worked well for what he had in mind for the evening. Scarlett knew they were going to dinner after the show, she just didn't know details. It was all part of the surprise he had planned for her. With Martina's help, he knew everything would come together perfectly.

Another text message came through.

Look for a woman with a spiked red mohawk standing near a door at the end of the hallway.

Antonio glanced around and immediately spotted the woman. He headed in that direction.

"Are you Antonio?" she asked when he approached.

"Yes."

She lifted a finger. "Give me a second." Disappearing inside the room, it took a few minutes for the door to reopen, and Scarlett appeared.

When she flashed him a smile, Antonio's heart did a giddy-up. He knew from the first time he'd met her that she'd been out of his league—sophisticated, worldly, and drop-dead gorgeous. The type of woman you'd see in a magazine or on the big screen. Every time since then, he thought the same thing, but it wouldn't stop him from shooting his shot with her.

It was clear he had caught her in the middle of getting ready. She was a woman who didn't need makeup to enhance her beauty. Yet, whoever had done up her face, adding just the right amount of eye shadow, blush, and probably a host of other products, had out done themselves. She was even more stunning if that were possible, even with the large rollers in her hair.

"Hi," she said.

"Hi, yourself. These are for you." He handed her the bouquet of roses and watched as she brought it to her nose to smell. "I wanted to wish you luck on the show."

"Antonio, this is so sweet. Thank you."

Stepping partly out of the doorway, Scarlett gently tugged on the front of his sports jacket. Pulling him close, she planted a kiss on him that had his pulse beating faster. The way she loved on his mouth made him even more confident about the decision to make her his forever.

"Thanks for being so accommodating this evening," she said when the kiss ended. "I'm looking forward to our date and by the way, you look extremely handsome."

Antonio glanced down at his clothing as if he didn't know what he was wearing. "Thank you. My woman dressed me tonight," he said, and they laughed.

That Sunday in Miami, Scarlett insisted on all of them going shopping. Not only had she purchased a few items for him, Bella, and herself, she helped him pick what she called key pieces to add to his wardrobe. That included the blue plaid sports jacket, the silk-like black T-shirt beneath it, and a necklace made of black beads, which he was wearing with a pair of blue dress pants.

Never in a million years would he have chosen the outfit for himself, but he had to admit, he loved it. He felt GQ in it and might let her pick out all his clothes going forward.

"All right, baby. I better let you go before Jada comes out. I can't wait to see you later. I'll meet you near the entrance at the end of the show."

"Sounds good, and thank you again, Tony," she said, blowing him a kiss before easing back into the room.

As he retraced his steps, Antonio's excitement for the evening continued to rise. He couldn't wait until the fashion show was over. He wanted everything to go as planned, and he needed her to say yes when he popped the question.

When he returned to the lobby, he saddled up to the bar and ordered a scotch. Guests were starting to arrive, and he gave a head nod to a few people he knew, then he saw a couple of his cousins.

"Ladies, how's it going?" he asked, giving each of them a kiss on the cheek.

"Hey, Cuz. What are you doing here?" Christina asked.

A painter by trade as well as a world-renown artist, she was dressed in her usual bohemian style. Her long, wild curls were held up with a colorful wrap around her head that kept them in place. It matched her long, flowy dress. Since they were kids, she always moved around life with a flower-child vibe. Peacefulness and calmness were a part of her and palpable whenever she was near.

"I never considered you a fashion show type," Charlee, Liam's wife said, checking out his attire.

Charlee was like Jada and Scarlett—a fashionista through and through. She might be very pregnant, but she could easily be one of the runway models. Pregnancy hadn't affected her dressing to the nines whenever he saw her. The bold, royal blue dress that hugged her body, huge stomach and all, stopped just above her knees and had a cape in the same color. What set the outfit off was the black, wide brim fedora that matched her purse and shoes.

Charlee fingered Antonio's jacket and smiled. "I have a feeling you had a little help pulling your outfit together. You're looking pretty sharp there."

Antonio chuckled. "What are you trying to say? I don't normally look sharp?"

They all laughed, and Charlee lifted her hands. "Hey, I'm just saying, you look good, Cuz."

"Thank you. Would you ladies like something to drink?"

Both said no just as someone announced the show would start in five minutes, and everyone should take their seats. When they entered the theater, Christina and Charlee were directed to the opposite side of the runway and he was escorted to the front row. That's when he saw Jada's husband, Zack. The retired NFL running back looked just as imposing in a suit as he did in a football uniform.

"What's up, man?" Zack said and stood, giving him a fist bump. "I heard you'd be joining me in here. So you and Scarlett, huh? Things must be serious if she has you coming to fashion shows."

"Yeah, things are going well."

Attending a fashion show was definitely something he never thought he'd do. But he knew if Scarlett asked him to climb Mount Kilimanjaro with her, he'd do it. As far as he was concerned, she could ask anything of him, and he'd try to make it happen.

The show started on time, and the first models wore fashions from one of the other designers. The music was banging, and there were plenty of *oohs* and *ahhs* from the audience as the models strutted down the runway. But there was only one model Antonio wanted to see, and he anxiously waited.

When Scarlett finally came out to model Jada's first outfit, Antonio almost swallowed his tongue. The sexy white dress barely covered her most precious assets, but damn if she didn't look hot in it. The halter dress was made of a slinky material with a deep V-neck that exposed the rounds of her breasts and much of her chest. With her sexy, elegant stride, the deep splits on both sides of the dress exposed long, shapely legs, and Antonio was left breathless.

When she stopped at the end of the runway and turned, he had a clear view of her whole back considering the dress was open to just above her fine ass.

Damn. He loved her in the outfit. Hopefully, Jada would consider selling it to him. Then again, he wouldn't be comfortable with Scarlett wearing it out in public, but she could wear it for him.

When she turned again, they made eye contact, and he flashed her a grin. She rewarded him with a sultry smile and a wink before walking back up the runway.

Oh, yeah. Tonight was going to be a night to remember.

Chapter Twenty-Two

As Antonio drove through the streets of Cincinnati, Scarlett gazed out the passenger window, still hyped from the show. She forgot how much she enjoyed modeling, especially runway modeling. Not only did she get to wear gorgeous clothes, but she also earned a nice amount of money for a few hours of work. Besides that, Jada was wonderful to work with, and they were kindred spirits when it came to fashion.

"Where are we going?" Scarlett asked when she realized they were in Antonio's neighborhood. "I thought we were going for Italian tonight?"

When they first discussed having dinner out, Antonio had mentioned an Italian restaurant with a view of downtown Cincinnati. Maybe he'd needed to stop home for something first.

"Change of plans," he said when he pulled onto his street and pushed the garage door opener. He didn't say anything further until he parked in the garage. "I thought we'd have dinner here tonight."

Surprised by the change, Scarlett tried to school her disappointment. She had her heart set on some gnocchi or chicken cacciatore and bread. Lots of bread and oil. She'd been thinking about food all day and how she'd planned to make up for practically starving herself for the last couple of days. Besides that, the white dress she was wearing was way too fancy to be worn to dinner at home.

Jada had insisted on Scarlett keeping the first outfit she had modeled in the show, and Scarlett had been looking forward to wearing it out. Then again, the way Antonio's gaze had eaten her up when she met him in the Art Center's lobby had been priceless. The dress had served its purpose. There'd been a moment when she thought the man would ravish her body right there in the main lobby.

After closing the garage's overhead door, Antonio turned to her. "I need to blindfold you."

His words were the second surprise Scarlett had received in a matter of minutes, and she sat stunned. When she thought of blindfolds, kinky stuff like whips and chains immediately came to mind, and she almost laughed. Why was she even thinking along that line? Antonio hadn't said a word about sex. Yet, that's where her mind had taken her.

Probably because my body wants more of him.

She couldn't wait to feel his mouth on her heated skin again. Or the way his large hands caressed every inch of her body, and the way his fingers ignited a—

"Scarlett?"

Scarlett's gaze leaped to his eyes. His brows had dipped into a frown and concern marred his handsome face.

"Is that okay?" he asked.

"Oh, sorry." She flashed an embarrassed smile as heat spread to her cheeks. Clearly, she needed to get laid again.

"Yes," she said, shaking off thoughts of getting naked and allowing excitement to take its place.

Giddiness bubbled inside of her when Antonio instructed her to face the passenger side window. As he carefully tied a scarf around her eyes, she couldn't stop the giggle that burst free. Her mind immediately started trying to figure out what he had planned. Maybe it involved whipped cream, chocolate sauce, and his huge—

Crap. There I go again.

She shook all sexual thoughts from her brain and instead tried to determine what type of surprise was in store. He'd had to work earlier and had been at the fashion show all evening. When did he even have time to do anything?

He probably had help.

Mahogany. She and Ben had returned from their honeymoon in Hawaii the other day, and if Mahogany found out Antonio was trying to do something sweet, she would've been all in. That's probably why she asked if Bella could spend the night. She claimed Jayden missed Bella and wanted her to go skating with him and Ben. Then Bella would also go to Jayden's baseball game in the morning. Scarlett had thought it perfect timing, now she knew it was all planned.

Antonio helped Scarlett out of the car and into the house, careful not to let her bump into anything. The moment she stepped across the threshold, instrumental Italian music played in the background and enticing aromas wafted to her nose. It smelled as if they'd stepped into an Italian restaurant.

She inhaled deeply. Oregano, basil, sage, and even the smell of fresh bread permeated the air.

Oh, yeah. She couldn't wait to eat.

"I hope you're hungry," Antonio said as if reading her mind.

"I am. I'm starving." She hadn't eaten anything since breakfast for fear she'd be too bloated for the outfits Jada had lined up. Good thing too since one of the dresses left her midsection bare.

After Antonio helped Scarlett into the kitchen, she started to take off the blindfold, but he gently swatted her hand away.

"Ow!" she said and chuckled.

"Sorry, but don't touch the blindfold. I'll remove it when I'm ready."

"Oh, okay," she said and let him slowly guide her farther into the house. He stopped and spun her a couple of times, and Scarlett cracked up. "Tony! You're making me dizzy. It's a good thing I haven't eaten anything, and my stomach is empty. Otherwise, you'd be cleaning up barf."

He had her by the waist, and her hands searched blindly for his arm, hoping that could help her head stop spinning. She was more than disoriented and had no clue of what room they were in.

"Wow, you're really doing up this surprise," she said, when she finally felt steadier on her feet.

"Yeah, I want tonight to be memorable."

"Well, whatever you're up to, I'm sure I'm going to remember it." As an afterthought, she added, "And I'm sure I'm going to love it."

"Okay, here we go." Antonio slowly removed the scarf, and when he did, Scarlett blinked several times as her eyes adjusted to the dimness of the room.

She glanced around, taking in the large space and feeling as if she had stepped into an Italian bistro.

"Oh, Tony. How..." she breathed, her hands going to her mouth as she took in the transformation of his family room.

Gone was his sectional, sofa tables, and all the other furniture that was originally in the space. Clear lights were strung from one wall to another, and there was a lamp in the far corner, giving the room a romantic ambiance. A table, covered with a white tablecloth, had two place settings along with four votive candles in the center that added to the romantic vibe.

Even though it might be a little warm to use the brick fireplace, there was a crackling fire going that made the whole space feel cozy.

"You thought of everything," she said as her gaze continued around the spectacular space.

There were also several large plants, almost the size of trees that had been brought in, and vines hung above the windows. Scarlett couldn't remember what type of artwork was originally on the walls, but even those had been switched out. Now there was a sunset in Venice painting, and another one with a large basket of bread with wine, cheese, and grapes on a plate in front of it.

The amount of work he had to have put into this surprise was so touching.

"Tony, I don't know what to say. This is unbelievable and amazing."

Scarlett gasped when she felt someone step to her left. Then she almost swallowed her tongue when she realized it was Martina. The woman seemed to come out of thin air, and what was she wearing? Scarlett took in her long sleeve white button-up shirt, black tie, black vest, and a long white apron over black pants. Across her forearm was a linen napkin and in her hands was a bottle of red wine.

"Oh. My. God," Scarlett said and howled. She laughed so hard she was sure the neighbors down the street could hear her, and she couldn't stop. Tears blurred her vision, and she stumbled backwards as she continued cracking up. Had it not been for Antonio, she was sure she would've lost her balance and crashed into something.

"Just so you know, I'm doing this under duress while you're over there laughing," Martina grumbled.

Laughing and crying, Scarlett struggled to pull herself together. She couldn't ever remember laughing this hard and for this long. Even Antonio, who rarely laughed, joined in.

Martina set the wine bottle on the table and picked up a pitcher of water from a nearby stand. "It's not that funny, and you two are going to owe me big time for this," she said and filled the water glasses before she left the room.

Wiping her eyes with the heel of her palm, Scarlett finally turned to Antonio.

"How in the *world* did you get her to go along with this?"

"She owed us," he said and pulled out the chair for Scarlett. "I told her this was the least she could do for freaking you out at the reception. She didn't agree initially, but she eventually came around."

"Tony, this is absolutely gorgeous," Scarlett said when he sat across from her. "No one has ever gone to such trouble for me before, and I'm... I'm... *Thank you*. Thank you so much for doing all this."

"It's my pleasure, baby, but I had a little help."

Martina returned and picked up the bottle of wine. She lifted Antonio's wine glass, poured a swallow into it, and nodded for him to taste it. He did with the seriousness of being in a fine-dining establishment.

It took all the control Scarlett could muster to not start laughing again. She had no idea how they could do any of this with a straight face. She'd seen actors who couldn't pull off what they were doing.

Once Antonio approved of the wine selection, Martina went about pouring both of them a glass.

"I'll be back to take your order shortly," Martina said and disappeared from the room.

"If I didn't know any better, I'd say she's had experience as a server," Scarlett said as she glanced at what looked to be a one sheet menu.

"She has. Remember, her husband has a couple of restaurants. When he opened the first one, Martina, for whatever reason, went through the training with the serving staff."

"Wow, so she helped out in the restaurant?"

"A couple of times but not because he needed her to. She said she'd mainly gone through the training in case he ever needed her to fill in."

"That's so sweet, and sounds so unlike her," Scarlett whispered and chuckled.

Antonio smiled. "Yeah, she's different with Paul. He's the only one who can keep her in line."

"Well, don't sell yourself short. I have a feeling she wouldn't do what she's doing if you didn't have some influence on her too."

"You guys might as well stop whispering. I can hear y'all," Martina said from the kitchen, and Scarlett lost it again. She laughed so hard she had to push away from the table for fear of knocking something over.

"Martina," Antonio ground out between gritted teeth. "You promised!"

"Fine! I'll be seen and not heard," she snapped.

It took Scarlett a good five minutes to pull herself together and once she did, she used the white cloth napkin to dab at her eyes. "I just can't with you two," she said, trying not to start up again, but man, they were funny without even trying to be.

"Once she serves dinner, she'll be out of here," Antonio said.

For the next part of the evening, Martina served them like a seasoned pro. Bringing out one course at a time. They dined on homemade bread, salad, chicken, and gnocchi, as well as pasta pomodoro and shrimp. Dessert was cannoli and semi-freddo. Scarlett couldn't remember the last time she'd eaten this good.

Throughout dinner, conversation with Antonio flowed as he shared funny stories about his family. He made growing up in a large, close-knit family sound fun, yet exhausting. He and Scarlett had been so deep in conversation at times, she had moments when she forgot they weren't in a real restaurant. She'd also forgotten Martina was still in the house until she appeared.

"Is there anything else I can get for you two before I leave for the evening?" Martina asked. Gone was the snark from earlier, and in its place was a professional server.

"Scarlett?" Antonio said.

"No, I'm good. This was absolutely amazing. My compliments to the chef," she said.

"Thank you. I'm glad you enjoyed everything," Martina said, looking pleased with herself.

"Wait." Scarlett sat up straighter. "You did all the cooking?"

"I did—except for the dessert. My cousin felt I owed him my time *and* my culinary skills. He's not the only Jenkins who knows how to cook. I do all right too."

"Well, I'm impressed. The food was outstanding, but I can't believe Antonio had you do everything."

"That's the least she could do. She's owed me for years for so many favors that I can't even count. Not once has she had to pay me back... until today."

Martina huffed out a breath. "He's right, but to be honest, we've had each other's back since he was a peanut-headed kid. Which is why, well before tonight, he was my favorite cousin. Now, after I've worked like a slave, I'm not so sure."

Scarlett grinned. Martina talked tough, but Scarlett could tell she and Antonio had a special bond. She noticed it whenever she saw them together. They often seemed more like brother and sister than cousins.

Martina grabbed the last items on the table and started to turn away but stopped and glanced at Antonio. "Just so you know, we're even. You can't ask me for shit else going forward." And with that, she was gone.

Scarlett stared at Antonio wide eyed before they both dissolved into laughter. Between great conversation, a fabulous meal, and all the laughs, Scarlett could honestly say this was the best date ever.

Once Martina said goodnight and left the house, Scarlett reached across the table and grasped Antonio's hand. "I can't thank you enough for the best date I've ever had. Tonight was so special and memorable."

"The night isn't over yet," he said, giving her a smile as he caressed the back of her hand with the pad of his thumb. They sat there in comfortable silence until he said, "I'll be right back."

When he returned a short while later, he reclaimed his seat and placed a manila envelope in the center of the table. But when he set a small velvet box next to it, unease crawled down Scarlett's spine.

Antonio folded his hands on the table and met her gaze. "We need to talk."

Chapter Twenty-Three

The envelope and velvet box sat between them like a king cobra snake waiting to strike. Then again, maybe that was too dramatic but still, Scarlett sat frozen in place afraid to move or say anything. She wasn't sure what was in the envelope, but she had a fairly good idea what might be in the small red box.

Pulse pounding faster, she swallowed hard, then lifted her gaze to Antonio who was watching her closely. The only sounds in the house were of the quiet hum of the refrigerator and soft jazz playing in the background. Seconds ticked by without either of them speaking.

Normally, she could get a conversation going between them, but Scarlett sat speechless. She should've known something like this was coming. It had been days since they left his father's office and agreed to put the adoption and marriage idea out of their minds. Well, she tried, even though the marriage of convenience suggestion had been swirling inside her head ever since Mr. Jenkins planted the idea. The weird thing was, she could totally envision a life with Antonio.

How was that possible? They barely knew each other. Yet, she knew without a doubt he'd make an amazing husband to her and a fantastic father to Bella. But she couldn't imagine a marriage of convenience. She really wanted to be in love before she said, "I do."

"While I was waiting for you to get changed after the fashion show, I heard from my dad," Antonio said. "Luke and Michael gathered a lot of information about Cynthia and her family. But my father was only willing to share a little of what was discovered. It appears Cynthia does have some health issues. I'm sorry to say she's been seen visiting one of the top oncologists in Coral Gables."

Scarlett sucked in a breath, but otherwise tried not to react for fear Antonio wouldn't tell her the rest. Yet, knowing her intuition was correct, that Cynthia was ill, weighed heavy on her. This explained all the talk about her will.

"It also appears Theodore and Alberta are separated, but they are keeping it very quiet. They have been seen socializing and attending events together and by all accounts they still look like a happily married power couple."

"Cynthia must not know," Scarlett murmured. "Then again, she probably does, but—"

"Who knows," Antonio said. "One good thing that Mike found was Alberta made sure Nina Tate, the person who killed Ezra won't be free for a very long time if ever. Nina's attorney requested the Florida parole commission give her early parole. Alberta knocked that down real quick by attending the hearing and told them the woman would die in jail if left up to her. She also—"

"She said that?"

"That's what I was told, but she also found proof that Nina's parents had paid off cops in two previous incidents when she was a senior in high school."

Scarlett's hand went to her chest. "What?" she whispered.

This was news to her. She hadn't attended the hearing because she no longer lived in Miami. Besides, the guilt she'd still been carrying at the time had been almost debilitating.

"Nina had received two citations, but they somehow disappeared from the database. One was for texting while driving. The other—though she tested under the legal limit—was for drinking and driving. That one resulted in an arrest, but it's unclear why it wasn't mentioned while she was standing trial for Ezra's death.

"Alberta filed for a new trial, but it's been pushed back a few times. Anyway, parole was denied and as of now, she's still expected to serve a minimum of fifteen years."

Heart pounding faster than it should, Scarlett sat stunned as she tried to process all he was saying. She still didn't want Alberta and her husband anywhere near Bella, but she was glad the woman was continuing to get justice for Ezra's death. It was the least she could do but hearing this brought back horrible memories of that night.

"Hey," Antonio said, and Scarlett jerked her head up when he gently touched her arm. "If you've heard enough, I can—"

"There's more?" she asked.

Yes, she'd heard enough, but she needed to know everything in order to determine what she might be up against in the future.

"There is and this next bit of information is a little troubling. It has to do with Theodore. Michael is looking a little deeper into some allegations regarding Ezra's father, but his initial findings make him believe they are true. Over the years, Theodore has been the subject of multiple sexual harassment lawsuits. The lawsuits have been settled in some cases and dropped in others. Recently, he was accused of accepting bribes and influence peddling, but denies all accusations.

"Alberta is Theodore's lawyer, and so far, he hasn't been charged with anything despite other politicians saying he's corrupt."

"Wait. I thought Alberta was a corporate lawyer."

"She is. She practices more than one area of law, including criminal law."

Wow. No wonder the woman had a bad attitude. She probably puts in a hundred hours a week.

"My dad also mentioned there are rumors floating around that Theodore's involved in an international bribery scheme, but right now those are only rumors."

Scarlett's head was spinning. She commended Alberta for fighting for justice for Ezra, but standing by Theodore, when it sounded like he had some corruption tendencies, was unconscionable. Yes, people should be considered innocent until proven guilty, but to even have his name mentioned in these instances is hard to ignore.

Either way, Scarlett believed Ezra and Cynthia regarding their personal experience and opinion when it came to Theodore and Alberta. She didn't want these people in their lives, especially Bella's life, and she needed to do whatever necessary to make sure it didn't happen.

Scarlett rubbed her temples. "God, this is a lot." It wasn't just about all that Antonio just told her. The sudden stress also had to do with the red box sitting in front of her like a blinking neon sign.

"Baby, I know it's a lot to process, but I don't want us to sit back and wait and see. I want us to take action."

He reached for the large envelope, and Scarlett's pulse pounded loudly in her ear. After removing the document, he handed it to her. At first, she just stared at the stack of papers before accepting them.

"This is a contract between you and me. A marriage contract."

Oh crap.

So much for tabling this discussion until... never. Of course, he couldn't drop the subject. Antonio was a take-charge person, one of many things she liked about him, but this? This...

"I love you, Scarlett."

Her gaze jerked to his, and the tenderness in his eyes matched his words, but... "Tony—"

"Let me finish," he interrupted. "I am *in* love with you, and I know you're the woman I'm supposed to spend the rest of my life with. I also know we've only known each other a short time, and I know we don't know everything about one another. That doesn't stop me from loving you and wanting to spend the rest of my life with you."

"I care about you," she said, her words sounding feeble compared to his declaration, but she really did.

She more than cared. So much so, it would break her heart if things ever ended between them. It didn't matter if it was only a friendship or something more. The thought of him not being in her life was scary as hell. He was a part of her. Maybe not in the way he wanted, but a part of her, nonetheless.

"I know you care about me," Antonio said with confidence and lifted the small red box. "I can see that in the way you look at me, and I feel it in the way you treat me. I also know you want to be *in* love before even considering marriage, but I'd like for you to make an exception. I want you as my wife, Scarlett, and I want Bella to be my daughter. Yes, this might start as a marriage of convenience, but I know you're going to fall in love with me at some point."

She quirked an eyebrow and couldn't stop the smile from spreading across her lips. His confidence, with a tad of arrogance, was sexy as hell. Instead of saying that, she let him continue.

"That contract lays out everything I'm promising, including adopting Bella and officially making her my daughter. I'll also cook for the both of you a minimum of four days a week, and I will support you both financially and emotionally. Whether you need me to or not. I promise you a minimum of two date nights a week, and a host of other things that are clearly laid out in the contract. Keep in mind, everything in the document is negotiable except for one thing."

Scarlett swallowed hard, almost afraid to ask. "And what's that?"

"We'd be married in every sense of the word."

Tears crept into Scarlett's eyes, and she quickly batted one away when it slipped down her cheek. Another one followed. Her heart felt as if it would explode from this man's kind gesture, his sweet words, and from the way he made her feel— loved.

God, this was too much.

She cared for him deeply. No, actually she loved him, but it wasn't enough. Was it? Scarlett couldn't believe she was seriously considering marrying someone who she wasn't madly and passionately in love with.

Antonio stood and moved around the table until he was next to her chair. When he dropped down to one knee and opened the red box, Scarlett's breath caught. The platinum twin pavé crossover diamond ring was breathtaking. It was the most beautiful ring she'd ever seen.

"Scarlett Rowsey, will you do me the honor of becoming my wife?"

Chapter Twenty-Four

"I told him I needed to think about it," Scarlett said as she sipped her coffee.

"When Antonio asked if I'd volunteer to keep Bella for the weekend, I had no idea he'd had this type of surprise for you," Mahogany said from across the small table. "And I was only gone for two weeks. How is it that your whole life has changed so much?"

She and Mahogany met at a coffee shop not too far from the house they were renting from Ben for their businesses. Scarlett had told her sister everything that happened over the last couple of weeks. That included her trip to Florida, the conversations with Cynthia, and even explaining how the marriage of convenience came to be.

"I don't know what to say."

Scarlett snorted. "Yeah, tell me about it. That's why I told Antonio I needed to think about it, and it's why I needed to talk to you. Voicing my thoughts out loud always seems to help give me clarity."

Mahogany nodded. "True. Same for me, but what are you

going to do? I have read plenty of romance novels that included a marriage of convenience trope. But I never met a real person who's been in this position, but it probably happens more often than not."

"Even if stuff like this happens all the time, I never in a million years thought I'd be considering a marriage of convenience. Oh, and you can't tell anyone about this, whether we go through with it or not. Antonio mentioned that, for now, we'll only tell you and Ben because we might need you two as witnesses if we move forward." Scarlett rolled her eyes realizing how wild this situation sounded out loud, and Mahogany chuckled.

"I won't say a word, especially since I'm assuming Antonio will be talking to Ben. That's assuming he hasn't already. You must admit, your man thinks of everything."

My man.

It had been so long since Scarlett had a man, hearing it like that sounded foreign, but she kinda liked it. She might like it more if marriage wasn't on the table. At least not like this. Not when she was considering marriage to ensure Bella had a normal upbringing in an extended family who would love and protect her. If she was honest, Scarlett had to admit there was a certain appeal to becoming Antonio's wife. She already knew she'd be well loved and cared for, but...

She glanced at the magnificent diamond ring that Antonio had slipped onto her finger the night before. Though she should've known the conversation about a marriage of convenience would come up again at some point, he had totally caught her off guard. His comment about them not waiting to see what happens if or when Cynthia passes away, and taking action now, made sense. But she was typically a wait and see type of person. It was a plus that he wasn't.

"That ring is everything," Mahogany said, cutting into Scarlett's thoughts. "Antonio clearly spared no expense, but how'd he know your ring size? It fits perfectly."

"It's the same size as your ring. I guess he was with Ben when he picked yours and figured our size would probably be close to the same." Once again, Scarlett stared at the jewelry. Her mind was blown that Antonio had proposed to her and in a spectacular way. He was a man of many surprises.

Mahogany picked at the large, buttery croissant on the plate sitting between them. They were supposed to be sharing it, but Scarlett couldn't eat. Her stomach was too nervous.

"If you're not sure you're going to marry Antonio, why are you wearing the ring?"

"Because he slid it onto my finger and asked that I wear it until I made a decision."

Mahogany shook her head and laughed. "Damn, my brother-in-law is good."

Scarlett couldn't stop the smile that broke through. "He's definitely thorough, and the contract he gave me is unbelievable."

"Really? What are some of the clauses included? Did you read all the way through it?"

"Three times. I've read that document three times, and it blows my mind at how thorough it is."

"Of course it is. Between Antonio and his dad, I'm sure nothing was missed. Give me the highlights."

Scarlett ran through some of the line items that Antonio had pointed out the night before. When she recited some of the other benefits, her sister laughed. Especially at the part when it said that she'd be entitled to a foot rub once a week. Scarlett found herself smiling as she discussed the contract. He really had thought of everything.

"There's even a line item that says I'd be allowed full access to the Jenkins family and all their resources. Then there was a special note added that said Gram would expect me to attend Sunday brunch."

Again, they laughed, knowing it was a big bonus, but also knowing that joining a large family would have its challenges too.

"He told me everything in the document is negotiable *except*—this will be a real marriage in every sense of the word."

The shock on Mahogany's face was priceless. After a long hesitation, she asked, "What does Antonio get out of this? The contract mainly covers what he'll do for you and Bella, which is amazing, but what about him?"

Scarlett released a long breath. "I asked him that when he brought me home last night because I feel like he'd be giving up everything by marrying me. It's a win-win for me, but for him..." She shook her head, still finding it all so unbelievable. "Anyway, he said he knows in his heart that I'm the woman he's supposed to spend the rest of his life with. That I'm *the one*. He said starting our life together with a contract instead of the natural way is a small price to pay to getting what he knows is divinely orchestrated."

"Wow," Mahogany said, seeming as stunned as Scarlett probably looked after he'd spoken those words. "*Divinely orchestrated*—that's deep. I remember Ben telling me that there's some type of myth in their family which says when a Jenkins man meets the woman he is supposed to spend the rest of his life with, he immediately knows."

Scarlett's mouth dropped open. "Seriously?"

Mahogany shrugged. "That's what he said. So far, it appears to ring true. All the guys seem to have similar stories of how they knew their wives were *the ones* they were supposed to marry. Maybe it's not a myth and there really is some truth to it. You must admit those men are wonderful."

Scarlett nodded. She had to agree, and it started with Antonio's grandfather, Steven Jenkins, the patriarch of the family. He was a big, powerful-looking guy who commanded attention the moment he walked into a room. And when he talked to you, it was as if you were the center of his attention. Scarlett remembered being in awe after he asked her about being a social media influencer. He seemed so engrossed in every word she spoke, and he'd been so easy to talk to. Heck, the whole family was great, and it would be a pleasure to be a part of it.

"So, what are you going to do?" Mahogany asked.

Every few minutes, Scarlett glanced at the diamond ring on her finger. Antonio, without knowing, had picked the perfect ring. A ring she would've chosen had she been there, and when he'd said he loved her, it had felt different from when Ezra told her. Scarlett couldn't figure out why, but maybe it was all about the delivery.

She couldn't help comparing this proposal to her first one, the one from Ezra. It was different in every way. Ezra had proposed out of the blue, probably even catching himself off guard. They were talking about the future, and suddenly he said, "Marry me." It hadn't been planned. There was no elaborate surprise, no magnificent dinner, and no ring. The proposal might have come out of nowhere, but Scarlett knew he'd been serious.

But the one thing that had been the same with both proposals were her feelings. Sort of. Antonio and Ezra both had a special spot in her heart, but like with Ezra, she wasn't in love with Antonio. Once again, she'd fallen into "like" with an amazing man, and Scarlett couldn't seem to get past that.

However, her feelings for Antonio were somewhat different. Probably because she was older and established. She and Ezra had been young and though they thought they were grown-up enough to discuss marriage, neither were in a place in life to make that type of commitment.

There was also more to consider this time around. She had to think about Bella and her well-being.

"We have something in common," Mahogany said, finishing off the croissant and dusting her hands over the empty plate.

"What's that?"

"Well, actually two things off the top of my head. We've both been proposed to twice, and we both have Jenkins men who are in love with us."

"Yeah, well you're in love with your Jenkins man."

"And I think you're in love with yours but don't realize it. *However*," Mahogany hurried to say when Scarlett opened her mouth to speak. "Maybe your heart hasn't informed your brain yet, and the words haven't left your mouth... yet. But the way you look at Antonio speaks volumes, Scarlett. You're in love with him."

Scarlett's heart stuttered, and she pounded on the table. She tried to ignore the attention that she'd attracted and leaned in. "How are you gonna tell me how I'm feeling? I know how I feel!" she snapped, the words coming out fast and forceful.

Mahogany lifted her hands. "Okay, okay. Calm down," she whispered-shouted. "I'm just telling you what I see and think. What do you need from me to help you with this decision?"

Chest heaving, Scarlett willed herself to calm down. Why the hell had she gone off like that? Sure, she and Mahogany didn't agree on everything, but they were best friends who talked about practically everything. Rarely did either of them go off on the other.

"I'm sorry," she said. "I'm so sorry. You just caught me off guard."

"It's okay. I'm sure your reaction has a lot to do with how serious this all is, and the fact that you probably didn't get much sleep last night."

She was right. Scarlett had drifted in and out of sleep,

unable to shut her brain down. There was so much to consider, but ultimately, she had to think of Bella. There were pros to marrying Antonio, even if it would be a marriage of convenience. But could she really marry a man who she wasn't in love with?

"If I were you, I'd say yes to Antonio. You have nothing to lose."

"Are you kidding me? What do you mean I have nothing to lose? I have everything to lose. My heart. My daughter's heart, and I might lose a *really* good friend. I love hanging out with Antonio, and I truly treasure his friendship. But that would be gone if I say no to this arrangement or if I say yes and this marriage doesn't work out. At first, I was thinking it would be a win-win to say yes, but the more I think about it, the more I'm not so sure."

Mahogany sat back in her seat. "Then say no. Don't marry him. I'm sure another woman will come along soon and recognize the gem he is."

Scarlett rolled her eyes, knowing what her sister was trying to do. Damn if it wasn't working. Antonio was a catch, and she'd be a fool to let him walk out of her life. Yes, he said that whether she said yes or no, he'd still be around, but she knew better. He'd be there for Bella, but that would be it.

Mahogany leaned forward again and folded her arms on the table. "The pros of this arrangement might outnumber the cons, but I understand this is not an easy decision. What is your heart telling you to do?"

Scarlett didn't even have to think about her response. "My heart is saying, yes."

Chapter Twenty-Five

Antonio wasn't sure what to expect when Scarlett had called him an hour ago and asked if he could come by her house. Now that he was there, he still didn't know where her head was at. He thought it would take days before she made a decision, but it had taken less than twenty-four hours. Since she invited him over, he was optimistic that she'd say yes. Otherwise, she could've just said no on the telephone.

With the open floor plan, he could see her in the kitchen. Wearing a fitted long sleeve T-shirt and a pair of skinny jeans, she made everything she wore look good and sexy. On her feet were a pair of thick socks. He rarely saw her this dressed down, and he loved the look.

"I want to add two things to the contract," she said when she strolled into the living room with two bottles of water and handed one to Antonio. Instead of sitting on the sofa, she perched on the arm of it.

Antonio struggled to keep his expression neutral. Especially since he wasn't sure what changes to the contract she wanted. He was glad it wasn't an outright no to his proposal, but whatever her contingencies may be, he wasn't sure if he could meet them. Though he would definitely try to give her whatever she wanted.

"What are they?" he finally asked.

"One, please remove the part about you supporting me and Bella financially. Since we're going to be a team, we'll figure out how to move forward financially together. Oh wait, it's going to be three things that need changing, like the part about an inheritance."

Antonio had his dad add that part in case Cynthia did leave her estate to Bella and Scarlett. It would be theirs, and he wanted to make sure she knew he didn't want or expect to have any access to it.

"If you're saying what's yours is ours, then it's only fair that what's ours is yours," Scarlett explained.

He was okay with them sharing what they currently brought to the table, but if Bella did receive an inheritance, he planned to make sure it was hers. That went for Scarlett too, especially as long as there was a contract between them. There was no doubt in his mind that she would one day realize she was just as crazy in love with him as he was with her. But some things took time, and Antonio was prepared to wait.

"We'll have to further discuss the financial part of our relationship. What else do you want changed in the contract?"

"I want an end date added to the contract. If we're not *in* love within a year—"

"You mean if you're not in love with me within a year," Antonio corrected. He knew his heart. He was in love with her whether she wanted to believe it or not.

"Okay," she conceded before continuing. "After a year, I'll agree to let you go. I love that you'll be Bella's father, but you and me..." Her words trailed off and her brows knitted together as if she was trying to find the right words. "Antonio, you're an incredible man. You deserve to be with someone who will love you like you deserve to be loved. I'm crazy about you, but I can't ask you to give up the rest of your life for me, especially when I'm not able to return your feelings."

"Yet," he added. For a reason he couldn't put his finger on, or maybe he was just being a hopeless romantic, he believed she'd fall in love with him. He also believed it would happen sooner than later.

She sighed loudly. "I know what you said about you getting me and Bella in this deal, but that's not enough. None of this seems fair to you."

"Shouldn't I be the judge of that?" he asked, then tugged on her hand and pulled her to him. When he positioned her to sit on his lap, he was glad she didn't refuse. "I think you're under-estimating the power you and Bella have over me. To be honest with you, I genuinely feel I'm the winner in all this."

She looked into his eyes and looped her arms around his neck. "I can already tell you're too good for me," she said quietly. "But to be honest, I'm looking forward to seeing where this goes. I really do hope everything turns out the way you're envisioning."

Antonio gently gripped her chin and pulled her mouth closer. "I promise you're not going to regret marrying me."

"I know I won't. I'm just hoping you won't regret marrying me."

Antonio wanted to erase the vulnerability he saw in her eyes. "I won't," he said, and covered her mouth with his.

Her lips were as sweet and soft as usual, but this kiss felt different from all the others. What they were sharing was more than just physical. They were sharing a promise. He would be hers. She would be his, and they were going to raise Bella together.

When the kiss ended, Scarlett rested her forehead to his.

"All we have to do now is tell Bella, but somehow I think she will be beside herself," Scarlett said smiling.

"I know I am. I can't wait to make this all official."

He also couldn't wait to prove to Scarlett that they were meant for each other.

* * *

Days later, Scarlett was in her office which also doubled as her studio, trying to get her nerves under control. Her pulse pounded loudly in her ear as she paced the large space, mentally preparing for the conversation she'd be having with Bella shortly. Thankfully, Antonio had agreed to be there when she broke the news about their upcoming nuptials.

The last few days had been chaotic, mixed with a huge dose of excitement. After she had given her conditions regarding the contract, she and Antonio talked it out and eventually came to terms they could agree on.

Then came the planning. Scarlett had never met anyone as organized as Antonio. Hoping she'd say yes, he had already developed a spreadsheet of next steps. It included suggested wedding dates, possible locations, and even move-in dates for her and Bella. The plan was for them to move into his home, which Scarlett loved.

They both agreed the sooner they got married the better. They had entertained the idea of flying to Vegas and eloping, but the timing wasn't good. They both had full schedules over the next few days and figured getting married in town would be better. Still, they didn't want a big wedding, nor did they want to marry at the courthouse.

On top of that, they had to decide who, if anyone, they'd include in their plans. Knowing that well-meaning friends and family would voice their opinion about them getting married suddenly, they decided to keep the news to themselves. They didn't want anyone to talk them out of something they didn't understand.

Instead, she and Antonio decided to have a very small ceremony with those who knew about the situation. Ben and Mahogany would act as their witnesses. While Antonio's stepmother, who'd gotten ordained as a minister a few years ago in order to officiate a friend's wedding, would marry them at her and Ben Sr.'s home.

Now, all they had to do was tell Bella what was going on. Scarlett had intentionally waited until the day before they got married to share the news with her daughter. Soon to be *their* daughter.

She shook her head. There were moments she still couldn't believe she was really going through with all this. But then she'd think about how her child would be cherished by Antonio, and all doubt would flee from Scarlett's mind.

"Hey, you ready?"

Scarlett startled when Antonio rested a hand against her back. She hadn't heard him enter the room.

"Bella and I are done cleaning the kitchen, and she went upstairs to grab her electronic tablet to show me something," he said.

He had prepared lunch for them, and it was wonderful how seamlessly he fit into their lives. Scarlett really felt she was making the right decision in moving forward with their marriage plans. They had considered telling Bella over lunch, but instead decided to wait until after they finished eating.

"I figured now might be a good time for all of us to talk."

"I'm ready," Scarlett said, slipping her hand into his. "You?"

He gave a curt nod. "I am, and I'll let you take the lead."

As they made it to the living room, Bella was bounding

down the stairs. "Okay, Uncle Tony, let me show you what the math app can do."

Scarlett smiled. Bella was a girly-girl, but she was showing interest in apps and anything computer related. Since her favorite subjects in school were math and science, it might not be too early to see about getting her into a STEM program for kids her age.

"Bella, before you do that, Tony and I want to talk to you. Come and have a seat." Scarlett and Bella sat on the sofa, and Tony sat across from them in one of the armchairs.

"Did I do something wrong?" Bella asked, her nervous gaze bouncing between them.

Scarlett put her arm around her daughter, pulled her close, and kissed the top of her head. "No sweetie. Tony and I have some good news to tell you." Scarlett glanced at Antonio, and he nodded reassuringly as she debated on where to start. Instead of giving some long, drawn-out speech about how they decided to spend their life together, she decided to keep it simple. "Tony and I are getting married."

Seconds ticked by before Bella's eyes grew large. "You are?" she asked excitedly, and Scarlett nodded. "Yay! Does that mean Uncle Tony will be my bonus dad like Aunt Momo is Jayden's bonus mom?" she said of Mahogany.

Scarlett was stumped because they hadn't figured out how to bring up the adoption part.

"Actually, Baby Doll," Antonio started, looking as if he was trying to pick his words carefully. "I know you have a dad in heaven, but I'd like to adopt you. I love you so much, and I want you to be my daughter. I want to be your real dad. Not your bonus dad." He glanced at Scarlett, and she smiled, appreciating the way he was leading into the conversation.

When Bella didn't respond and looked confused, Scarlett added. "When Antonio and I get married, my name will change to Scarlett Jenkins, and your name will change too. It'll be Bella Jenkins, and Antonio will be your father. We'll all be a family. Do you understand?"

Scarlett couldn't think of a clearer way to explain it to a seven-year-old. She'd explain more about the adoption when the time came, but right now, she wanted to make sure her daughter was okay with her marrying Antonio.

"Bella," Antonio said and reached for Bella's hand, and gently tugged her to him.

That's when Scarlett realized tears filled her daughter's eyes. *Oh no.*

Scarlett's heart slammed against her chest when Bella's bottom lip trembled, and tears began sliding down Bella's cheek.

"Oh, sweetheart. Why are you crying?" she asked, trying to keep her own tears at bay.

"*Because...* Because I always wanted a daddy who wasn't in heaven." Bella threw herself at Antonio and wrapped her arms around his neck. "I'm glad you're going to be my real daddy."

Scarlett let her own tears fall. She didn't think Bella would have a problem with her and Antonio getting married, but her child's words hit hard. Since Bella never mentioned wanting a father, she thought her daughter was okay with it being just the two of them.

"I love you so much," Antonio was saying to Bella when Scarlett watched as the two of them embraced. It was clear by his glossy eyes that Bella's declaration had touched him too.

"I love you too." Bella's words were muffled against Antonio's shoulder, but then she lifted her head. "Now my real daddy will be in the daddy-daughter dance show."

Antonio sputtered a laugh, and Scarlett grinned.

"Which reminds me, *Daddy*," she said with a laugh and

moved over to where they were, then perched on the arm of the chair, "Practice starts next Friday. I hope you're ready."

Giving her a watery smile, Antonio had one arm around Bella and slipped his other around Scarlett. "I'm more than ready." He kissed Scarlett's lips, then kissed Bella's cheek.

Any doubts Scarlett had about their marriage of convenience was squashed and replaced with hope. More than ever, she was looking forward to what the future would bring for the three of them.

Chapter Twenty-Six

"Well, Mrs. Jenkins, are you ready to step into the next chapter of our lives?" Antonio asked Scarlett as they approached the door to their hotel suite.

She glanced up at him and her gaze was as soft as a caress.

My wife. The woman he planned to spend the rest of his life with, and he couldn't be happier than he was in that moment.

His gaze raked over her, and Antonio had never seen her look more radiant than she did today. She wore a stunning, strapless white dress with pearls and gemstones covering much of the top part of the garment. The skirt of the dress was soft like silk and molded over her hips and stopped just above her knees. If the outfit didn't have her looking sexy as hell, her high-heeled shoes, which had to be at least four inches tall, added to her allure and made her shapely legs look incredible.

"I'm ready, my handsome husband," she said and giggled. "I'm sorry. I know I keep saying this, but I can't believe I'm married!" she whispered-shouted.

Antonio laughed, something he'd been doing a lot of today. He never knew he could be this happy. Between marrying Scarlett and starting the adoption procedures for Bella, his life was perfect.

"All right, let's do this," he said and handed Scarlett the keycard.

She shrieked, then burst out laughing when he swung her up into his arms.

"I don't think I'll ever get used to you carrying me around," she said, then cupped his cheek before kissing him slowly. "But I like it."

"Yeah, I like it too," he admitted. "So get used to me holding you close like this."

Scarlett wrapped her arms around his neck. "If you insist." She smiled, and his heart softened even more, if that were possible. "Have I told you how much I love seeing you in a tuxedo?" she asked and adjusted his bowtie.

"No, I can't say you have."

"Well, you look smoking hot."

"I am hot. Hot for you," he said, and they laughed. "I know. My comebacks still need work."

She grinned, then kissed his cheek. "Well, it wasn't as cheesy as some of them. You're getting better."

"Gee, thanks. Shall we go in?"

Scarlett nodded and unlocked the door. Careful not to bump her against the doorjamb, Antonio angled his body and carried her into the suite. The door slammed behind them, and he continued forward to where the hallway opened into a large living space.

"Oh, this is beautiful," Scarlett said when he set her on her feet. She gravitated to the small kitchenette, and on the counter was a bouquet of flowers and a huge fruit basket.

She plucked the card from the flowers. "We're thrilled you

two found each other. Thanks for allowing us to be a part of your special day. We love..."

Scarlett stiffened and the last of her words trailed off.

"Who are they from?" Antonio asked, thinking they were from Ben and Mahogany. He glanced over Scarlett's shoulder at the card.

He should've known they were from his parents. They'd gifted them with the hotel suite for their wedding night. Unfortunately, the gifts reminded Scarlett that she hadn't let her mother in on the plans. Antonio knew she regretted that decision, especially when Ben made a toast and said something about how the family was growing. Had it been up to Antonio, Mrs. Amelia would have been there, but it had been Scarlett's decision not to tell her mother about what was going on.

"I'll have to make sure we send a thank-you card to your parents. They've done so much for us," she said quietly.

A knock sounded at the door, and Antonio assumed it was their luggage being delivered. He dug into his pants pocket for his wallet as he opened the door.

"Your luggage, sir," the bellhop said and brought in the two small suitcases.

After tipping him, Antonio double locked the door before returning to the living room. While Scarlett stood gazing out of the floor to ceiling windows, he carried their bags and the fruit basket into the bedroom.

Since their honeymoon consisted of one night in a luxury suite, he wanted to make full use of the time and space. He glanced into the huge bathroom and spotted the oversized jacuzzi tub and a plan formed in his mind.

A short while later, Antonio returned to the living space and found Scarlett looking through the refrigerator.

"Did you know there's food and drinks in here?" she asked. "Are your parents behind that too?"

When she finally looked at him, her eyes went wide as she let the refrigerator door close. "Wow, you look... naked. I like." She grinned and started toward him.

He still had on his boxer briefs, but the lust in her gorgeous eyes made him feel as if he were wearing nothing. He loved that he could turn her on so easily and planned to take full advantage.

"Come on. Let me see if I can take your mind off everything except me," Antonio said, guiding her into the bedroom and then to the master bathroom.

"Oh, wow. This is so romantic," she said, glancing around at the large tub full of bubbles.

Antonio had also carried a black, wrought iron stand from the bedroom and set it next to the tub, and it held the basket of fruit, as well as two glasses and a bottle of champagne. To add to the romantic vibe, a love ballet played through his phone speaker, and he had dimmed the lights. Whoever had thought to add the dimmer fixture switch to a hotel bathroom was a genius.

Standing behind her, Antonio wrapped his arms around his wife and kissed the side of her neck. He liked it when she wore her hair in an updo. It gave him easy access to her graceful, scented neck.

"Though I think this dress is stunning on you, let's get you out of it."

He unzipped the garment and helped her step out of it. When she turned to face him, his breath caught in his throat. She gave him a full view of her luscious body in the sexiest, skimpiest, see-through underwear he'd ever seen, and her sky-high heels only added to the vision.

He almost dropped her dress to the floor but thought better of it. Instead, he rushed out of the bathroom, tossed it in a nearby chair, and returned within seconds.

Scarlett started laughing. "I would've dropped it to the floor," she said as she approached him looking like a damn sex goddess.

"Umm... wow," Antonio said, unable to form a complete sentence.

He had planned on them taking a relaxing bubble bath while he fed her grapes, strawberries, and sipped champagne. That idea was out. There was no way he'd be able to do either with her looking like a wet dream.

"You... Damn, Scarlett."

She flashed him a grin, and her gaze went to his erection that had tented his boxer briefs. His body was always ready for action whenever she was around. And when she looked at him the way she was doing now, all he wanted to do was take her to the nearest bed and have his way with her.

She boldly slipped her hand into his underwear. "I can tell you like what you see," she said as she began gliding her soft hand up and down his shaft and stroking him slowly.

Antonio gasped for air as she increased the pressure on his dick. He was so aroused, there was no way in hell he'd be able to take much more of her touch, but he didn't want her to stop. It felt too good as she continued gliding her hand up and down, squeezing and gently tugging his length to the point of him seeing stars.

When he felt his control slipping, he reluctantly gripped her wrist. "I'm already about to lose it," he rasped, his breathing shallow as he struggled to get air into his lungs. "If you keep doing that, this—this will be over quicker than either of us want."

Ignoring his words, she continued what she was doing—wreaking havoc on his dick, and he stumbled back, bumping into a nearby wall.

"Aww hell," he ground out as his hips moved on their own accord with each stroke of her hand.

This was not what he had planned. This was not how he wanted things to go the first time they got together as husband and wife.

"Okay," he growled, and jerked out of her hold.

Breathing hard, he spun her around and backed her to the wall, catching her totally off guard if her wide eyes and mouth hanging open were any indication.

"I had planned on a nice romantic bath, but you've shot those plans to hell," he said gruffly, as he quickly removed her shoes, tossing them behind him, then made quick work of stripping her out of her underwear.

Scarlett yelped when he lifted her, her back braced against the wall.

"I want you so damn bad," he ground between gritted teeth. He had barely pulled his dick from his briefs before he was buried balls deep inside of her.

"Oh, yes," Scarlett cried out as she held on to him, her arms tightening around his neck as he thrust in and out of her.

Antonio's lips found hers, and as their tongues mated, he thrust into her like a man possessed. In the back of his mind, he feared he'd hurt her with the way her back was plastered against the wall, but he couldn't stop. His pace increased as he pumped his hips, going deeper each time he drove into her.

One of her hands gripped the back of his neck as their kiss grew more intense, more frantic with each lap of their tongues. The erotic moans and the way she whimpered into his mouth, let him know she was nearing her release.

He dug his fingers into the bottom of her thighs, hanging on to her as his own orgasm lingered nearby. She was so damn wet, and as her juices coated his—

He ripped his mouth from hers. "Oh shit! Condom!" he panted.

"Don't you dare stop!" Scarlett screamed. Her frantic words and how good it felt to be deep inside of her lit a fire in him that he couldn't extinguish.

Flames of passion licked at every nerve in his body. His wife had him so hard and out of control, Antonio couldn't stop even if he wanted to. Intense heat charged through his body as he drove into her over and over again, going deeper with each thrust.

"I—I'm coming," Scarlett cried. Her interior walls tightened around him as her body bucked, and he lost it. He came right along with her with such force, it shook him to the soles of his feet.

Shuddering, they held on to each other tightly as their chests heaved, and they struggled to breathe. Scarlett's head rested on his shoulder while his forehead was plastered against the wall. Antonio couldn't move. He could barely think straight. Still buried inside of her, he had Scarlett pinned, but even knowing that he couldn't move.

"Baby," she gasped, her breath hot against his heated skin. "That was... that was..."

"So not what I had planned for us, but it... it was mind-blowing," he said, still unable to move.

"Exactly."

Antonio didn't know how long he held her there before he was finally able to breathe normally. He slowly lowered Scarlett until her feet touched the floor, but he didn't release her.

"I'm sorry about the condom."

"It's okay, I'm on the pill, but I guess this is yet another thing we'll need to talk about, huh?"

"Yeah, but not today. I'm not done with you."

With an unexpected burst of energy, Antonio scooped her

up, loving the way she squealed. Carrying her to the bedroom, he already knew making love to his wife was going to be his new favorite pastime. And since they had the rest of the day and all night, trying a few different positions was definitely in order.

* * *

Hours later, as they lounged in the oversized tub, Scarlett marveled at how every muscle in her body ached. It was a delicious ache brought on by several rounds of the most intense sex she'd ever had. The pleasure Antonio had given to every inch, every dip, and every curve of her body had Scarlett ready for more. The man knew how to please her sexually.

She was sitting in front of him, wrapped in his warmth as bubbles came up to her chin. If only they could stay like this forever. For the last few days, she'd been imagining what it was going to be like being married to Antonio. So far, the experience was exceeding her imagination. First their small, intimate, but beautiful wedding was more than she could've asked for. Her sister and Makena had come through big time.

Mahogany had helped her find a dress and shoes at the last minute for her and Bella. While that happened, Makena took care of the backyard setting, music, and even a small wedding cake.

And Antonio. The man had made her feel like a queen in the way he catered to her every need and desire. He had even rented a limousine that only added to the fairytale-like day. The driver was great, and Scarlett felt like royalty as he drove them around the city while she and Antonio munched on snacks and drank champagne.

The day had been perfect.

"Are you ready for tomorrow?" Antonio asked as he ran a soapy washcloth over her tender breasts and sensitive nipples.

Scarlett closed her eyes and moaned. "I can't think straight when you touch me like that." Especially when his hardness was pressed against her lower back. She might be sore, but he made her feel so good, she'd be open for another round with him.

"Oh, sorry," he murmured close to her ear, and stopped with the washcloth.

Her eyes popped open. "What are you doing? I didn't say stop."

Antonio laughed, and Scarlett smiled. She loved this laid-back side of him. Hopefully, she could keep him like this. Not that she didn't adore his more serious in-charge persona, but she loved his laugh, and his smile, and his cute dimples.

He wrapped his arms around her, ignoring the way some of the water splashed onto the floor. Thankfully there was a large, absorbent bath rug next to the tub.

Kissing the side of her head, he said, "Are you ready for Sunday brunch tomorrow?"

"Not really," she said honestly.

Mahogany was tasked with inviting their mother to brunch. Scarlett was sure she'd attend since she had gotten close to several members of the Jenkins family. By having her there, Scarlett and Antonio would be able to share their news with everyone at one time.

It was going to be a big day. Not only would they announce their marriage, but they'd also be celebrating Bella's birthday. Her actual birthday wasn't until Tuesday, but Antonio wanted to celebrate it early. He wanted her to get the full Jenkins family treatment. Apparently, the kids' birthdays came with a huge cake and lots of presents. Once again, he'd gotten Martina's help with that.

"Which part of tomorrow are you concerned about?" Antonio asked, probably already knowing the answer.

"When my mother finds out about us, I don't know if she will ever forgive me. I should've listened to you."

He had wanted to fill her mother in on everything, but Scarlett honestly hadn't thought it would be a good idea. Now, she had to reap the consequences of her decision.

"My mother thinks you're amazing, Antonio, but I was afraid she'd say something that would change my mind about our arrangement. Actually, I know she would've. She would've thought logically and would've said something like—*You're overreacting. Bella's other grandparents would never do anything to harm her.*" And Scarlett hadn't wanted to hear it. Maybe she had overreacted, but she believed Cynthia and her concerns about Alberta and Theodore.

"Well, whatever happens, just know I'll be right there with you," Antonio said, tightening his hold around her.

Snuggled in his arms made her feel cherished and safe. Like he could protect her from the big, bad world.

"It'll be okay," he said.

"Yeah, I hope you're right."

Chapter Twenty-Seven

Antonio parked on the side of his grandparents' massive home and shut off his truck. Scarlett had been mostly quiet on the ride there, and he knew she was nervous. Who wouldn't be? His family was a lot on normal days, but when there was big news shared, chaos often broke out. Antonio just wished he could promise her that no one would butt into their business. He couldn't.

"We don't have to go in if you don't want to," he said and reached across the center console for her hand. "We can go home and save the announcement for another day."

"Thanks, but I know we need to get this over with. You have a cool family, but this is one time I wished there weren't so many of them. There has to be at least twenty cars lining the long driveway," she glanced out at where they were parked, "and another five over here. That's a lot of people for Sunday brunch."

Antonio didn't have the heart to tell her that more might show up before the day was over. He had intentionally arrived later, hoping everyone would be too distracted with eating to notice when they walked in. All he had to do was tell a few people in the house, and the news would spread like a wildfire on a windy day.

He brought Scarlett's hand to his mouth and kissed the back of it. "Ready to make a move?"

She glanced at the brick home and released a long breath. "As ready as I'll ever be."

Kids' laughter and boisterous talking came from the back-yard where there was a large jungle gym and clubhouse. He and his cousins added to the structures every year. The kids' outdoor space could rival any public playground. The family was growing so fast with all his first cousins having kids every few years. Soon, this new generation of Jenkins would outnumber his generation.

Hand in hand, he and Scarlett entered through the front door and were greeted by the mouthwatering smell of something rich and savory. Usually his grandmother, some of his aunts, and a few of his female cousins did the bulk of the cooking for Sunday brunch. No doubt they had outdone themselves as usual.

Scarlett held on tightly as they strolled down the long hallway where tons of family photos graced the walls. Antonio headed toward the kitchen, surprised they hadn't come in contact with anyone yet. Which meant people had already started eating. The house was so big, the family was able to spread out. To keep things civilized, his grandmother had arranged for there to be a couple of different food stations on the main and lower level.

As they reached the opening to the kitchen, loud talking and laughter flowed from the room. It sounded as if there was a party going on, and Antonio glanced down at Scarlett. He was still debating on whether they should share their news this way, but she smiled and gave a slight nod.

When they entered, there were five or six people, including his grandmother, who were hustling around the kitchen. One person was at the stove, another at the sink, and the others busied themselves with setting out food.

"You said we wouldn't need any more fried chicken, which was why I made a turkey tenderloin," one of his aunts was saying.

"I don't think we're going to have enough cornbread," someone else said.

There were tons of food dishes on every flat surface. It looked as if family members had already dug in based on some partially empty serving dishes. Folks were probably already camped out in the basement or dining room.

"Hey, baby. Glad to see you two," Gram said over the loud talking and headed toward them. Dressed in a colorful kaftan housedress, her customary attire for around the house, she greeted them with a smile. "Welcome back, Scarlett." She hugged and kissed her cheek before doing the same to Antonio. "I hope you guys are hungry."

"I am," Antonio said, "but we have an announcement." But the moment he opened his mouth again to speak, Bella ran into the kitchen.

"Mommy, Daddy! You're here!" she yelled and leaped into Antonio's arms.

It was as if the world stopped spinning. All eyes were suddenly on him. Nobody moved. Nobody spoke, and he wasn't even sure if anyone was still breathing. No doubt they caught the "daddy" part of Bella's greeting.

Well, here goes.

Antonio wrapped his free arm around his wife and pulled her to his side. "Scarlett and I got married yesterday."

The silence in the room was deafening. Then everyone started speaking at once and moved in on them like a colony of

bees swarming toward their new home. Antonio hated attention, and the questions being thrown at them at rapid-fire speed
were exhausting. Without looking around, he could feel more
people had entered the kitchen determined to find out what
was going on.

"*She must be pregnant.*"

"*Yes, our family is growing! I love it.*"

"*What the hell?*"

"*Someone should've warned her about this family.*"

"*Another cousin...*"

Everyone talked at once, and Antonio sighed. Maybe he
should've let Martina spread the word before they got there.
She had offered the week before when she helped him pick out
Scarlett's ring, but he'd told her to keep her big mouth shut.
Apparently, she had listened.

As if thinking about her had conjured her up, she entered
the kitchen grinning. "So, I guess you guys heard the news."
Her presence and words only added to the frenzy and incited
more questions.

He'd had enough, and poor Scarlett looked even more over-
whelmed than before.

"Stop!" Antonio yelled, and once everyone settled down,
he said, "Yes, we're married. We got married yesterday."

"*Married?*" The word was snapped out by someone nearby,
and Scarlett stiffened against him.

Dammit. That one word had to have come from her
mother. This wasn't exactly how Scarlett had wanted Mrs.
Amelia to find out. They turned slowly and faced Scarlett's
mother. The expression on the older woman's face was a
mixture of shock and disappointment, but disappointment
won out.

"Mom, I can explain," Scarlett hurried to say and pulled
away from Antonio.

"Why is Grandma mad?" Bella whispered in Antonio's ear.

Antonio moved quickly. "We can go and talk in Pop's office down the hall," he said of his grandfather's office, hoping it was empty. There wasn't a Sunday that went by when someone didn't end up in there to hash out grievances with another family member.

Before walking out the door, he started to set Bella on her feet, but she clung to him. "I want to go too," she said, almost pleadingly.

Antonio groaned. He still struggled with saying no to her despite Scarlett always accusing him of spoiling Bella.

"Bella, sweetie, I need your help," Gram said from the other side of the huge center island.

Antonio could've kissed his grandmother. No one could resist her requests, and he bet it would be the same with Bella.

"I have these cupcakes that need pink frosting. I thought you'd probably want to frost them. Can you?"

Bella bit her lower lip, then nodded. "Okay."

Antonio set her on her feet and whispered in her ear. "Thanks for helping Gram. I have a surprise for you later."

A slow grin spread across her mouth, and his heart melted like usual. "You do?"

"Yes, so go help. Then after me and your mom finish talking to your grandmother, I'll be back."

"Okay." She kissed his cheek and then hustled over to Gram. Antonio blew his grandmother a kiss and smiled when she winked at him.

When he reached the hallway outside of the kitchen, he found Scarlett and Mrs. Amelia in a heated discussion. They might be whispering, but it didn't stop others from listening in. There were family members peeking out of the dining room, and no doubt there were others peeking out from somewhere nearby.

He gently grasped Scarlett's hand and rested his hand on Mrs. Amelia's back as he escorted them toward the front of the house to his grandfather's office. Thankfully, no one was in there, and he ushered the women inside before closing the door.

"What is going on?" Mrs. Amelia snapped and stood in front of Scarlett. "I know you didn't just wake up one morning and decide, oh, today I think I'll get married. How could you not tell me?"

The hurt in her tone cut right through Antonio, and he saw it had the same effect on Scarlett. Her eyes watered, and he knew he had to do something.

"Mrs. Amelia, I asked Scarlett not—"

"Don't," Scarlett said just above a whisper as she swiped at her cheeks. "Antonio, don't lie for me. Mom, it's true. Antonio and I are married."

Chapter Twenty-Eight

After closing the office door behind Antonio, Scarlett almost wanted to call him back in. But this was something she needed to do by herself. Her mother deserved to hear everything from her. Yet, the hurt on her mom's face was almost too much to bear. Still Scarlett needed to tell her everything and hoped she understood.

"Are you pregnant?" her mother asked before Scarlett made it back to the sofa where she was sitting.

"No, Mom, I'm not pregnant."

The question reminded her of when she'd had to tell her mother over eight years ago that she was pregnant. It had been weeks after learning of Ezra's death and turned out to be one of the most difficult times in Scarlett's life. She'd only gotten through that time with the help of her mother and Mahogany.

"Then please explain to me why you eloped. What was the big hurry to get married, and why didn't you tell me?"

Scarlett almost groaned out loud. If her mother was hurt now, she'd be devastated to learn they hadn't eloped. That they'd had a small, intimate wedding with their immediate family... with everyone except for her.

Scarlett felt worse.

"Just so you know, the decision to not tell you was all me. Antonio thought I was wrong, but I did what I thought was right at the time."

Her mother sat on the edge of the sofa cushion and looked at her confused. "Why would you think you couldn't tell me? We've always been able to discuss everything. Ever since you were a little girl, you've known you could talk to me. What's changed?"

"You're right. You are the most amazing mother who has been there for me at every turn. Because of that, I've tried to never do anything to disappoint you or anything that would embarrass you."

Basically, Scarlett had tried to be perfect. The perfect child who never gave her parents any trouble and who always did what was expected. The only time she had let her mother down was when she'd had to tell her she was pregnant out of wedlock.

"I didn't tell you because of the reason why I got married. I didn't want you to talk me out of it. I didn't want you to think less of me for the decisions I made that I thought would be best for me and Bella."

Scarlett shared everything, including conversations with Cynthia and her run-in with Alberta. She begged her mom not to share the information with anyone. She wanted everyone around them to think she got married for the usual reason people married—love. Not because she was trying to shield her child from Ezra's parents. Parents who had caused emotional trauma and abandonment issues within their son. Grandparents who she didn't want anywhere near Bella, and she had just proven the lengths she'd go to see to that.

Hearing herself say everything aloud made Scarlett realize just how impulsive she'd been, but she was standing by her decision. She felt deep in her heart that if she'd had to choose a father for her child, it would've been Antonio.

Ultimately, if this ended up being the stupidest thing she'd ever done, or the worst decision she ever made, she'd have to live with it. It gave her comfort that there wasn't a person on the planet who hadn't done something wild and unpopular at some point in their life. And that's what she told her mother.

Scarlett's mother sat back on the sofa and crossed her legs at the ankles. Casually dressed in a yellow blouse and dark pants with short heels, she looked her cool and confident self. But Scarlett knew she had hurt her.

"I'm so sorry, Mom. Not including you was one of the hardest decisions I ever had to make. If I had a do-over, I'd make a different choice where you're concerned. I wanted you there beside me, standing in support of my decision, but unfortunately, it's too late. I'm so sorry if I disappointed you. I hope you can forgive me."

Her mother met her gaze and frowned. "Of course I forgive you. You're my daughter, my heart. I have always loved you and your sister unconditionally, and there is nothing that will ever change that, Scarlett.

"You were right. I would've tried to talk you out of getting married. Not because I don't think you love Antonio, but because of the reason you decided to marry him."

Discomfort clawed through Scarlett. She hadn't mentioned she wasn't in love with Antonio. And to set her mother straight would just cause more questions, more drama. Besides, she didn't want anyone, besides Antonio and her sister, to know she'd married him though she wasn't in love with him.

It was okay for people to think less of her, but Scarlett

didn't want anyone to think less of Antonio or to judge him for marrying someone who didn't love him.

"I would've loved to witness you getting married, but..." She shrugged. "Like you said, it's too late. You're a grown woman who can make her own decisions. Just know I'll always support you, and I'm glad you found someone like Antonio. He's a wonderful man who will treat you and Bella right. I'm also glad he'll be Bella's father. She's a lucky girl to have two parents who love and cherish her so much."

Scarlett smiled for the first time since arriving for Sunday brunch. She and Bella were both lucky to have Antonio in their lives, and she hoped he felt the same.

* * *

Scarlett's emotions were all over the place as she freshened up in one of the bathrooms. She was thrilled to be at the covenant Sunday brunch with her new family. On the other hand, she still felt awful about disappointing her mother.

After freshening up in one of the bathrooms, Scarlett made her way to the kitchen, hoping it had cleared out some. Talking to her mother, and apologizing over and over, had been emotionally exhausting, but she was glad she'd done it.

Thankfully, only Gram, Makena, and a couple of Antonio's aunts were in the kitchen. One being, Martina's mother, Carolyn.

"Hey, sweetie. You doing okay?" Makena asked, giving Scarlett a hug and a squeeze.

"Yes, I'm fine. Thank you for asking," she said to her mother-in-law, then turned to Gram. "Mrs. Jenkins, thanks so much for distracting Bella for us earlier."

Gram kissed her cheek. "It was my pleasure. I'm thrilled to

have you join our family, and I love having another great-grand-daughter to spoil. Bella is a sweetheart."

"Hi, we haven't met. I'm Mary, one of Antonio's aunts." They hugged, and Scarlett learned she was visiting from Chicago. Her and her three sons, who owned a tech company, were thinking about moving back to Cincinnati.

Mary was the spitting image of Gram except younger. They both wore their hair long and pulled back from their face, had smooth brown skin, and friendly smiles. While Carolyn looked like a perfect size six, her sister and mother were a bit thicker around the waist and hips.

"Even though Antonio didn't give us much time to plan Bella's celebration," Gram said, "I think she'll be happy with what we have planned."

"Wanna see her cake?" Carolyn asked, and before Scarlett could respond, she brought it from the pantry.

Scarlett's mouth fell open as Martina's mom set the three-tier cake, that looked like something straight off one of the food channels baking shows, on the counter. "Wow."

It was big and beautifully decorated with pink, yellow, and white flowers at the bottom of each tier. The cake topper was a black ballerina wearing a pink tutu and looked so much like Bella, Scarlett almost thought it was her.

"Yeah, Martina has skills. She really should give up construction and open a specialized bakery," Gram said, and that news shocked Scarlett even more.

"Wait, MJ cooks and bakes?"

Mary snorted. "Girl, yeah. She's not just a pain in the ass, she's actually..." Mary's voice trailed off. "Oops, sorry, Mama. That slipped. Anyway, MJ's very talented."

"Clearly," Scarlett said.

They explained what they had planned for Bella's celebration. It included gathering everyone into the ballroom, playing some kid games, then singing happy birthday to Bella before cutting the cake.

"She is going to love that," Scarlett said, though she knew, like Antonio, Bella didn't like being the center of attention. But the gesture was one of the sweetest things anyone had ever done for her child. "Thank you all for welcoming me and Bella to the family. This means so much."

Gram smiled warmly and patted her hand. "Thank you for making Antonio so happy. I have never seen him smile as much as he does when you and Bella are around."

Guilt stabbed Scarlett in the chest. What would his family think of her if they knew why Antonio married her? Hopefully, they'd never find out.

A short while later, Scarlett loaded her plate with barbecue chicken, the most delicious looking mac and cheese she'd ever seen, and collard greens. There were so many different types of food, but she was determined not to overeat. Still, she planned on hitting the gym in the morning, especially since she wanted a slice of the pecan pie. Then there was Bella's cake that she'd have to taste.

She took her plate and a bottle of water to the dining room where Mahogany was eating with a few of Antonio's cousins.

"Get up, Toni. Make room for the family's new rebel," Martina said, nudging her cousin and laughing.

Scarlett rolled her eyes and sat across from Martina and next to Mahogany. "I'm almost afraid to ask what she's talking about."

"She's ranked you into the Jenkins family thug category for not telling Mom you were getting married," Mahogany volunteered.

Scarlett sighed. "I make one mistake, and it sounds like I'm going to hear about it for the rest of my life."

"Pretty much," Christina said with a laugh from the far end of the table.

"Mixing up salt and sugar is a mistake," Martina continued. "Not inviting your own mother to be a part of your nuptials is straight up gangster. Especially when yo momma looks like she don't take shit from nobody."

A few chuckles went around the table, and Scarlett couldn't help but join in. Her mother was petite with the kindest demeanor of anyone Scarlett knew except for maybe Gram. She rarely raised her voice, even when they were growing up. So, Martina's depiction of Amelia Rowsey was comical.

"*Sooo,* are you pregnant?" Toni asked, and Scarlett groaned while the others laughed. "Hey, I'm asking because everyone else is thinking it."

Toni Jenkins-Logan was one of the managers at Jenkins & Sons Construction, as well as a master plumber by trade. Considering she was part of a male-dominant career, she looked more like a college student or maybe a schoolteacher. Then again, the T-shirt she was wearing—which read, *I'm a plumber. We take care of sh#%*—probably put her more in the gangster category that Martina alluded to.

"Not that it's any of our business, but why the secret nuptials?" Christina asked. "And if I'm being too nosey, just say so. I don't want to be another MJ."

Scarlett glanced at Martina who kept eating and didn't look put off at all. Someone as bold as her, with no filter, probably didn't offend or embarrass easily.

"It was the way Antonio and I wanted it," Scarlett said. She and Antonio had agreed to keep their responses similar to that.

"You're right, CJ, it's none of your business," Martina said, pointing her fork at her cousin. "I can't believe you asked her that."

The cousins stared at Martina as if seeing her for the first time, and Scarlett wondered why.

"Oh. My. God. You knew about them getting married!" Toni accused, glaring at Martina. "And the reason must be huge if your big mouth didn't tell everyone."

"You're right!" Christina added. "Otherwise, she'd be giving Scarlett a hard time right about now."

Martina went back to eating as if Toni hadn't spoken, and Scarlett wondered just how much MJ knew about her situation. And when the woman winked at Scarlett on the sly, she knew in that moment that Martina knew way more than she was letting on.

"Now I really want to know what happened. If Martina is being hush, hush, it means this is juicy," Toni said, and Christina agreed.

"Antonio is my favorite cousin. Even if I knew why he got married without telling anyone, I wouldn't tell y'all nosey asses. Y'all always trying to get into someone's business."

"Nosey?"

"Seriously?"

Toni and Christina said at the same time.

"You're the one who is always in everybody's business," Toni snapped. "You're the last person who can call someone nosey. Now, spill it, Scarlett. What are you hiding? We're going to find out eventually."

"All right, leave Scarlett alone. We wouldn't want to scare her away from the family, would we?" Jada asked as she sashayed into the dining room with a small plate of food and looking like she just stepped off the cover of Vogue magazine.

Scarlett wondered if she ever dressed down because the woman looked as if she was going out on the town, not having brunch with the family. Her hair was pulled on top of her head in a messy, but cute, ponytail with long tendrils framing her face, but it was her outfit that was the real showstopper. The hunter-green, bodycon, one-shoulder dress was gorgeous against her dark skin. She wore her own designs, and Scarlett planned to see if she had the outfit in red.

"All, hell. Who let her bougie ass back in the house," Martina grumbled. "Shouldn't you be in Paris or whatever hell the fashion capital of the world is these days?"

"Shut up, MJ," Jada said without missing a beat as she sat at the head of the table and to Scarlett's left. "The only reason I'm not going to tell you what I think about you is because I saw little Bella's birthday cake. You did your thang girl. It is too cute."

Everyone started talking at once, giving Martina props on her cake decorating skills. Scarlett didn't know how they could hear each other considering how loud they were talking.

Jada leaned over to Scarlett. "And *that's* how you redirect this group and get the attention off yourself."

Scarlett grinned. "Noted. Thanks."

Considering the way the visit had started, Scarlett could admit she was looking forward to future Sunday brunches. Especially if she wasn't the center of attention.

Chapter Twenty-Nine

Antonio watched as Bella measured the baking powder for the peanut butter chocolate chip cookies she was making for dessert. His little sous chef impressed him at every turn. For the last few weeks, since she wanted to learn to cook and bake, he had her helping him in the kitchen. Yes, preparing meals took longer with her assistance, but his dad had taken the time to teach him to cook. Now it was Antonio's turn to do the same with his daughter.

My daughter, he thought with a smile as he watched Bella add the next ingredient into the dough. She wasn't legally his yet, but in Antonio's heart she was his.

"Daddy, guess what?"

"What?"

"Gram sent me another birthday gift even though my birthday was weeks ago. She said it didn't arrive on time."

"What did she give you?"

"It's a... I'll just show you."

Bella dusted off her hands and left the kitchen. She was still talking about her *epic* Jenkins family birthday party. It had definitely left an impression on her. Even though she'd started out shy that day, she had soon warmed up to everybody. Especially when they started playing birthday games.

Antonio was proud of how his family always came through, and he appreciated the way they had welcomed Scarlett and Bella to the family.

Bella returned to the kitchen carrying a white, yellow, and pink birthday bag.

"It's an apron, and it came with a chef's hat and look what it says." She pulled the hot-pink apron out of the bag and held it up. "It says, *Chef in Training.*"

Antonio chuckled. "That's perfect, but why aren't you wearing it now?"

She smacked her lips and gave him a look that said he should know why. "Because I don't want to get it dirty."

"Wait, isn't that the whole point of an apron—to keep your clothes from getting food on them? It's meant to get dirty."

"Not if I don't wear it," she said and left the kitchen again.

Antonio shook his head and laughed. *Women.*

A short while later, they worked together rolling the cookie dough into balls and placing them on a cookie sheet.

"You can put them in the oven right before we sit down for dinner," Antonio said just as the timer on the stove sounded.

Bella hurried across the room to turn it off. "Should I take the baked chicken out now?"

"Yes, if you think you can handle it."

Bella was still timid when it came to removing items from the oven, but she was getting better. He made sure the pans were light enough for her to hold.

She nibbled on her lower lip, looking unsure. "I think I can handle it, but can you help me?"

"Of course. Grab your oven mitts."

Antonio was keeping his promise to Scarlett, regarding

cooking at least four times a week despite his work schedule being hectic. He had accepted the VP position, and for the most part, he loved the job. What he didn't like was having to take work home at night. Most days he could leave the office at six, but that also meant he couldn't always get everything done.

Bella slid her hands into the small oven mitts he'd bought her while Antonio grabbed a couple of potholders. She slowly pulled out the pan, and he hovered close, trying not to jump in.

She set the dish on the cooling rack and grinned. "Done."

They fist bumped each other, and Antonio turned off the oven, needing it to cool off some before they baked the cookies.

"Oh, it smells good in here," Scarlett said, strolling into the kitchen. When she slid her arm around his waist, Antonio pulled her in for a hug and kissed her.

"You taste like strawberries," he told her.

"It's a new lip gloss that I'm testing out. I think I like it."

"Me too." He kissed her again.

"Okay, so I have some bad news." Scarlett moved away from him and leaned her back against the counter. "I just heard from Sue, and she said the daddy-daughter dance has been canceled. Or at least postponed."

"Oh, no, but we practiced so much," Bella said with her bottom lip poked out.

Though Antonio loved the idea of dancing with her, he hated that the organizers wanted the fathers to wear tutus. Of course, they all would do anything for their daughters, but he was glad he wouldn't have to embarrass himself.

"I'm sorry, baby, but the weather is too bad. They don't want anyone to get caught in the storm."

In that moment, the windows rattled, and the lights flickered, but they didn't go out. Antonio had already pulled out his tornado preparation bag. They were also prepared if the lights went out. He always kept battery operated lanterns in every room.

"Do the weather people still think we're going to have a tornado?" Bella asked nervously and glanced at the windows. "It's really windy."

It was. Last Antonio heard, the winds had gotten up to forty miles per hour. The house was solidly built, but that hadn't stopped him from hearing creaks here and there, along with the windows shaking.

"There's still a tornado watch, but it hasn't turned into a warning," Scarlett said. "I was thinking. After dinner, maybe you and your dad can do your performance for me. I can video-tape it and take pictures of you two. What do you say? Because I was really looking forward to seeing it."

Her wicked smile and the gleam in her eyes meant what she really was looking forward to was seeing him in the stupid tutu. Hell, he didn't even know they made those things that big.

"Yes! That's a great idea," Bella said, grinning. "Is that okay, Dad?"

Antonio sighed dramatically. "Fine. I guess if I have to."

They had practiced for weeks, and though he loved hanging out with Bella, he wasn't too broken up about the performance being canceled. Thank goodness for small miracles.

The lights flickered again, and he pulled a few candles from the pantry. "How about we eat by candlelight tonight?"

His girls agreed, and they went about their usual dinner-time routine. Bella set the table, and he laid out the food. Scarlett usually had cleanup duty but assisted wherever needed.

As they prepared for dinner, Antonio felt a peace deep down in his soul. He finally had everything he'd ever wanted, and he couldn't ask for a better life.

* * *

Since Scarlett had planned to make up Bella's face for the performance tonight, she went ahead and did it even though they'd be performing at home. They were in the master bathroom. The bathroom Antonio had remodeled days before she and Bella moved in, and now Scarlett had a makeup vanity that she loved.

They had gotten into an easy routine as a family, and it felt as if the three of them had been together forever. She never knew marriage could be so much fun and make her feel so complete. It was all because of Antonio. He was turning out to be everything she didn't know she wanted or needed.

She had Cynthia to thank.

Scarlett smiled recalling the woman's reaction when she told her about marrying Antonio. *That's the best news I've heard in a long time.* She hadn't seemed all that surprised, and Scarlett wondered if Cynthia had manipulated her by putting the adoption idea in her head. She probably knew there couldn't be an adoption without them getting married, but Scarlett wasn't complaining. Marrying Antonio was one of her best decisions ever.

"Can you do my makeup for when I go to Chanelle's birthday party next Saturday?" Bella said of Nick's oldest daughter. The kids in the Jenkins family welcomed Bella, but she really enjoyed hanging out with Nick's two little girls.

"I'll let you wear makeup sometimes around the house, but not in public. You're too young. Maybe a little lip-gloss occasionally, but that's it until you're fifteen."

Bella smacked her lips and huffed. "But that's a long time away."

"Exactly. Baby, you're beautiful without makeup. You don't need it."

"Daddy said you're beautiful too. So you don't need makeup either."

Caught off guard by her daughter's words, Scarlett wasn't surprised Antonio had said that. Some women wished their husbands complimented them more, but hers actually did. She also appreciated that he was honest. He wasn't one of those men who only told her what she wanted to hear. There'd been several occasions when she ended up changing clothes after asking his opinion about an outfit. There used to be a time when she dressed for her pleasure. Now, she also dressed for his.

"Okay, are you ready for the show?" Scarlett asked Bella while tidying up the vanity.

"Yes! I'm ready. Let's do this."

Scarlett laughed and followed her downstairs. Antonio had already moved furniture around to create a stage for them, and all Scarlett needed was her camera equipment.

Twenty minutes later, she was dabbing at her eyes. Bella and Antonio had three dances they were going to perform, and when they danced to "One Call Away" by Charlie Puth, Scarlett felt the lyrics were perfect for the two of them.

Bella looked like an adorable ballerina in pink and white as she did a pirouette and pranced in front of her dad. Antonio, bless his heart, gave Bella his full attention, preparing for when he had to lift or spin her. He looked handsome in the white button-down shirt and black pants, and Scarlett didn't blame him for not wearing the pink tutu. Still, it warmed her heart that he would have if Bella had insisted.

There were moments like this that Scarlett was so glad Antonio was in her daughter's life... in their lives. She didn't realize what they'd been missing until he came along. Sure, she and Bella were happy with just the two of them, but Antonio made them feel more like a family.

Scarlett had the video camera set up on a tripod to catch the whole performance. While that was happening, she took pictures. She brought her camera back up to her eye and snapped several shots of Antonio lifting Bella. He held her up high and her daughter stretched out her arms as if she were flying. The trust she had in Antonio was clear as he danced around the makeshift stage while holding her up in the air.

God, this man. He was meant to be a father.

Scarlett startled when a loud crackle sounded outside, followed by roaring thunder that shook the house. Then there was a loud *boom* that rocked them seconds before the lights went out and the music stopped.

"I'm scared," Bella said, her voice trembling.

Scarlett couldn't help but chuckle as she felt her way to the fireplace mantel where Antonio had set a lantern. She turned it on and lifted it up, aiming it toward Bella and Antonio. "Well, I guess that's it for the show, huh?" she asked

"That wasn't the end," Bella said with attitude. "It was just getting good."

Scarlett and Antonio laughed.

"It was," he agreed. "Maybe we can pick up where we left off later or another day. For now, how about we hang out in the basement for the rest of the evening? We have everything we need down there in case this storm gets worse."

What he meant was in case this storm resulted in a tornado. This was one time when Scarlett was glad he was well-prepared. Not only did he have supplies, but the rec room in the basement was cozy. There was a sofa sleeper, and Antonio had taken an air mattress and extra lanterns downstairs earlier —just in case. They'd be able to entertain themselves with games or shooting pool, and Scarlett was glad they'd have a distraction. Like Bella, she hated storms.

"I loved the show," Scarlett said. Antonio still had Bella in his arms, and he reached for Scarlett's hand. "Your dad is a good dancer."

"Yep, he is. At practice, he was better than all the other daddies," Bella said proudly and rested her head on Antonio's shoulder.

"I'm sure he was."

Scarlett could barely make out his expression in the dim lighting, but he squeezed her hand. She hoped he felt how important he was to them and how much they adored him. Because Scarlett couldn't imagine her life without him.

Chapter Thirty

Frustration charged through Scarlett as she called Antonio one more time. He was supposed to meet her and Bella at the house so they could go to the concert in the park, but he hadn't shown. Knowing he was probably trying to do that "one more thing" at work, she'd decided to head to the park and hopefully meet him there.

"Mommy, is my dad coming?" Bella asked from the back seat as she unfastened her seatbelt.

"I'm not sure, honey. He hasn't called me back." She'd been trying to reach him for the last forty minutes. After leaving two messages and a text, she didn't bother leaving another.

Tonight was the last day of the summer's free concerts in the park. They had already missed several of them over the last few months because of his hectic work schedule. She had hoped they could finally get one in. Apparently not. At least not as a family.

As Scarlett was getting out of the car, her cell phone rang, and relief flooded through her. At least until she realized it wasn't Antonio.

"Hey, Sis," she answered and moved around to the trunk to pull out the stuff they'd brought with them. "You guys here yet?" The plan had been to meet Mahogany, Ben, and Jayden there, have a little picnic, and enjoy the music.

"We are, and we found a great spot not too close, and not too far from the stage."

Mahogany gave her directions on where to find them before Scarlett disconnected the call. As she and Bella placed the picnic basket, chairs, and blanket into the wagon, Scarlett debated on calling Antonio again. But why bother? It was clear work had become more important than her and Bella.

He'd been working long hours, promising it was only temporary. She wanted to be supportive in his new role as VP. She also understood how hard it was to get acclimated to a new position. Still, enough was enough. He had missed three events because of work. It wouldn't be a big deal if he hadn't committed to them, but he had and then flaked on each one. This time was worse because he hadn't even called.

"Well, let's go find your Aunt Momo, Uncle Ben, and Jayden," Scarlett said and started on the long walk.

When she reached the area where her sister said they'd be, it took a moment before she spotted them. Now she needed to get her attitude in check. This was the first time she'd been truly mad at Antonio, and she didn't want to take her frustrations out on anyone else.

"Hey, you guys made it," Ben said as he approached them and took over pulling the wagon. "Where's Ant?"

Scarlett sighed. "Probably working. He's not answering my calls."

Without responding, Ben pulled out his cell phone and made a call. After several rings, he made another call with the same results. "I tried his cell and his office. After I help get you guys situated, I'll call around and see if I can find him. It's not like him not to answer calls."

Scarlett hadn't been worried until that moment. What if something happened to him? Ben was right, Antonio was good about calling if he was going to be late and getting messages to her. She couldn't ever remember him not answering when she called, but lately he'd been so distracted, she wasn't sure what to think.

Antonio was doing too much. He'd been coming home exhausted because he was trying to be everything to everybody at work. Then because of the promises he'd made to her, he came home, cooked, and tried to spend as much time with her and Bella as possible. Something had to give. He couldn't keep going like this, not just because she wanted to see more of him. But also, because he had workaholic tendencies, it wasn't good for his health.

For the next hour, they enjoyed the local band who played everything from Boys II Men hits to some of Phil Collins most notable songs. The lead singer was talented, and he and the band helped take Scarlett's mind off the fact that she still hadn't heard from Antonio.

Bella, who had been lying on the blanket next to Jayden, stood up. Scarlett assumed she had to use the bathroom.

"Mommy, can you call Daddy again? I want him to come here with us. He's missing the concert."

"I know, sweetie, but I already left messages for him."

"I just received a text from Nate," Ben said while glancing down at his phone. "Antonio is at a meeting with one of our biggest clients."

"Oh, okay. Thanks for letting me know." Scarlett was glad that he was all right, but it didn't explain why he hadn't called them back.

Ben stood. "Hey, who wants ice cream?"

Scarlett could've kissed him. There were several food trucks nearby, and with him taking the kids, it would give her and Mahogony a chance to chat.

"Everything okay with you and Antonio?" Mahogany asked when the kids and Ben left.

"Except for him putting work before us, everything is wonderful." Scarlett fiddled with her wedding ring. "He's the sweetest, most attentive man I've ever met. I feel so blessed to have him in my life." She sighed and glanced at Mahogany who smiled knowingly at her. "How did you know you were in love with Ben?"

After a short hesitation, her sister said, "I'm not sure how I knew, but I remember when it happened. It was that day I was literally running after him, and then I fell down the stairs. We didn't know each other, not really. But even though I might've cost him a *major* job, he didn't think twice about taking me to the hospital. More than that, he waited for me."

Scarlett smiled. Her sister was a klutz on any given day. It was no surprise that an accident helped her snag her man. "And you lived happily ever after," Scarlett said and laughed, remembering that day as if it were yesterday.

"Exactly," Mahogany said, laughing. "But seriously, if you're asking me that question, I assume your feelings for Antonio have changed."

"I'm not sure if they've changed, but our connection is even more intense than I ever thought possible."

"Why are you so hesitant to admit you're in love?"

Scarlett looked at her sister and frowned. "Because I don't know if I am. That's why I'm asking you how you knew."

Mahogany huffed out a breath. "I'm not sure what to tell you except, when it happens, you'll know."

Scarlett hated that response. It was like a non-answer as far as she was concerned. When it happened, would she really just know?

* * *

Antonio strolled into his office, mad that he had left his phone there. It wouldn't have been a big deal, but what was supposed to be a drink with one of their long-time clients, had turned into dinner. He hadn't expected to be out so late and knew Scarlett was probably wondering why he wasn't home yet.

"I should've planned today better," he muttered.

Actually, he hadn't planned to meet with the guy in the first place. Nate was the one who had agreed to discuss business over drinks, but then something came up, and he'd asked Antonio to fill in. The worst part was Antonio hadn't been able to suggest meeting on a different day. Mr. Smith was only in town for the day and wanted to discuss upcoming projects.

Well, at least that was done, and Antonio could get home to his girls.

When he approached his desk, he spied a large white envelope that hadn't been there when he left. There was a note saying it had been delivered by messenger, and then he noticed it had come from his father's law office.

Excitement bubbled up inside of him, and a smile spread across his face as he opened it. He hoped it was what he thought it was—the final decree confirming he was Bella's father. Since he and Scarlett were married and Ezra was deceased, Luke felt the adoption wouldn't take as long to be finalized. Looks like he was right.

Antonio pulled out the document and did a fist pump in the air. Bella was officially his daughter. In the envelope was also a new birth certificate for her, which was a surprise. They'd been told it would take longer to receive it, but apparently, whatever his legal team had done to speed up the process, worked.

This is cause for a celebration.

He shoved everything back into the envelope and grabbed his cell phone from the charger. A quick glance at the screen and he froze. Unease prickled down his spine and fear nipped at every cell in his body. He had missed numerous calls from Scarlett and Ben.

Something must have happened. Just when he started to call Scarlett, he remembered.

Oh no. No, no, no. How the hell had he forgotten their plans for the night?

"Damn, damn, damn!"

He rushed out of the office, locking the door behind him before jogging to the elevator. When he glanced at his watch, he realized it was too late to head to the park and growled under his breath. Scarlett was going to kill him.

He sent her a quick text letting her know he was on his way home.

"Damn work," he grumbled and jumped into his car.

It was always work. His life lately was centered around his new VP position, but no way would he risk his marriage for a job. He couldn't screw this up. He had waited too long to have the family he had always dreamed of. He couldn't let this new position or anyone else get in the way. Scarlett and Bella had to always come first.

By the time Antonio arrived home and pulled into the garage, he was exhausted. He had already been tired before realizing he had messed up royally tonight. But trying to figure out how to make things right with his girls had used up what little energy he'd had left.

After leaving the office, he stopped at the store, picked up flowers, and bought apology gifts. He just hoped it would be enough.

Walking into the house, he stopped in the kitchen and hung up his keys. "Hello," he called out loud enough for them to hear him even if they were upstairs.

He immediately heard Bella's footsteps running overhead, and he smiled. Even if Scarlett was pissed, Bella would give him some grace. He loved her at this age, where she always seemed excited to see him when he walked through the door. He'd heard people at work talk about their teenage daughters, and he already knew he wasn't looking forward to that stage in her life.

"Daddy! You're home," she said and ran to him, hugging him tightly. "Where were you? Mommy was trying to call... Oooh, are those Twizzlers for me?"

"Yes, they are, and these are too." Antonio handed her a small bouquet of wildflowers. "I'm sorry I missed the concert. I totally forgot about it, and then I ended up working late."

"It's okay. These are pretty. Thank you," she said and gave him another hug.

This wasn't the first time he had brought her and her mother flowers. Yet, it was the first time he was using them as part of his apology.

"Since it's a little late, you can only eat two Twizzlers tonight."

"How about three?" she countered, grinning up at him, and of course Antonio gave in.

"Where's your mom?"

"Upstairs," Bella said absently as she dug into her candy.

Antonio kissed the top of her head and went in search of his wife. When he made it to their bedroom, the door was closed, and he braced himself for an argument. They didn't disagree on much, but he knew tonight would be different.

He entered the bedroom and found Scarlett on the bed, propped up against the headboard while thumbing through a magazine. She spared him a glance but didn't speak. Clearly, it was going to take more than flowers and chocolate to get back into her good graces.

"I'm sorry," he said, and strolled around to her side of the bed, then sat on the edge of the mattress.

He set the envelope with Bella's adoption papers on the nightstand, and still, Scarlett said nothing. She acted as if he wasn't even there, and Antonio eased the magazine from her grasp, afraid she might knock him upside the head with it.

"I am so sorry, sweetheart," he said and handed her the flowers and dark chocolate. "I know I messed up, and I promise it won't happen again."

Scarlett released a noisy sigh. "Tony, it was bad enough that you didn't show up for the concert, but not calling to let me know you were okay is unacceptable." She brought the flowers to her nose and inhaled. "These are lovely, and they smell amazing. Thank you."

"You're welcome."

He turned his back to her, and leaned forward, his elbows on his thighs. As he stared down at the floor, exhaustion settled over him. He felt like he could sleep a week, but first, he had to make things right.

"I don't have a good excuse for forgetting the concert. It totally slipped my mind. As for missing your calls, Nate was supposed to have drinks with one of our clients, but he had an emergency at home. At the last minute, he asked me to fill in."

"And you couldn't call to say you'll be late?"

He shrugged. "I was caught up in the moment. This is one of our biggest clients who's used us for every property he's purchased in Ohio. In my rush to get to the restaurant, I forgot my phone in the office. We were only supposed to have a drink, but it ended up being dinner."

When Scarlett didn't say anything, Antonio glanced over his shoulder at her. She was eating the chocolates he'd brought her. That was a good sign, then she looked at him. Those big, beautiful brown eyes did it to him every time. All the love he felt for her seemed to multiply. She was everything to him. How could he have let work dominate so much of his time over the last three months?

"Something has to change," she said between bites before setting the chocolate on the nightstand. "You can't keep going like this. Half sleeping, barely eating, and now you're missing family outings. At this rate, you're going to work yourself to death and for what? I get that this new position is your dream job, but ten, and twelve-hour days, six days a week is too much."

She reached over and cupped his cheek, and Antonio leaned into her touch and closed his eyes. She was right about everything. Changes were needed, and he had to make them sooner than later. He had the authority to hire some help, and he needed to take the time to do it.

When he opened his eyes, Scarlett leaned forward and kissed him. He wrapped his arms around her waist and brought her in even closer, loving on her mouth, her sweetness. Yeah, he couldn't allow a job to mess up what they'd been building.

When the kiss ended, she rested her forehead against his. "I forgive you, but you need to know I can handle a cancellation from time to time, but I can't handle you not calling. First, I was mad at you, but then I was worried something had happened."

He gave her another quick kiss. "I know, and I'm sorry I worried you. It won't happen again."

He straightened and grabbed the envelope. "I received some good news today."

"Is that what I think it is?"

Antonio nodded and handed her the document. "I was thinking we could tell Bella the news together."

Scarlett skimmed through the papers. "This is awesome, and they were able to get the birth certificate already." She set everything aside and wrapped her arms around his neck. "It's official, my dear. You have a daughter."

Antonio grinned as warmth spread through him. Every day, he felt like the luckiest man alive, but in this moment, the feeling had multiplied. How was this his life? Months ago, he was at his brother's wedding feeling sorry for himself, and now? Now he had everything he had longed for.

"Thank you for coming into my life and making it a thousand times better," he said to Scarlett before kissing her deeply. Antonio tried to put everything he felt for her into that kiss. He loved her so much.

"We should probably have makeup sex," he said against her lips, and Scarlett laughed.

"I wouldn't say no to that."

"Okay, but first, let me go get Bella so we can tell her the good news. Then you're all mine."

Scarlett smiled at him so sweetly, Antonio was sure his heart cracked open. He had never loved a human being the way he loved her, and it was exciting and a little scary. If she never fell in love with him and decided to leave one day, he didn't think he would ever recover.

"Actually, that won't be necessary. She already knows you're her dad. She doesn't need a piece of paper to tell her that. Besides, I'm going to be a little selfish right now because I want you all to myself."

"Is that right?"

"Yep. So let the making up begin."

Chapter Thirty-One

Days later, Scarlett woke with a start when her cell phone rang at seven in the morning. Eyes barely opened, she snatched the device from the nightstand.

"Hello," she said groggily, then glanced to the other side of the bed which was empty. That was no surprise. Antonio was probably already out for his morning run, which he did faithfully.

"H—hi, Scarlett, it's Nancy."

Scarlett stilled. Nancy never called that time of morning, unless...

"It's Cynthia. She... she died in her sleep, and..." Nancy's words trailed off, and she started crying.

Scarlett closed her eyes and covered her mouth with her hand unable to hold back her own sobs. Even though she knew this day would come, sensing it would be soon, she still couldn't believe her friend, Ezra's grandmother, was gone.

God, she hated this. Death might be inevitable for everyone, but she still hated it.

She sat up in bed, pulling the comforter up over her bare breasts, and wiped at her eyes. Neither her nor Nancy spoke for a few minutes, both trying to pull themselves together. Scarlett couldn't believe Cynthia was gone.

"I'm so sorry to call you like this. I thought I could do this without crying. Apparently, not," Nancy said.

"It's okay. It's a hard loss for all of us. How's everyone else doing?" Scarlett asked about the house staff. They adored Cynthia, and no doubt this was going to hit them all hard.

"Everyone is doing as well as expected. We could tell her health was declining, and when she gave us all huge, life-changing, bonuses a couple of weeks ago, we knew this day was coming soon."

Scarlett let the woman talk, sensing she needed it. She shared a couple of stories about Cynthia and how much the woman meant to her. Nancy and the others adored Cynthia as much as she did. Losing her was a huge loss for all of them.

"She gave me an envelope last week and said not to open it until she was gone. She never shared what was wrong with her, but her health declined fast over the last week. Anyway, in the envelope was a short list of people she wanted me to call and let know about her death. You were at the top of the list."

"Thank you for calling me," Scarlett said, and then unease swirled around her. "What about her daughter? Is she on the list?"

"No. I assume Cynthia's attorney will notify Alberta."

Scarlett nodded, not that Nancy could see her. "You're probably right."

Now all Scarlett could think about was the fallout that might happen if Cynthia followed through on what she'd said about her estate. Bella would be a wealthy little girl, and Alberta was going to be furious.

She and Nancy chatted for a little while longer. Scarlett

already knew there wouldn't be a funeral. Cynthia didn't want one, not even a memorial service. She'd said she didn't want folks that she hadn't seen or heard from in years to be crying over her. And she wanted those she'd been close with during her last days, to remember her the way they last saw her or spoke to her.

"Included with the list of people," Nancy continued, "she wrote these words: Tell everyone not to cry for me. Tell them that I'm happy, and I finally get to be reunited with my two favorite guys. I can't wait to see and hug them. To all of you, I love you. Thank you for being such an important part of my world. Remember, live life to the fullest and love hard."

A fresh wave of tears assaulted Scarlett as her heart broke. She might have lost a dear friend, but heaven got another angel.

* * *

The moment Antonio entered the bedroom with a cup of coffee for Scarlett, he knew something was wrong. Normally, she'd still be in bed, even if she was awake. After checking their bathroom and then Bella's bedroom, and not finding Scarlett, he retraced his steps. Back downstairs, he went to the room at the back of the house that she used to create content for her social media sites. That's where he found her.

"Hey, what are you doing up so early?" he asked as he entered, then pulled up short when she turned to look at him with red-rimmed eyes. She had a small stack of photos in her hand. "What's wrong? What happened?"

Antonio moved across the room, set her coffee on the work desk. The pictures were of her, Ezra, Cynthia, and Cynthia's late husband.

"Cynthia's gone," she said with a watery smile. "Nancy just called me."

"Ahh, baby, I'm sorry." He pulled her into his arms and held her tight. "I'm so sorry for your loss. What happened?"

They sat in the upholstered double chair tucked in the far corner of the spacious room as Scarlett explained that Cynthia had died in her sleep. He'd only met the woman once but had talked with her via FaceTime a few times when Scarlett was on the phone with her. He liked Cynthia, and he loved how much she adored Scarlett and Bella. On more than one occasion, she reminded him that he'd better do right by her girls.

"I'm worried," Scarlett said. "I asked Cynthia more than once not to leave Bella everything. I begged her to leave her estate to the house staff and Alberta, but I don't think she listened. I have no doubt her staff will be well taken care of, but Alberta and Theodore..." Her words trailed off.

She didn't have to complete the thought. Antonio was a little concerned too. He didn't know how things would shake out regarding Cynthia's estate, but like Scarlett, his main concern was for the safety of their daughter.

My daughter.

There were days it still blew his mind that he had a daughter, and she was a Jenkins. He hoped his and Scarlett's concerns about Ezra's parents were unwarranted, and he'd be open to them getting to know her. She was a special little girl, and they'd love her if they got a chance to meet her.

But it would have to be on his and Scarlett's terms. If they tried to use their daughter in their political aspirations, or if they tried to go after her inheritance, then they'd have to deal with him. Antonio would use every means at his disposal to keep them from her and out of her life.

Chapter Thirty-Two

S carlett sipped her latte as she gazed around the mall's food court. Seemed like it had been forever since she and Bella had a girls' day of shopping. It was needed. At least for Scarlett. The last few weeks had been a little stressful with work and coming to grips with Cynthia's death. She didn't realize how much she'd miss the outspoken woman.

That last thought brought a smile to her face, and she glanced across the table at Bella. Her sweet daughter had only agreed to spend this Saturday shopping with her because Antonio was hanging out with some of his cousins this afternoon. Normally, he would be doing the dad thing, shuttling Bella around to dance class or gymnastics, but they had a weekend off. So, she suggested he hang with the guys while she and Bella indulged in a little retail therapy.

"Where should we go next? I was thinking maybe we could find a birthday present for grandma Amelia," she said to Bella, who was sitting across the table from her eating chicken nuggets and watching a group of girls at a nearby table.

Soon that would be her little girl hanging out with friends

at the mall. Scarlett knew she had to let her grow up, but she wasn't looking forward to the teenage years. Bella was already showing some independence. Soon, she'd be a moody teenager who wanted nothing to do with her old mom.

Scarlett grimaced at the thought. In the meantime, she would take every opportunity for them to hang out.

"Grandma has everything," Bella finally said. "What could we get her?"

"Good question. At first, I was thinking we could buy her a new handbag and matching shoes, but the last time we did that, she said it was a waste of money."

Her mother insisted she didn't need to keep up with the latest fashions. That her handbags and shoes were still in good shape and in style. Scarlett on the other hand didn't think there was such a thing as too many shoes and purses.

"What about a spa day?" Bella suggested. "She likes getting her nails done. We could get her a gift card or something."

"You're brilliant! Maybe we all can go somewhere together for a spa day. Oh, we can plan a girls' weekend away and invite your Aunt Momo too."

"Yes! That would be fun."

Her daughter still didn't know she was a multimillionaire. Scarlett had told her about Cynthia's death, and Bella had been shocked, saying she'd just seen her great-grandmother not too long ago.

"I'm sad she's gone," Bella had said. "But maybe she'll see my other dad, Ezra, while she's in heaven."

It was a sweet thing to say, and Cynthia would've loved the sentiment. The woman adored Bella. Not only had she left her a huge inheritance, but she had also left a ton of money to Scarlett and Antonio, as well as the mansion, which blew their minds. That meant she hadn't left it to Alberta. Scarlett didn't want it. She had decided to sell it and split the proceeds with Cynthia's staff.

But Makena, Antonio's stepmother, who was an estate planning attorney, suggested she think about it for a while before making any final decisions. In the meantime, Makena had moved the property to a trust, and the staff would be able to live in the home rent free for another six months. That would give Scarlett and Antonio time to decide what to do with the place.

After doing a little more shopping, and accumulating more shopping bags full of stuff, Scarlett and Bella decided to head home.

"I really like my new shoes," Bella said of her high-top yellow Converses as she jogged to keep up with Scarlett.

"I'm glad, baby. Does that mean you have a new favorite color?" Scarlett led the way to the exit leading to the parking garage. "You have a lot of pink in your... Bella, watch where you're going," she said when Bella, who wasn't paying attention, almost ran into a lady and her kids.

"Oops, sorry," she said to the woman who was pushing a baby stroller that was the size of a small boat. "Oh, you have two babies."

The woman slowed and smiled at Bella and Scarlett. "Yes, they're twins."

"They are precious," Scarlett said as she looked into the stroller that held baby boys who couldn't have been more than three months old. Her heart melted when the smallest of the two smiled at them. "Oh, my goodness, they are too cute," she cooed, and a sudden twinge of longing seized her. Though she'd love to have a couple of more kids, she hadn't thought much about it, until now.

She chatted with the woman for a few minutes while Bella

baby talked with the two cuties. When they started back on their way to the garage, Scarlett was still thinking about babies.

"I wouldn't mind having two little brothers," Bella said, surprising Scarlett. She never mentioned wanting a sibling.

"Really? You wouldn't want a little sister?"

"Well, maybe I can get a brother and a sister. Maybe we can ask Daddy." Bella grinned up at Scarlett, knowing she'd said the right thing. Antonio insisted on giving their daughter everything she wanted, and Scarlett already knew he wanted more kids.

"Maybe," she said noncommittal as she readjusted the bags in her hand to dig for her keys. "But if that happens, you're going to be a big sister, which is a huge responsibility. Are you sure—"

"Scarlett? Bella?" Someone called out, and Scarlett glanced to her left and saw a man smiling at them. He was around her age and walking toward them.

He didn't look familiar, but the way he was grinning at her made it clear he knew her.

"I'm sorry. Do I know you?" she asked as he approached. Even from several feet away, Scarlett could smell cigarette smoke on him that was masked beneath cheap cologne, and she subconsciously took a step back.

"Yeah, I'm Jake, Ezra's friend." The mention of Ezra's name relaxed her a bit, but she searched her memory and still came up blank. She knew all of Ezra's closest friends. Maybe this guy was an acquaintance.

"You and I met at a frat party during me and Ezra's junior year at the University of Miami. Then we met again when a group of us had dinner and shot darts one night in South Beach. You look exactly the same. How've you been?"

An unexpected dread slithered through Scarlett. Something wasn't right. Something felt off, but she couldn't quite put her finger on it. Yeah, she and Ezra had gone to their share of parties and hung out, but still he didn't look familiar.

Then something else came to mind. What was a friend of Ezra's doing in Cincinnati? More importantly, how'd this guy know Bella? Ezra never knew he had fathered a child.

Warning bells blared through Scarlett's mind. "I'm sorry. We really need to be going. Take care of yourself," she said, and started backing away.

Her car was across the aisle and three cars over, and she mentally kicked herself for having her hands full of bags.

"Hey, I'm not trying to make you uncomfortable," the guy said with his hands out in front of him. "I was surprised to see you is all. I was sorry to hear about what happened to Ezra."

When he started moving forward, Scarlett managed to tug on Bella's shirt, trying to keep her close.

"Jake, I need you to stop right there," Scarlett said, trying to sound normal despite the fear clawing through her. "I need to get my daughter in the car."

"Mommy, who is that?"

"Hey Bella, I was a friend of your dad's."

Scarlett pushed her car remote and unlocked the doors as she approached the front of the car. "Come on, Bella, get in the car."

"Ezra's not my real daddy," Bella said.

The words had barely left her child's mouth when the guy charged toward them and snatched Bella's arm.

"Ahhh! Mommy!" Bella shrieked, and her bags fell to the ground when the man picked her up and took off. "Mommy!" she screamed, the sound cutting through Scarlett like a serrated knife plunging into her heart.

She didn't think. She dropped her bags and ran after them. "Let her go!" she yelled and then lunged. She went for the man's face, clawing at his skin with everything in her.

He cried out, twisting and turning, trying to shake her off him while still holding on to Bella. He swung her daughter to the right, then the left, hitting Scarlett and knocking her off-balance.

Her heart lodged in her throat when she hit the ground hard, falling onto her hands and knees, but she popped back up and chased after him. "Stop!" Tears blurred her vision, but she grabbed the back of his shirt and pulled, barely slowing him down as her arms screamed in pain, and she struggled to hang on.

Don't let go. Don't let go.

The words blared through her mind. She couldn't let go. She couldn't let him take her child.

The guy stopped abruptly, and Scarlett slammed into him.

"Get off me, bitch!" he roared and backhanded her.

An explosion of pain burst through her face, her head snapped back, and her sight blurred. But she shook her head, fighting to stay upright as she charged after him again. Once she was close, she threw herself at the man's retreating back and grabbed his waistband.

The guy growled, swinging Bella back and forth while dragging Scarlett along. She kept screaming.

"Hey! What's going on over there!" someone yelled in the distance, and footsteps ran toward them.

"Help! Please! Help me!" Scarlett's arms were burning with pain as the man continued dragging her. This time when she slipped, he stumbled and almost went down, losing his grip on Bella.

"Bella, run, baby! Run!"

The man cursed and kicked out, almost catching the side of Scarlett's head, but she let go of him in time to protect her face.

"Hey! Get away from her," someone yelled, sounding as if they were closer.

The attacker took off down the garage, and Scarlett lost sight of him when he cut through parked cars.

She scrambled to her feet and looked around frantically. "Bella!"

"Mommy," she cried, running toward her with a woman hurrying behind her.

Scarlett grabbed her child and cried. She barely noticed the pain pulsing throughout her body as she held her baby girl. "Ohmigod. Ohmigod."

A couple of people surrounded them, saying that security was coming. Others promised everything was going to be all right. But there was only one person who could make her feel everything would truly be okay.

Still holding on to Bella, Scarlett pulled her cell phone from the back pocket of her jeans. Her hand was shaking, and she barely managed to speed dial her husband.

Antonio answered on the first ring. "Hey, baby," he said, and at the sound of his voice, Scarlett burst into tears.

Deep sobs racked her body, and she shook violently as tears blinded her eyes and choked her voice. A heaviness clogged her chest, and she was barely aware of someone taking the phone from her. Bella's cries stabbed through Scarlett, but still, she couldn't pull herself together.

Someone put their arms around her. "It's okay, honey. You're safe now."

"Her husband said he's on his way," someone else said.

My husband.

All she needed was her husband.

Chapter Thirty-Three

Feeling as if she'd been hit by a Mack truck, Scarlett kept dabbing at her eyes and couldn't stop sniffling. Her face throbbed, exhaustion weighed her down like a two-ton boulder, and her nerves were raw. This had been the worst day of her life, and she couldn't wait until it was over.

With an arm around Bella's shoulder, they sat together on a bench in the mall's security room with their shopping bags at their feet. The space was small, and thankfully, the security guy keeping an eye on them stood outside the door instead of inside the room.

Scarlett appreciated the time alone, though she couldn't stop thinking about what they'd just gone through. Everything happened so fast, and each time she remembered the way that man snatched Bella, she started crying all over again. Her throat was sore, her voice was hoarse, and her tear ducts should be dry. Yet every few minutes a rogue tear slid down her cheek.

God, I just want to go home.

They'd been in the room for a few minutes, but it felt like hours. They'd answered questions one right after another until

Scarlett told the security guy that she was done talking. She didn't want to see anybody. She didn't want to answer any more questions. She didn't even want to be there. All she wanted was for her husband to arrive and take them home.

She kissed the top of Bella's head, and her daughter burrowed deeper into Scarlett's side. She hadn't said a word since they walked into the room. They both had experienced something that Scarlett wouldn't wish on her worst enemy, and she prayed they could move past it.

"Where's my wife and daughter?" Antonio's anxious voice filtered into the room, and Scarlett and Bella popped up from their seats.

When Antonio appeared in the doorway, Bella took off running and leaped into his arms. Scarlett, on the other hand, couldn't seem to get her feet to move. Her heart split wide open, and her pulse pounded loudly in her ears at the sight of the man who consumed her thoughts. The man who had loved her unconditionally from day one. The man who had given up his life for her and her daughter.

Her husband.

The first person she thought to call after the incident. The only person she wanted to see or be with, and the man she loved with all her heart.

Oh. My. God. I'm *in* love with my husband.

The thought paralyzed her. She couldn't move. Her thoughts were jumbled, and her emotions were all over the place, but the one thing she was sure of was that she was deeply and madly in love with Antonio Jenkins.

"Tony." Scarlett rushed to him and yielded to the uncontrollable sobs that shook her to her core. She thought all her tears had dried up, but apparently not. But she hated that, with her crying, Bella started back crying.

"Oh, baby," Antonio said, his voice raspy as he held her and Bella close.

Being in the safety of his strong arms felt like home. This was where she was meant to be. Nowhere else but with him.

Scarlett had lost all track of time and had no idea how long they stood together in that spot. Voices could be heard nearby, and there was some commotion around them, but she kept her face buried in Antonio's chest. His strong and protective presence soothed her like nothing else ever could.

"That—that man tri—tried to take me," Bella said. "I hit him, but he wouldn't let me go."

Fear and anger returned to Scarlett. She could have lost her baby... her heart.

"He—he hit Mommy," Bella said in a small voice, and Antonio stiffened. His grip didn't loosen, but it was as if he was frozen in place. Though her ear was against his chest, she couldn't even hear his heart beating anymore.

"Come here, sweetheart," someone said, and Bella was taken out of Antonio's arms.

It sounded like Mr. Jenkins, and that was confirmed when Bella said, "Hi, Papa."

After a few minutes, the room went quiet, and Antonio loosened his hold but didn't release Scarlett. She was grateful. She just wanted to be held.

"You scared me to death," he mumbled against her hair. His voice was gravelly as if he'd been yelling a lot. "It would've killed me if I lost you two." He kissed the side of her head and Scarlett melted into him.

"I love you, Tony. I love you so much. I don't know what I would do without you." The words spilled from her mouth until he pulled back slightly.

Still sniffling, she lifted her head and dabbed at her tears with the heel of her palm. Her cheek and just below her right eye throbbed, but she was too grateful to be there in one piece to really care.

"I love you, too, baby. You're everything to me." He placed a tender kiss on her lips, then lifted her chin with the pad of his finger. Scarlett closed her eyes when he cursed. She didn't know what he saw, but his anger was palpable.

"Your cheek is swelling. Why the hell didn't they give you some ice," he grumbled, but she didn't respond. She just wanted to go home.

As if reading her mind, he said, "Let's get you out of here."

When he started to lead her away, Scarlett noticed the room had indeed cleared out, including her shopping bags. Her anxiety picked up when she thought they'd be going back to the parking garage. But she settled down when Antonio led her outside where an SUV sat idling at the curb.

Antonio opened the back door, and as Scarlett climbed in, she laid eyes on Bella.

"Hi, Mommy. Papa bought me Twizzlers," she said, holding up the licorice.

"I see." Scarlett couldn't help but smile.

Kids. They were so resilient.

She glanced in the front seat. Liam was their driver and Mr. Jenkins was on the passenger side. They both gave her a nod, but neither spoke. Thank goodness. She was all talked out.

Scarlett rested her hand on her daughter's thigh, needing to touch her. Apparently, Antonio needed something similar. He linked his fingers with Scarlett's and held on tight.

She glanced at him, but he didn't smile. Worry filled his eyes, and she sighed before laying her head on his shoulder.

Later. There'd be plenty of time to talk later.

* * *

I love you, Tony. I love you so much. I don't know what I would do without you.

Those words played through Antonio's mind as he paced his living room like a caged animal. Scarlett had finally told him what he'd been wanting to hear but on one of the worst days of his life. Still, he loved hearing them.

But right now, emotions warred within him. Every few minutes, he felt as if he was going to explode. Or hit something. Yeah, he definitely wanted to hit something. Better yet, he wanted to hit somebody, like the asshole who thought it was okay to hit his wife and try to take his daughter.

Just the thought had him gritting his teeth and balling his fists at his side.

"Son, have a seat before you wear a hole in the carpet," his dad said.

He'd been shocked when his father walked into the security office at the mall. Apparently, Luke had called him.

Antonio shook his head as he thought about how the afternoon had played out. He and Liam had met Luke at the gym and were getting ready to play basketball, but then Scarlett called. When he heard her voice and she started crying hysterically, he hadn't known what to think. He thought for sure she'd been in an accident or something serious had happened to Bella.

He was pretty sure his heart had stopped beating while the room around him spun. One minute he was standing with the phone pasted to his ear and the next, the guys were helping him into a nearby chair. Antonio had never been so scared in his life.

It wasn't until some unknown woman got on Scarlett's phone, filled him in on what little she knew, that he'd been able to breathe again—a little. After hearing Scarlett crying, he'd been in no condition to drive. Liam drove him and Luke to the mall. Once they got there, Antonio had run to the security office, anxious to get to his girls.

He had been glad to see his father, especially when he'd been able to distract Bella for a while. It all worked out in the end. While Liam drove them home, Luke had driven Scarlett's car to the house.

Bella's laughter floated up the stairs from the basement, and it made Antonio feel a little better. When they arrived home, several people were there including Ben Jr., Mahogany, and Jayden, as well as Mrs. Amelia and Makena. Now, the women were upstairs, and Ben Jr. was downstairs entertaining the kids.

Antonio sat on the sofa next to his dad and felt as if he had run a marathon. For the last hour, his emotions had been all over the place.

"Does Craig know anything yet?" he asked of his cousin-in-law, Toni's husband. The former Cincinnati police detective was a law enforcement consultant and still had contacts at the police department.

"Not yet, but he's working with the mall's security, as well as the cops to figure out what happened. He's going to do everything he can to find the guy."

What type of person was brazened enough to snatch a kid from her mother like that? From a mall parking garage. Antonio knew human trafficking was real, but this? Trying to snatch his kid? This was a little too close to home.

Ben, Bella, and Jayden appeared in the living room.

"You need to hear this," his brother said, his tone serious, which made Antonio straighten. "Sweetheart, tell your dad what you told us."

When Bella didn't speak or move from her spot, Antonio inched to the edge of the sofa cushion.

"Come here, Baby Doll. What do you want to tell me?" He

stretched his hand out to her, and she hurried over, throwing herself into his arms. "Talk to me. Tell me what's going on."

"That man said he was a friend of my dad, Ezra. I told him that Ezra wasn't my real daddy."

Shock blasted through Antonio, and he glanced at his father whose eyebrows were raised. They all had to be thinking the same thing. The guy had targeted Scarlett and Bella.

"What happened after that?" He watched her carefully. She was eight, and he wasn't sure if she was remembering correctly, but what if she was? What if this person intentionally went after them?

"He..." she choked out, tears suddenly filling her eyes. Antonio's heart was breaking, but he encouraged her to keep talking. "He got mad at me and grabbed my arm really hard."

When a tear slipped down her cheek, Antonio wiped it away with the pad of his thumb and kissed her. "Thank you for telling me. I'm not going to let anything else happen to you. You're my baby, and I'm going to always protect you. Okay?"

She nodded. "Okay, but I'm not a baby," she said with a little attitude, and a small smile spread across her adorable face.

He chuckled, loving that she could be tough while also being sweet. "Yeah, but you're *my* baby. Remember that."

"All right, shall we go back down and finish shooting pool?" Ben Jr. asked, and Antonio mouthed a thank you to him.

"Can we play a video game instead?" Jayden asked. "Bella's not good at shooting pool."

"Yeah, but I'm getting better, and one day I'm going to beat you," she retorted and followed them back down the stairs.

Antonio glanced at his dad. "You caught that?"

"I did, and I think you're going to need to get Scarlett talking."

Just then, Makena and Mrs. Amelia came down the stairs, and Antonio and his dad stood.

"Is she okay?" Antonio asked.

"She's tired, and I think she's getting a little hungry though she insists she can't eat anything," Mrs. Amelia said.

"I'll take care of that," Antonio said.

"Good. I'm gonna catch a ride with your mom and dad. Call me if you guys need me for anything."

"I will." He hugged her, then kissed her cheek. "Thanks for being here for us."

"Always," she said.

When they left, Antonio fixed Scarlett a plate from the leftovers in the refrigerator. He also poured her a glass of wine and took it upstairs.

When he reached the bedroom, Mahogany was at the door. She held up the ice pack that he'd given Scarlett when they arrived home.

"Hey, I was about to head downstairs to put this back in the freezer. Also, I told Scarlett if you guys need me to keep Bella for the night, just—"

"No," Antonio said, the word coming out harsher than intended, but he wasn't letting Scarlett or Bella go anywhere without him. At least not until he got his nerves under control. "I mean, I need her home tonight."

Mahogany nodded. "I understand. I'll be downstairs. Holler if you guys need anything."

She closed the door behind her, and Antonio set the tray of food down. He made quick work of kicking off his shoes, then climbed onto the bed.

"How do you feel?" he asked, scooting next to Scarlett while holding the tray on his lap.

"Tired, but I can't shut my brain off. It's like the whole thing keeps playing through my mind every time I close my eyes."

"Okay. Well, how about we eat while you fill me in on what happened, and then we'll get in bed so you can get some sleep."

He cut a piece of the grilled salmon and fed it to her. Then some brown rice. "Bella said the guy who tried to take her mentioned Ezra's name. Is that true?"

Scarlett wiped her mouth with a napkin and nodded. "Yeah, he knew us."

He listened as she told him everything the guy had said and the moment she realized something wasn't right. Antonio tried to keep his emotions at bay and his expression neutral, but inside, he was freaking out. His family could've been killed or seriously hurt.

"Tony, there's only one way he could've known about me and Ezra... and Bella," Scarlett said, her voice shaking.

He put his arm around her and kissed the side of her head. "Yeah, I think it's safe to assume Theodore and Alberta know about Bella. But what they don't know is they've messed with the wrong family."

Chapter Thirty-Four

Anxiousness swirled through Scarlett as she and Antonio were led to an observation room at the police station. The cops thought they'd caught the guy who tried to snatch Bella, and they wanted Scarlett to pick him out of a lineup.

She'd been a nervous wreck the past week and driving her family crazy. She couldn't help it. She didn't want to let Bella out of her sight, and she couldn't seem to shake the fear that she had experienced that day at the mall.

So when Monday rolled around, and it was time for Bella to go to school, Scarlett had a panic attack. She freaked out, refusing to let Bella leave the house. If it weren't for Antonio, their child would never be allowed out of the house again.

Now, the day had finally come when she could gain back some of her power. She was getting ready to come face-to-face with the asshole who had thought it was okay to snatch a kid.

"Right in here," the police detective said as he escorted her and Antonio to a small dark room. Before he closed the door, Luke entered.

Scarlett hadn't expected to see him today even though he and Craig had played a large role in catching this guy. Luke had interviewed witnesses who had been in the mall's parking garage that day and got a lead on the vehicle that was used. While Craig had tapped into some of his connections in various divisions of law enforcement. He'd been able to go through mall security tapes, as well as the city's video footage in the surrounding areas.

They'd found the vehicle the man was using, but of course the car had been reported stolen days before. Still, they managed to pull a partial fingerprint from the gear shift and learned the perp had been in the system. There was a warrant out for his arrest in West Virginia.

"They're bringing them in now," the detective announced just before several men were escorted into the small room on the other side of the one-way glass.

Each man fell into step, then faced forward so Scarlett could see them. All of them held a large, square card with a number on it.

"All right, Mrs. Jenkins. I just need you to look at each man and let me know if anyone looks familiar."

Scarlett knew immediately as her gaze ran over the guy who she had wrestled with. The one who had backhanded her. He looked younger than he had the other day, and it was clear he was nervous as he shuffled from one foot to the other.

"Stand still," the police officer in the room with the men barked.

The scumbag she wanted to see behind bars was around five-ten with a slight build. Had he been any bigger, she might not have been able to stop him. The thought terrified her. What if he had gotten away? What if he had taken her child, and she never saw her again?

She wanted his ass locked up for the rest of his life, even though she was told that might not happen.

"Number three," she said, anger lacing her words as she stood with her fists balled at her sides.

She wanted to leap through the glass and beat the crap out of the asshole for terrorizing her and Bella. Well, mainly her since Bella seemed to have recovered within a day. That first night their daughter had slept with them because of a nightmare. Since then, she'd been fine.

It was a different story with Scarlett and Antonio. Scarlett was still trying to rein in her fear and her anger. Those first few nights, every time she closed her eyes, she saw number three's face. Or she heard her daughter's screams. Antonio had suggested she talk to someone, a professional who could help her work through her fear. Scarlett was giving it another week or two, hoping she'd be able to help herself. If not, she'd take his advice.

As for Antonio, he was staying close to her, even working from home. Though he seemed okay with Bella going to school, he was the one taking her and picking her up every day. It was a small private school, and the principal had let him hire a team of three undercover security specialists. They were tasked with being on the school grounds whenever Bella was there and until the threat was over.

Scarlett was confident that their lives would go back to normal soon. At least she hoped.

The detective pushed a button on the side of the wall. "You can escort everyone out except for number three," he said into a microphone.

"I want to talk to him," Scarlett said and started for the door, but the detective blocked her path.

"Sorry, that's not going to happen," he said apologetically.

"We have to do everything by the book to ensure this guy pays for what he did."

Craig had already explained the guy might get off with a slap on the wrist. He could be charged and fined, but he probably wouldn't receive any jail time since he hadn't kidnapped Bella. He only attempted to.

Stupid laws.

If they couldn't put him behind bars in Cincinnati, she hoped whatever he'd done in West Virginia would land him in prison for the rest of his life.

"We'll be questioning him," the detective said. "We'll get everything we—"

"I should be the one to question him since I'm the one who needs to know why he came after our child." Scarlett knew she sounded crazy, but she was serious. He hadn't been working alone and deep down, she really believed Ezra's parents were behind all of this. "I want to know who sent him, and then I want to beat the—"

"Ma'am, I understand, and I sympathize with what you went through, but we can't let you near him."

"Well, let him go, and I'll meet him outside," Antonio said with so much steel in his voice Scarlett feared he really would go after the man.

"Which is why I'm here," Luke said and stepped forward. "As your attorney, I'm here to make sure neither of you do anything stupid, and what you're suggesting is just that. So, we'll let the detective do his job, and he'll get back to us."

Scarlett growled under her breath, catching all the men off guard. She wanted answers, her own answers, and she wanted that man to pay and to suffer the way she had.

"As a favor to Craig," the detective continued, "I can let you guys hang out in the observation room, and you can listen in while we interrogate him. But that's all I can offer."

"Good. When?" Antonio asked.

A phone buzzed, and they all looked around until they realized it was Luke's.

He pulled the device from the inside pocket of his suit jacket and glanced at the screen. "Actually, you guys, we need to leave."

"Why? What's going on?" Antonio demanded.

"Ben Sr. needs us at the firm ASAP."

"All of us?" Scarlett asked, wondering what was so important that they had to stop what they were doing and leave. Her father-in-law was one of the busiest people she knew. For him to summon them to his office like this meant it had to be important.

"The two of you," Luke said simply, as if it was the end of the discussion.

"Did he say why?" Antonio asked, looking as if he had no intention of leaving.

Luke glared at him. "Dude, it's been my experience that when my boss, *your* father, tells me to do something, life goes a lot better when I just do it. Hasn't that been your experience, too?"

Antonio huffed out a breath and slipped his arm around Scarlett. "Yeah. Let's go."

* * *

Antonio was still fuming when they arrived at his father's office. He knew how much Scarlett wanted to sit in on the interrogation at the police station. Hell, he did too. He wanted to know why the guy tried to kidnap Bella. He wanted to know what his endgame was, and he wanted to know if he was working with anyone else.

They'd probably get those answers, but Antonio wanted to hear it from the guy himself.

He had texted his dad before they left the police station asking if they could stop by his office in a couple of hours, instead of now. His father said he wanted them there immediately. It wasn't like him not to give a reason why, and that concerned Antonio.

"Hi, Antonio, Scarlett," Claire, his dad's assistant, said with her usual warm smile. "Mr. Jenkins wants you to meet him in conference room C. I'll escort you." She moved from around her desk and started down the hallway with them by her side. "There's already water in the room, but would either of you like something else to drink?"

Antonio glanced at Scarlett. "Nothing for me, but what about you, sweetheart?"

"No, I'm good. Thank you."

As they walked with Claire, Antonio nodded and waved at a few of his dad's staff and attorneys until he reached the conference room. Claire knocked twice on the closed door before pushing it open.

"Right in here," she said.

They stepped in but they both pulled up short.

"You!" Scarlett roared and started to charge forward, but Antonio stopped her with a hand on her arm. "Tony, that's her! That's Cynthia's daughter, Alberta. She's probably the one behind what happened to Bella."

Antonio turned to his father. "Dad, what the heck's going on?"

"Come in and have a seat," Ben Sr. said calmly and stood. He pulled out the chair next to him for Scarlett, and Antonio sat on the other side of her. "Let me officially introduce you to Attorney Alberta Upton, Cynthia's daughter."

"We know who she is. What we don't know is why she's here," Antonio bit out.

"She's here because she believes her husband was behind the attempted kidnapping," Ben Sr. said.

"Your husband and not you?" Scarlett snapped. "I wouldn't be surprised if you both were behind it. I already know you're a horrible person because you made it clear the first time I met you."

"I didn't *know* who you were when I saw you at my mother's home," Alberta shot back. "If you knew how many people have tried to take advantage of her kindness, you would've reacted the same way."

"No, I wouldn't have! I tend to give people the benefit of the doubt until I get to know them."

Alberta nodded. "Fair enough. My apologies. I wasn't at my best that day."

Scarlett was vibrating with anger, and Antonio reached under the table and sought out her hand. Holding it, he caressed the back of it with his thumb in hopes it would settle her down.

She didn't like Alberta for several reasons. One being she hated that the woman hadn't spent more time with Cynthia. She also couldn't understand how Alberta could stand by her husband, Senator Theodore Upton, despite all the negative press surrounding him.

Ben Sr. cleared his throat. "Attorney Upton has—"

"Alberta, please," Cynthia's daughter said and turned her attention to Scarlett. "Even though I made an ass of myself the last time we met, I hope you'll give me a chance to explain why I'm here. And whatever you think of me, it's probably true. I have a lot to repent for, but I also want you to know I had *nothing* to do with your daughter's attempted abduction."

"Alberta reached out to me when she obtained proof that her husband was involved in what happened to Bella."

"Do you two know each other?" Antonio asked his father. "How did she find you?"

His father shook his head. "No, we've never met, but she knew of Scarlett and eventually that led to me."

"She's lying. She doesn't know anything about me!" Scarlett bit out.

"Actually, I do. I had you investigated the day after I met you at my mother's house."

Scarlett released a humorless laugh. "Of course you did. Like mother, like daughter. Clearly a person's privacy means nothing to either of you."

"Scarlett, after that day at my mother's house, when you were visiting, I remembered you. I first saw you at Ezra's college graduation. During that time, he didn't share anything with us about his life. Not who his friends were. Not his plans for the future, and not who he was dating. The only reason we knew about the graduation was because of my mother. When I saw you and Ezra together there, I assumed you were dating. Then when I saw you again at my mother's house months ago, and she mentioned you being a friend of Ezra's, I wanted to know who you really were."

"I assume that means you know everything about Bella," Antonio said as anger stirred inside of him.

"I do. I know Bella's my granddaughter, but that's not why I'm here. I'm here to right a few wrongs. First of all, Theodore is my soon-to-be ex-husband. We're legally separated, but not divorced... yet."

She stared down at the oak conference table and released a long sigh before continuing.

"Scarlett, I know Ezra and my mother have probably said a lot about me, and unfortunately, I'm sure most of it is true. But let me give you a *little* history about me and my relationship with Ezra's father."

Antonio watched her carefully. She was a lawyer. She was used to putting on a show and trying to make people believe what she wanted them to believe.

"Theodore and I married when we were very young, and I fell crazy in love with him. I loved his drive, his intellect, and he was the most charming man I'd ever met. My mother hated him from day one, and in hindsight, I should've listened to her concerns. But she and I had always been on opposites sides of everything. So, I assumed she only hated him because I was in love with him."

Alberta took a small sip from her glass of water and set it back down on the table.

"I'm only telling you this to give you some insight into my frame of mind in the early years of my marriage." She met Scarlett's gaze. "I have two regrets in my life that I'll never be able to forgive myself for. One: abandoning my son. I was so in love with his father and all that we were trying to build. I didn't realize how bad things were between us and Ezra until it was too late."

Antonio stiffened, recognizing some of his own past in her words and how like Ezra, he'd grown up without a mother.

"What's the other regret?" Scarlett asked.

"I regret not apologizing to my mother before she died. She was right. I was a fool to fall for Theodore's charm."

Sadness showed in her eyes, but just as quickly, it disappeared.

"I've had someone tracking Theodore for a while. A couple of years ago, I hired a private investigator because I thought he was cheating on me. He was, but he was doing so much more than that. At the time, I didn't do anything about it publicly because we both had a lot to lose. We had invested so much into our marriage, even though Theodore had stepped out on me, I thought we could get our marriage back on track.

"Then sexual harassment accusations started piling up along with other political indiscretions. It was too much not to think that some of it, if not all of it, was true. But I couldn't divorce him at the time. Not showing a united front when we were in public would've cost me in every area of my life, especially with my career. So though we were sharing a house and looking like the happy couple, we were living two separate lives.

"But after seeing you at my mother's bedside months ago..." Her voice shook, and her words trailed off as she looked away. Seconds ticked by before she returned her attention to Scarlett. "I knew I had to make some changes, especially when I found out she was dying. Of course, it was too late to try to repair the damage to our relationship, but I tried."

She sounded like she was telling the truth, but Antonio wanted to hurry her along. He didn't, though. Mainly because whatever else the woman planned to say might help give Scarlett more closure as it related to Ezra and Cynthia.

"I hated the person who I had become. Years ago, it was all about becoming the best damn lawyer I could be. Then when Theodore decided to go into politics, we were positioning ourselves to be that 'it' power couple. Then I got pregnant with Ezra, and that threw us into a tailspin because we never planned to have kids."

She shook her head.

"I made so many mistakes. I didn't realize what horrible parents we were until it was too late, and I didn't know how to fix my relationship with my son. But after he was killed, I thought if I fought to get justice for his death, then I could somehow forgive myself for not being the mother he deserved.

"After that, my marriage slowly started crumbling, and here

we are. The main reason I haven't divorced my husband yet is because he would have the right to half of everything I have. He's broke, and I'm not giving him a dime. Instead, I'm biding my time because Theodore is being investigated by the FBI for several crimes. I've agreed to work with them and help build a case against him."

Unbelievable. The more Antonio learned about Ezra's family, the more he disliked them. Well, he disliked this woman. As for Cynthia, he owed her so much for the role she played in getting him and Scarlett together. Her tactic might have been unconventional, but it had worked. He not only got the woman he couldn't live without, but he also was blessed with Bella.

"What exactly does this have to do with my daughter's attempted kidnapping?" Antonio asked, his patience thinning.

Alberta stared at him for the longest. Clearly, she didn't like the way he referred to Bella as his daughter. Too damn bad. She was his, and there wasn't a damn thing this woman could do about it.

He'd give her credit, though, for showing up, but she'd have to lay out solid proof for him to believe she had nothing to do with what happened the other day. Yes, the cops had arrested the man who snatched Bella, but Antonio knew someone else was behind it all. Someone who'd done their homework and found Scarlett, and someone who knew Bella was Ezra's biological child.

"Before I started working with the FBI, I had hired a private investigator to keep tabs on Theodore. I'm a true believer that it's important to keep your enemies close, and that's how I've viewed him for the last couple of years."

"Wait, you want us to believe you've had your husband under surveillance all this time?" Scarlett asked, disbelief coloring her words. "Yet, you and your law firm defend him at every turn whenever he gets into trouble."

Alberta sighed loudly. "Again, keep your enemies close. Besides, I have to play the role of doting wife. It's all a front until we gather enough evidence for his numerous crimes and put him in prison for the rest of his life."

"So what wrongs are you trying to right by being here?" Antonio asked. "And what do you get out of it?"

Chapter Thirty-Five

This was like a bad movie plot that was getting worse at every turn. Scarlett couldn't believe she was sitting across from Ezra's mother, a shrewd businesswoman. She had hoped to never see her again, but if Alberta could shed some light on why Bella was attacked, then she'd hear her out.

"To answer your question," Alberta said to Antonio, "I want to do everything I can to make sure Theodore is held accountable for trying to kidnap *your* daughter."

Good, she's acknowledging Antonio as Bella's father.

As Bella got older, Scarlett would make sure she knew more about Ezra and Cynthia, but her feelings toward Ezra's parents were the same. She didn't want them anywhere near Bella.

"How do you know Theodore is behind the attempted kidnapping? More importantly, why should we believe anything you say?" Antonio asked.

Scarlett could hear the skepticism in his voice, but at least he hadn't shut the woman down. Then again, that probably had everything to do with Mr. Jenkins. He wouldn't have changed his schedule for this woman unless he believed she knew something.

Antonio glanced at his father who hadn't said much in the last few minutes. "Do you believe her?" he asked.

His dad nodded. "I do. She has documentation, recordings, and pictures to support what she's saying." He slid over several photos of Theodore at a restaurant talking with an older man. "I wanted to give you two an opportunity to hear Alberta's story."

"I don't blame you for not believing me. I haven't given you reason too," Alberta said, not seeming slighted in the least bit. "But everything I've shared with you is the truth. Les Allen, the guy in the photo with Theodore at the restaurant, is a fixer of sorts. He's done much of Theodore's dirty work over the years and has a lot to do with why Theodore is not in jail yet. They both have a law degree and have masterfully skirted around the law for years."

Scarlett glanced at the photo of the two men huddled across from each other in a restaurant booth. If she'd seen either of them on the street, she wouldn't have categorized them as criminals. They looked like harmless businessmen discussing their next deal.

"The recording your father has is a copy of the conversation that the two men had at the restaurant. They were discussing the kidnapping and how it fell apart."

"I don't understand," Scarlett said. "Why? Why would he try to have Bella kidnapped?"

"Money. Theodore is broke. I didn't tell him when I found out we had a granddaughter. My mother was right in keeping you two a secret. I wouldn't want our crazy lives to spill over onto you guys in any way. But when my mother died, Theodore thought I would inherit the bulk of her estate. As you know, I didn't. According to that recording," she nodded to the small recorder in front of Mr. Jenkins, "Theodore not only knows Bella is his granddaughter, he knows she inherited my mother's estate. In the conversation he had with Les at the restaurant, he calls Bella by name and refers to her as his grand-daughter."

"My God," Scarlett said, her head spinning from this information.

"What was his endgame?" Antonio asked.

Mr. Jenkins lifted the recorder off the table and held it up. "According to the recording, to kidnap Bella and demand a ransom."

"This is unreal," Scarlett breathed. "What type of lowlife would put a child through that type of trauma? It's hard for me to reconcile in my mind that Ezra was the product of someone who could do something so heinous. Your son was so kind, thoughtful, and loving. He was an amazing man. Yet, his father just tried to kidnap a child."

Antonio slid his arm around Scarlett's shoulder and placed a kiss against her temple. She was so grateful to have him in her life. He'd been her rock throughout all of this, and it scared her to death knowing she could've been going through all this alone.

But Cynthia...

Scarlett would be forever grateful for Cynthia. In her own way, she had masterfully pushed her and Antonio together. Surely, she hadn't known what the outcome would be, but Scarlett was grateful for her, nonetheless.

"So what happens now?" Antonio asked, glancing between Alberta and his father.

"Now it's in the hands of the authorities," Mr. Jenkins said.

"Theodore is probably being arrested as we speak," Alberta added. "Him and everyone else who was involved."

Scarlett nodded and thought about the guy who had tried

to take Bella. He was just a pawn in all this, but she hoped he rotted in hell.

"Wait, Alberta what's the other wrong that you're trying to right?" Scarlett asked. She hoped this woman wasn't going to ask to be in Bella's life because that would be a solid, NO.

"I wanted to apologize to you for the way I treated you months ago. It sounds like you really cared about my son."

"I did, very much so. I just hate he never knew about Bella, but he would've loved knowing she and Cynthia had a relationship."

Alberta nodded. "I'm glad you allowed my mother an opportunity to get to know her great-granddaughter. I'm sure it meant the world to her. Ezra was her everything, and when he died, a part of her died too."

"Yeah, I know." Scarlett thought about how much of a blessing Cynthia had been, and her generosity would change Bella's life forever.

Silence fell over the room until Scarlett asked, "Are you planning to contest Cynthia's will or Bella's inheritance?"

Alberta shook her head. "No. For one, I know my mother well enough to know it's ironclad." She smiled sadly. "And two, she left me more than I deserve. She gave me her forgiveness by way of a letter. She said a lot of things that we both should've said before she passed away."

"I'm sorry for your loss," Scarlett said.

"Thank you, and I'm sorry for yours. Despite the way I behaved, I could tell that day you were at my mother's house how much you truly cared for her."

"She was one of my best friends," Scarlett admitted.

Alberta glanced down at the table. "Then you knew how sharp she was. She must've found out that I was separated from Theodore and planning to divorce. In the letter she left me, she told me if my divorce was final within six months after she dies, there would be a sizable inheritance waiting for me."

Shock rocked Scarlett and she couldn't help but chuckle. "That sounds like something she would do."

Alberta grinned, and it transformed her features. Scarlett could see so much of Ezra in his mother's face.

"She might've been pissed at me for the last twenty-five, thirty years, but her unconditional love shined through." Alberta shook her head and this time she smiled fondly. "She always said she and I were like oil and water, but we were more alike than she thought."

"I can see that," Scarlett said. "She was very sharp and listening to you today. I can totally see some of Cynthia in you."

"I know I don't deserve to know or spend time with Bella, and I'm not asking to. But can you tell me about her?"

Scarlett smiled. She didn't know if she'd ever trust Alberta to be around her daughter, but the least she could do is tell the woman how amazing her granddaughter is.

"She's a lot like Ezra..."

* * *

Hours later, Scarlett sat on the sofa, toed off her house shoes, and tucked her legs beneath her. She laid her head back and stared at the ceiling. *What a day.* It was ten o'clock at night, and her mind was still whirling over everything that had transpired in the last fifteen hours.

The visit to the police station. Learning who was behind the attempted kidnapping. Getting to know Ezra's mother. All of it felt as if she'd fallen into an alternate universe. Never in a million years would Scarlett have thought this could be her life.

"I think tonight calls for something stronger than wine,"

Antonio said when he strolled into the family room carrying two glasses and a bottle of Hennessy.

So exhausted from the day's event, neither of them had felt like cooking, and they'd opted for ordering a pizza. Of course, Bella had been thrilled. According to her, pizza was her favorite meal. Add that to eating it in front of the TV while watching a Disney movie, and she'd been the happiest kid in town.

Now that she was in bed, they could finally sit back and unwind. Alberta had been correct, Theodore and his accomplices were in jail. Scarlett could now breathe. She'd probably still be on edge for a while, but at least the people who tried to destroy her world were behind bars.

Antonio set the liquor bottle and glasses on the table, then poured them each a drink. When he handed Scarlett one of the glasses, she smiled. Memories of the last time she'd drank hard liquor came to mind.

Talk about coming full circle.

"Does this moment remind you of anything?" she asked Antonio as he sat on the sofa and pulled her against his side.

He chuckled. "Yeah, it was about six or seven months ago, and the beginning of when you changed my life forever. Actually, that's not true, I think the beginning was when you invited me to travel to Miami with you and Bella."

"I bet you're sorry you said yes," she said with a laugh.

He kissed the side of head, and Scarlett snuggled deeper into him.

"On the contrary. Who knew that would be the start of something amazing? What a ride, baby. In seven months, you have changed my world for the better in every single way." He held out his glass. "Here's to many, many more adventures with you," he said, and she tapped her glass to his before taking a small sip.

"Tony, I never thought I could have a life like you've given me." Scarlett sat up and set the glass on the table before turning to him. "I love you more than I thought I could ever love a man. I can't even imagine my life without you."

"Same here, baby," he said and tossed back the rest of his liquor, cringed, and then set his empty glass on the side table. "Now, come here."

Antonio lifted her to his lap, and Scarlett wrapped her arms around his neck just as he kissed her sweetly. This man. This incredibly sexy, sweet, and gentle man was all hers.

As he kissed her, his tongue tangling with hers, and his large hand caressing her body, Scarlett couldn't help thinking that she was the luckiest woman in the world.

When the kiss ended, she cupped his cheek and smiled at him. "You were right."

He frowned. "About what?"

"About being able to make me fall *in* love with you. I didn't think it was possible, but you proved me wrong and now I'm crazy in love with you Antonio Jenkins."

They kissed again, and Scarlett knew this was just the beginning for them. They were going to have an amazing life together.

Epilogue

"**M**y boy," Antonio breathed as he stared down at the most amazing human being resting in the crook of his arm—his son. His heart had practically exploded at the first sight of him. The miracle of birth was mind-blowing, but when that birth was your own child, it was unbelievable.

Antonio glanced up as Mrs. Amelia approached him. Scarlett had insisted she wanted him and her mother in the delivery room. Her mom had been honored, and Scarlett was happy that she could have her be a part of this momentous experience.

"He is so precious," his mother-in-law said, staring down at her new grandson and lightly brushing a finger over his dark, curly hair. "Chase Armani Jenkins. The name fits him perfectly."

Antonio agreed. They had wanted to honor Cynthia in some way and had planned to name their first born after her. But once they learned they'd be having a boy, they opted to make his middle name, Armani, which was Cynthia's last name.

"May I hold him?" Mrs. Amelia asked and reached for Chase.

Antonio reluctantly gave him up. He might as well get used to doing that, considering the size of his family. Though they wouldn't all get to hold him today, he was sure there would be a lot of passing the baby at Chase's first Sunday brunch.

Antonio moved back over to Scarlett whose eyes were barely open. His heart knocked against his chest when she gave him a tired smile.

"How do you feel?" he asked and brushed several micro braids away from her face.

"Like I just gave birth to an eight-pound, nine-ounce, stubborn little boy who took his time coming out."

Antonio chuckled. "I have to admit, watching him be born was *epic*," he said, using one of Bella's favorite words.

"I'm glad you enjoyed yourself," Scarlett deadpanned, and he laughed. "But seriously, thank you for being here with me. I wouldn't have wanted to go through giving birth to our baby boy without you."

Antonio planted a lingering kiss on freshly glossed lips. He really did like that they tasted like strawberries. "Sweetheart, there's no other place I would've wanted to be than right here by your side. Also, if you want to give me more amazing gifts like this, I'm here for it. Say maybe two or three more boys or girls?"

"*You wish*." She sputtered a laugh, and he joined in. "Talk to me in a year, and then maybe I'll think about it."

A knock sounded on the door just before Bella and Jayden burst into the room.

At ten years old, Bella was the spitting image of her mother. It was wild watching her grow up so fast. His smart, funny, beautiful daughter was still the light of his life, but it was bugging the hell out of him that she was catching the attention of little boys now. Thankfully, Jayden, who attended the same school, was helping Antonio scare them away.

"We came to see our new nephew," Mahogany announced when she strolled in with Ben Jr. and their one-year-old daughter, Viridian.

"Auntie Momo said we could see Chase just for a minute," Bella said and hurried to the chair that Mrs. Amelia was sitting in. "Ohhh, he's so little, and he's *sooo* cute," Bella cooed. "I can't believe I have a little brother. I love him!"

"Look, Chase is trying to open his eyes," Jayden announced, and they all glanced down at the baby. "He looks like my sister. They have the same eyes."

Antonio had to agree. It appeared that Chase and Viridian had inherited their grandfather Ben Sr.'s light-brown hazel eyes. But it was still a little early to tell if Chase's would stay that color.

As everyone *oohed* and *ahhed* over Chase, Antonio went back to Scarlett's side. Her eyes were closed, and he stood there admiring her beauty.

There were days he just stared at her in awe, amazed that she was his wife, his better half, his life partner. For so long, marriage and having a family seemed like a dream that would never come true, but it did. He had everything he could ever want, and it started with a marriage of convenience. Antonio never knew his life could be this fulfilling.

I'm so blessed.

He bent down and brushed a light kiss over his wife's lips. "Thank you for growing our family," he whispered, and her eyes eased open.

"Well, I had a little help," she said quietly and flashed him a smile that he felt straight to his heart. "I love you so much, Tony. I'm glad you're my husband and the father of my babies."

"I love you more, sweetheart, and it's an honor to be your husband and your babies' daddy."

They both laughed before he touched his lips to hers again. Their union might have started unconventionally, but it had turned into a love story that would live on for generations to come.

***

If you enjoyed this book by Sharon C. Cooper,
consider leaving a review on any online book site, review site or
social media outlet.

Join Sharon's Mailing List

To get sneak peeks of upcoming stories and to hear about giveaways that Sharon is sponsoring, go to https://sharoncooper.net/newsletter to join her mailing list.

Other Titles By Sharon

Atlanta's Finest Series
Vindicated (book 1)
Indebted (book 2)
Accused (book 3)
Betrayed (book 4)
Hunted (book 5)
Tempted (book 6)
Committed (book 7)

Jenkins & Sons Construction Series
(Contemporary Romance)
Love Under Contract (book 1)
Proposal for Love (book 2)
A Lesson on Love (book 3)
Unplanned Love (book 4)
Bid on Love (book 5)
The Cost of Love (book 6)

Jenkins Family Series (Contemporary Romance)
Best Woman for the Job (Short Story Prequel)
Still the Best Woman for the Job (book 1)
All You'll Ever Need (book 2)
Tempting the Artist (book 3)
Negotiating for Love (book 4)
Seducing the Boss Lady (book 5)
Love at Last (Holiday Novella)
When Love Calls (Novella)
More Than Love (Novella)

Reunited Series (Romantic Suspense)
Blue Roses (book 1)
Secret Rendezvous (Prequel to Rendezvous with Danger)
Rendezvous with Danger (book 2)
Truth or Consequences (book 3)
Operation Midnight (book 4)
Casino Heat (book 5)

Finding Love Series
Legal Seduction (Contemporary Romance)
A Dose of Passion (Contemporary Romance)
Model Attraction (Contemporary Romance)

Stand Alones
Something New ("Edgy" Sweet Romance)
Sin City Temptation (Contemporary Romance)
A Passionate Kiss (Contemporary Romance)
Soul's Desire (Unparalleled Love series)
Show Me (Irresistible Husband series)
His to Protect (Harlequin Romantic Suspense)
His to Defend (Harlequin Romantic Suspense)

Sharon C. Cooper

Business Not As Usual (Romantic Comedy)
In It to Win It (Romantic Comedy)
Kiss Me (Irresistible Husband – Contemporary Romance)
Mr. One and Only (Baes of Juneteenth)
Fiancé for Hire (Men for Hire)

About the Author

USA Today bestselling author Sharon C. Cooper loves anything involving romance with a happily-ever-after, whether in books, movies, or real life. She writes contemporary romance, as well as romantic suspense and enjoys rainy days, carpet picnics, and peanut butter and jelly sandwiches. Her stories have won numerous awards over the years, and when Sharon isn't writing, she's hanging out with her amazing husband, doing volunteer work, or reading a good book (a romance of course). To read more about Sharon and her novels, visit www.sharoncooper.net

Website: https://sharoncooper.net

Join Sharon's mailing list: https://bit.ly/31Xsm36

Facebook fan page: http://www.facebook.com/AuthorSharonCCooper21?ref=hl

Twitter: https://twitter.com/#!/Sharon_Cooper1

Subscribe to her blog: http://sharonccooper.wordpress.com/

Goodreads: http://www.goodreads.com/author/show/5823574.Sharon_C_Cooper

Pinterest: https://www.pinterest.com/sharonccooper/

Instagram: https://www.instagram.com/authorsharonccooper/

Bookbub: bookbub.com/profile/sharon-c-cooper